ɔ be

Mayra Lazara Dole

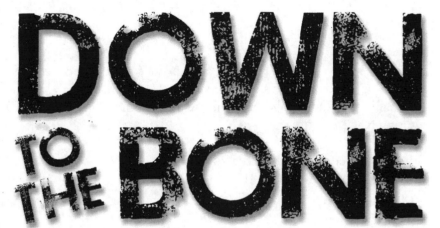

DOWN TO THE BONE

Bella
BOOKS

2012

First published by Harper Teen 2008
First Bella Books Edition 2012

*This first Bella Books edition has been augmented with substantial
additional text and contains editorial changes from the original.*

2011002073

Printed in the United States of America on acid-free paper
First Edition

Editor: Katherine V. Forrest
Cover Designer: Kiaro Creative

ISBN: 978-1-59493-317-2

To Mami and Damarys, the two loves of my life.

About the Author

Mayra Lazara Dole loves papayas (slang for you-know-what but she's honestly talking about the fruit), pineapples, finger bananas and long, cascading hair. She was born in Havana and raised in exotic Miami. The author was kicked out of an all-girl private school at thirteen due to a sizzling confiscated love note written to her by her girlfriend about their first time. She worked as a librarian assistant, ESL tutor and landscape designer until she became a full-time writer. Mayra lives in Miami with her beloved partner (aka: Astro Maniac)—she's obsessed with astronomy, astrology and the occult and drives Mayra nuts! Dole started her writing career with picture books depicting two rebel eight-year-old girls (for sure they'll be MAJOR lesbos when they grow up), and the first Cuban American critically acclaimed lesbian YA novel in history. She's written essays, short stories and poetry for literary and lesbian magazines and for Hunger Mountain—the Vermont College Fine Arts journal of the arts. Mayra's magical realism short story, *Inside the Inside* (CORNERED anthology / Running Press) and *Run for Your Life!* (THE LETTER Q anthology / Scholastic) will also be published in 2012. Oh, and she's been a Lambda Literary YA judge, something she loves and is very proud of.

Author's Note

I'm grateful to Bella Books for allowing me an updated, literary version of *Down to the Bone*. I LOVED rewriting the novel and hope new readers and old fans enjoy this second edition.

Gracias!

Mayra

I—The Kiss

Today, the morning rose like a loaf of sweet banana bread. I left the house ready to start living life juicy bite by juicy bite.

It was the last day of school and we were free before lunch. And if *that* wasn't the best news ever, it was also my two-year anniversary with Marlena, the love of my life. Her summer vacation started yesterday. She was expecting me at her place to celebrate (if you know what I mean). I couldn't *wait* to get out of the mind-numbing last class to visit her.

I was certain that soon Marlena would be in my arms. After a few hours of fun, we'd transform into all the colors of the spectrum until that kaleidoscopic nanosecond where we'd turn luminous, phosphorescent and fly . . .

But instead, I got myself into a hellish nightmare.

The instant my teacher opened her mouth and hissed like a cobra, I should have run for my life. If only I'd seen what was coming, I would still have a place to live.

I've just arrived at the beach by bus to clear my head and

figure out where I'm headed.

I look around me.

There's a light aqua sky. The sand is filled with people who seem joyous, as if their lives haven't just been ruined.

A girl with a cap and surfing shorts slams congas with her palms: *Dún-prak, checke prak!*

Girls in bikinis with hair flying all over the place clap and shuffle their feet to the beat.

I stand on the pier, looking down, watching my puppy, Neruda, chase sand crabs. She runs after them and barks. She gets close, and they disappear into their burrows.

I wish my life were so easy.

Just last night, my mom, Marlena and I visited my grandmother in Ft. Lauderdale. She'd finally healed from an appendix operation but still needed help with chores. I didn't allow my grandma to move a muscle. After the three of us whizzed around the apartment vacuuming, mopping and making a racket washing and drying dishes, *Abuela* said, "Your mother and I will finish the kitchen. Go on. You girls go have some fun."

And boy, did we have a blast!

Marlena and I shut ourselves in the basement filled with packaged foods and canned goods (in case of the impending nuclear explosion, of course!) to "watch TV."

I dipped Marlena in honey and tasted her, bit by bit.

Before you knew it, we were heading back home to pick up my little brother at a friend's house. Everything was so perfect.

I grab Pedri's picture from my shoulder bag. His shiny smooth face and sweet harmonica smile gives me hope. "Shyly," he wrote on the back in his broken English, "you are a big, littol, eskinny, fat, tall, short cooko monthster. I love U berry much! Pedri."

I walk down to the sand to get Neruda. I throw my towel under two coconut palms leaning against each other like secret lovers. The sun sparkles through fan-shaped greenery. Water laps gently along the shore.

I breathe in the salty smell that reminds me of my mom's

meals. She fried fish every Friday night. I'll probably never eat her home cooking again. I'll miss helping her slice, chop and mash as we prepared dinner together while listening to music. Mami's always been generous with food. Recently, for Marlena's mom's birthday, she made a mouth-watering lemon pork dinner. Neighbors were invited for a feast that ended with guava shells and cream cheese, Tania's favorite desert.

It kills me to think I've destroyed my mom's life, and if I'm not careful, I'll probably wreck Marlena's as well.

Marlena and I met a couple of years ago when she moved a block away. She wasn't allowed to go out much. That's why we became homework buddies. I got her hooked on magical realism, anime PC games, karaoke and snorkeling. She turned me on to dystopian novels, poetry and chess.

A year later, without warning, our friendship came to a screeching swerve.

We were at the movies eating buttered popcorn from the same bucket. Our fingers met and lingered for an awkward moment. She spent the night. After I shut off the light and plunked down on my side of the bed, there was a minute of hesitation as we kissed each other's cheeks and said good night.

I had no clue what would transpire between us the following day. I remember it as if it just happened this morning:

Galloping rain and blasting thunder shakes my house. Pedri is spread on the orange living room sofa, watching cartoons. My mom and her boyfriend Jaime sit in the mango-smelling dining room, talking and drinking after-dinner cafecitos.

Marlena and I are sprawled on my bed after dancing our heads off, listening to a mixed CD of Jaipongan, Middle Eastern and Nu Soul.

She tells me, "My parents won't allow me to date until I turn sixteen."

"Woah." I shake my head. "That's two years away. I wish they weren't so strict and let you come to parties with me."

She smoothes my hair away from my face and plants a kiss on my forehead. "It's okay. At least they let me come here and spend the night." Her black eyes sparkle. "I don't need to go out weekends. Dancing with you is what kissing a girl must be like: the best feeling in the world."

My heart bangs in my chest. Kissing a girl?

With a flick of the finger, she changes the music to a slow romantic bolero and just lies there searching my eyes.

I bolt from the bed, rush to the music shelf, grab a djembe CD and put it on. Heart-thumping beats vibrate the walls.

I hoist my hip-hugger button-down jeans and mess up my long, straight, sun-streaked hair so it's crazy-wild. "Come on!"

Marlena jolts out of bed and lands in front of me. She tries to mimic my wild freestyle footwork and bouncy rhythm, but her feet get all tangled up. I rotate my hips before stepping into a twirling cha-cha-cha. "Sleek or what?"

"You're incredible!"

The CD ends and for a second there's sharp silence. We stand face-to-face. A whooshing wind dives in through the bedroom windows, making her long, mahogany curls wave around in the breeze. Her violet eyes seem liquid under the dim light. A beautiful sweetness pours over me.

The walls around me fade. I feel like I'm swimming inside her. Something different is happening within me. She leans into me. Her velvety lips touch mine, and I get goose bumps all over. I feel as if silvery threads of rain are covering my entire body. I'm turning into the sea, becoming one with her, melting.

We kiss for a long, long time . . .

The memory is snapped out of me when the girl stops banging the congas. The sounds are vacuumed away and it seems as if the world has stopped breathing.

I stare at the rolling waves for comfort, but can't stop my mind from buzzing with thoughts.

I woke up way too early this morning from the anticipation and excitement I was feeling about getting together with Marlena. With one eye open, I reached for my cell on my night table and texted her:

happy 2 yrs! i love u love u love u. can't wait to kiss u kiss u kiss u & u know what else . . .

I lowered the shades and fell back asleep. Soon thereafter, a thudding electrical storm that soaked the city woke me up just in time to catch the bus for school.

My room turned hazy and dark as I stumbled around searching for clothes to wear. I was dying to take a taxi to Marlena's and get tangled up under the covers with her, but I didn't allow myself that luxury.

Instead, I left for school.

Bad move.

By the time noon approached, I could barely contain myself from running out of class.

Ms. Alegre—better known as Fart Face—was up on the board writing the name of textbooks we'd need next year. What kind of a senseless thing was *that*?

I was finishing reading all the sweet, luscious texts Marlena sent me last night after my mom dropped her home—my iPhone was hidden inside my math book. Memories fly to me as if in a 3D film:

. . . tomorrow is our happy 2 yrs! remember our 1st time? ur fingers . . .

A looming presence stands before me. "Shai. Didn't you hear my question?"

I look up. Gray-haired, wrinkly Fart Face tears the cell out of my hands.

She faces the students. "Class. Would you like to hear what's in Shai's highly important texts?"

She can't read my personal texts to the entire class. She can't!

Everyone, except my best friend Soli, blasts, "Yeah!"

"Please give it back," I plead. I try to grab my cell with force out of her hands, but she instantly pulls it away.

Fart Face puts on a disgustingly fake smile and walks slowly to her desk. "So these texts are that good, huh?" She speaks to the class. "I'm sure you'd love to hear everything, but I'm afraid I'll need to use the word 'bleep' in place of X-rated words."

She sits poised on the chair, lowers her reading glasses, and begins: ur the greatest kisser and lover ever, Scrunchy.

love BLEEP BLEEPING w u.

tomorrow, when u come over after school, we can BLEEP BLEEP 4 hours.

i love when u BLEEP, BLEEP me.

The guys whistle and shout, "Way to go, Scrunchy!"

"Scrunch-Munch is a beast!" Roberto cheers.

"Scrunch-Munch! Scrunch-Munch!"

I lower my head and wring my trembling hands. Fart Face walks toward me in almost silent steps. She stops a few feet away from my desk. "Wait until your mother finds out. She'll just *love* it."

She turns to the class.

"Should I continue reading, or are these texts too dull and dreary?"

"Read on!" Everyone, except Soli, goes nuts. She sits wagging her head.

"No! Please, stop," I beg with my heart in my mouth.

"Quiet!" Fart Face stomps her foot and shuts me up. "Maybe next time you'll learn to pay attention in class."

I want to run out of here, but my feet are glued to the floor.

She clears her raspy voice and continues. *ur BLEEP, BLEEP and more BLEEPS . . .*

Soli widens her eyes as if telling me, "Grab the cell and run!" But I still can't move.

i love 2 feel ur body BLEEP under me.

i go crazy about the way ur BLEEP feels when—

Ryki interrupts and teases, "Who's your secret lovey-dove, huh, Scrunchy?"

My body feels as if a Mack truck is parked on it. I stare out the windows. Lightning bolts threaten the dark sky. The scent of humiliation surrounds me. I gulp hard to try and release the tension, but it doesn't help.

I think about a white horse picking me up and galloping me full speed out of here. I know my mom will kill me. I'm trapped by Fart Face's rasping voice, hurting my ears, stabbing me slowly. She's really enjoying this.

I cover my ears with my hands.

ur my life. i'll love you till eternity. so glad we're girls my beautiful Shai Sofía . . .

The room becomes hushed.

Caro and her girlfriend Maribel smile. "Hey, I didn't know you were lesbo too! Let's go to Papaya's this Friday for the all girl, alcohol-free, dance night!"

Karina, better known as Butchie, shouts with a fist in the air, "Yeah!"

I feel darts shooting at me from my friend CC's eyes. "You're a tortillera? You should have told me instead of lying so much about phony guys you liked and a boyfriend in Spain."

Marlena made me promise not to tell a soul about us. I took it too far by fibbing so much. I owe CC, and all my friends, an apology when the time is right. I hope they accept it.

Bookworm Margarita speaks up. "Give Shai a break. She wasn't ready to tell you. Don't be so dense."

Half the class supports me. "Who cares?" Telia says. "Let's get to-gether tomorrow night at Pizza Girls and have a big party for Shai and her girlfriend."

"Woooh hoooooo!" a bunch of people cheer. "Party! Party!"

I try to crack a smile, but the sides of my mouth won't cooperate. My mom will soon find out what I've really been up to every day after school.

Olivia, my friend since fourth grade, scrunches up her face. "Count me out." She sticks her index finger in her mouth, as if she were about to puke.

Soli comes over and puts an arm around my shoulder. She says to the class, "This is for the jerks: So what if she didn't tell you bunch of morons about her private life?" She gives attitude just by being her curvy self, with those cantaloupe boobs and perky butt.

Gustavo lets out a gutsy laugh. "I have no problem with lezzies. Let's have a threesome!"

"A manage a trios!" Some of the guys get all riled up, laughing uproariously, clapping and stomping their feet. "Let's do it! Threesome! Threesome!"

"Shush!" Fart Face reprimands. She juts her long pointy chin at Soli. "Go back to your seat, Soledad."

Soli squeezes me harder to her.

Fart Face untangles Soli's arm from around me and raises her voice, "Shai, follow me."

2—Tazer

Some people think going from your usual source of strength—fun and laughter—to vulnerable, without armor, helps you grow. Bull! I'd rather have my life back, filled with excitement and no worries, dim-witted as that may seem.

A girl who looks exactly like a cute surfer guy walks from the water to an empty towel close by. She's wearing a vivid green T and long bathing trunks. Her straight bleached blond hair is buzzed all over, and streaks of dyed purple bangs hang over her eyes. The sleek dark sunglasses, sitting on top of her head, make her look hip.

I hope she's not coming toward me. A condemned person can't celebrate life and new friendships like she used to. I just need to be alone to figure out where I'm going to live and what's about to become of me.

As she nears, Neruda dashes to her. She vigorously pets my pup's fuzzy head. "Hey cutie," she says in a mild Cuban accent. Neruda is all over her, slobbering her chiseled, dimpled chin and nipping at her tiny earlobes.

"Neruda!" I call to her. She flies to me and I grab her. "Sorry." I look away into the horizon. I don't want her to start a conversation. What I'm going through is too intense. I can't share it with a stranger. What do I tell her, "Hey, hi! Great to meet you! Today, I have several names: Shamed. Mortified. Disgraced. Embarrassed. Dishonored. You can call me any of those, or better yet, make up one of your own!"

But how do I tell such a friendly face I need silence, and total concentration, to help unburden myself from all I'm going through?

"No problem. I love puppies. Neruda's my favorite poet. What a brill name for a dog." She recites a few of her favorite Neruda lines verbatim. I'm amazed she seems to enjoy him as much as I do but stay quiet about it.

She dries her face, wrings the bottom of her T, and slips on white sneakers. She brings her purple towel closer to me and plops on it. "I'm Tazer."

"Hi. I'm Shai." I try hard to smile.

"S-h-y?" Tazer slides her glasses down to her nose, and her hazel eyes look up over them.

"Sounds the same but it's spelled, S-h-a-i." I clutch my hair with both hands and stare away from her, into nothingness.

"Beautiful name. It doesn't sound Cuban."

"Thanks. My mom loves America because it's given us so much. That's the reason she gave me an English sounding first name."

"Epic. You okay?" She catches on.

"Fantastic." Sarcasm usually has restorative powers but it's not working for me right now.

"What happened?"

"Just had a beautiful fight with my mother." I feel my chin trembling. I clutch Neruda in my arms and squeeze her tightly against me.

"That's terrible. Why?"

"Because she's a case." I kiss Neruda's head and stare at the frothy ocean waves. *What have I got to lose by telling an unfamiliar person something about my messed-up life? Maybe she'll have valuable insight that'll help me reflect on the destruction humanity brings upon itself and say things like, "Consider yourself lucky. Most artists' work becomes more and more powerful with suffering and pain."*

Suddenly, words just pour out and I can't stop them.

"In second grade, I brought home a picture book called, *Birthday in the Barrio*, about rebel eight-year-old Chavi and her best friend Rosario. My mom read the author's blog where she stated that in her next novel, the girls are twenty-year-old lesbian girlfriends. She tore the book into pieces, threw it in the trash and said, 'Authors like these plant seeds in girls' minds about choosing different lifestyles when they're all grown up. Girls can do anything they set their minds to. You could be president, but no one will hire you for the job if you turn into a woman uninterested in men. I don't want you transforming into one of *those*.'"

"*Qué loca.*" Tazer totally gets it.

"Well . . . she's a great mom except for some things. Right now, she wants to tear up my life and throw it away in the garbage."

I hate talking about my mother that way. I should present Tazer with a complete history of all the great moments my mom and I have shared, like the day we entered a daughter and mother singing contest and won, or how we usually walk hand-in-hand, singing together, in harmony, whenever we're out and about.

A sympathetic ear to relieve what I'm feeling might be a good thing, though. But maybe not. I don't want Tazer to think my mom is disposable just because of one character flaw. I really shouldn't tell her what Mami just did to me.

A bunch of wild green parrots startle us as they circle the palm trees above us. I stand to catch a clearer view. "How beautiful. I have four in the backyard of my house." I want to change the subject from me, to anything at all.

Neruda growls and barks up at them. Tazer lifts her, belly up, and pets her chubby stomach. "We've got a family of owls in my backyard."

It would be rude if I didn't at least ask her *some*thing about herself. She'll just think I'm one of those narcissistic, egocentric, *plástica* Cubanita chicks who don't give a royal rooster's butt about anything but themselves.

I lift my dorky, navy blue school skirt and stretch down my tank top. "Where do you live?"

She sets Neruda down on my towel. "With my dad, in Gables by the Sea." Gables by the Sea is one of the wealthiest places in Miami. "My uncle, who's been here twenty-five years, got my father into becoming a realtor. They struck it rich during the real estate boom. I miss my family in Cuba. I lived in an apartment building with my grandparents, uncles, aunts and cousins. There were nineteen of us. Now I have everything, but I don't have them."

"That's sad." She nods. I tell her I live in Little Havana. "But we're moving soon to a ritzy neighborhood in Coconut Grove. My mom just got married. She wants to move up in the world." I tell her this so she gets it that I can relate. "I'll miss my old neighborhood, too."

Suddenly, I miss Pedri, my home, my friends, and everyone who now sees me as a lying, untrustworthy jerk. My chest fills up with pain.

Tazer talks about her fun life at Coral Gables High, and having headed the LGBTQI Center there when she's interrupted by a girl far away waving her hands and yelling, "Taze!"

"I'll be right back. That's my friend Zoe." She takes off.

As I watch her dash away, I flash back to our principal, Mrs. Superior-Sicko, a cockroach of a woman, with bloodshot, steely eyes, paper-thin lips and tangled eyebrows. She stood with feet planted close together as she read the texts to my mom. I wanted to tear my cell out of her hands but she'd have destroyed me.

I can't shake the memories of Fart Face walking her ogre self into the principal's office, dragging me behind her.

She calls my mom at work and in Spanish, says, "Mrs. Amores, we have a problem with your daughter. She's in the office. We need you here immediately."

That call is my death. My legs feel like they're made of clay. To any mother, reading vivid, detailed texts of her daughter being with another girl will horrify her. I'd rather fry in the chair than for this to happen.

My hands won't stop trembling. I've got to pee. Sweat drips down my back from my neck as I wait for Mami to come through the door. No one is talking to me. But they're talking about me with my cell in hand. They're desperately trying to figure out Marlena's name and number so they can call her parents.

"The callback number was turned off. This is preposterous. We can't allow two bad apples to spoil our private school's impeccable reputation. We won't let such indecency here."

In a quavering voice, I raise my hand. "May I please use the restroom?" I'll make a mad dash out of this dreadful school and run for my life after I pee.

Mrs. Superior-Sicko grits her teeth. She scratches her bulbous nose. "The restroom? You should have thought about the consequences of these atrocious texts, young lady." Her ears and neck flush a dark pink. A thick blue vein on her forehead pops out. Her eyes drill holes into mine. "Hold it until we resolve this matter."

I try to sit but they won't let me. My legs are weak.

Before you know it, my mom rushes through the door and they're reading the texts to her.

. . . your breasts on my . . .

Mami's face goes from rosy to deathly pale as she burns holes into my pupils with her stare. "Those texts are obscene. This is so embarrassing. How dare *you have a relationship with a girl in this school behind my back?"*

Mrs. Superior-Sicko glares at me. She points a fat finger toward the middle of my forehead. "If you'd like Shai to stay in our school, you must keep watch over her so she doesn't meet up with that girl again. They must end this sexual relationship and filthy texting, today."

"It's not disgusting like you all think."

Fart Face comes to me, shoving the cell in my face. "Shai, you know this school accepts homosexuality. We even have a Straight and Gay Alliance. This isn't about sexual preferences. The same rules apply to straight kids. This issue has to do with having sex at your age. Reading, writing, sending or receiving these types of explicit texts during class is not allowed. Who's the girl you're having sex with? You're both responsible for this unacceptable behavior."

I want to blurt, "It's your favorite niece, Alicita, the perfect genius you're always yacking about." But instead, I zip my lips tightly.

My mom digs holes in my eyes. "I didn't even know you liked girls." She looks to Fart Face. "Shai wears dresses. She slow dances at parties with boys. As far as I knew, she loves the opposite sex. I've been fooled by my own daughter?" She turns to me. "We were so close."

Mrs. Superior-Sicko gives me an ultimatum: "Tell us who the girl who wrote those texts is, or you'll be expelled." I'm still mute. She continues with hatred in her eyes. "Whoever she is, her behavior needs to be stopped. I won't allow girls, boys, gays, straights, giraffes, whatever, to write or read graphic, explicit, sexual texts in class."

The ticking sound of the grandfather clock blasts out like a bunch of loud shots, over and over again, driving me crazy.

"Who is the nasty girl?" My mom's jaw tenses. "Go bring her to us right now."

"She's not nasty!" No one's going to find out it was Marlena. I'll let them keep believing she's in this school. I don't give a royal banana if they keep me prisoner here for years. I'll never talk!

Mami utters, "I'm deeply sorry. I raised her to be polite. She's never given me trouble. Shai's been a great girl and, as you know, an A student. I don't know what's gotten into her and why she won't cooperate."

"I'm not shocked," Fart Face affirms. "This type of sexual behavior shouldn't be happening at such a young age, but unfortunately, it's common."

Mrs. Superior-Sicko's jaw is tight as she digs holes into my pupils. "Well, Shai Amores, I see that you will not cooperate. You're lucky today is the last day of school and you've graduated. But you're not welcome back next year." She blinks her crusty bug eyes. "Get your books and go home."

Mami stays behind, talking with the Torturers. I don't want to see her face when I get back. Maybe I can run into the street and get hit by a car. No. No. Pedri will suffer if I die.

First, I dash to the bathroom to pee. Then, I walk into the class. Some girls stare at me with question marks in their eyes. A few guys make fun of me. "Hey, Muff Diver!" They sing out, "Shai e-eats octa-pussy! Shai lo-oves octa-pussy!"

"Shut up, jerks!" Soli chews them out.

The room fills with the buzzing sound of gossip. I don't understand. Some of these kids have been my friends all my life.

Soli hugs me and kisses my cheek. "Things'll be okay. I'll call you soon." Lucky for Soli, everyone knows she's boy crazy, otherwise they'd think she was the texter. I don't want Soli to let go. I'd like her to slap me awake and tell me my mom hasn't read those intimate texts and this isn't real.

I kiss her cheek. "Later." The lump in my throat from knowing what's awaiting me is killing me.

I grab my book bag and see smiles on the faces of Margarita, Julian, Sasha and Hernando. "Hasta luego, Shai."

"Bye," I wave back then say goodbye to everyone else. Most of the class waves back but my friends look away.

"Liar!" CC yells after me.

I hear Soli shouting, "Leave her alone, asswipe!"

I close the door behind me, knowing what my life will be like from now on.

I'm snapped out of my memory when Tazer reaches me.

"I'm back. Zoe's a friend from school. I always see her here. I let her know I'll catch up with her next week." She plops on her towel.

Gusts of wind have the coconut palms swaying. Sweet smells of fried plantains fill the beach. A vendor walks over to us selling *pastelitos, platanitos maduros* and sodas.

Tazer buys two *pastelitos de guayaba* and freezing cold Maltas. I thank her, and we sit in the shade of the tree sipping the soda that reminds me of Pedri. When he was a baby, I'd pour condensed milk in a glass bottle, add Malta, shake it, and feed it to him; it's still his favorite. I sink my teeth into the pastry. "So what do you do for fun?"

"Surfing, skateboarding, chilling with friends at the car

races, reading, writing plays, going to the theatre and clubbing every weekend with my fake ID." She swallows, wipes *pastelito* flakes off her skinny chicken lips with her hand, and throws me a gleaming smile. "What about you?"

"I love collecting ancient music and watching foreign films, especially Cuban, French and Italian. I like Japanese animation, too. I'm hard-core into drawing, painting murals, riding bikes, swimming, reading and things of that nature. I've got a fantastic part-time job doing landscapes, on weekends. Marco, the boss, will soon be hiring me full time."

My brain feels like it's about to explode. The words I see flying around me have nothing to do with happiness. They must have been what Pandora saw when she opened the infamous box: Chaos. Cataclysm. Superficiality. Absurdity. Futility. Pointlessness. Sadness. Brutality.

I can't stop visions of what's just happened. I'm trying hard to listen but everything gets jumbled up and reverted back to when I was in my mother's *cacharro* on our ride home.

The fumes are making me nauseous. My mom puts her foot to the pedal, grips the wheel, and prays, "Ay Jesucristo, give me strength." She makes a promesa: *"If you save my child from the filth of this modern life, I'll never cut my hair for as long as I live."*

Old-fashioned Cuban mothers always make weird promises like that. I mean, why would Jesus give three and a half coconuts if my mother let her hair grow down to her heels?

I try to reason with her: "Let me explain."

She yanks my hair. "Explain? You're a disgrace to our family name. If your father were alive, he'd die. Tell me who that degenerada *girl writing you those X-rated texts is!"*

The buildings thin out around us as we speed through the school district. My mom makes a left turn. She leaves behind squat structures and drives into a well-manicured neighborhood filled with three-story mansions. The villas lose their usual grasp on me and give way to a dark blur where nothing makes sense. I've lost Mami's trust. My life is changing as quickly as the landscapes flashing by.

I stare out the window, still mute. I can't tell on Marlena. That will start World War III.

The rest of the ride is silent. We get home and walk into my mom's dark, hairspray-smelling room. She pulls up the shades and the light blinds me. I cover my eyes with my forearm.

"So that's what you've been doing every day after school before I get home from work, eh?" Mami shakes her head in disgust. "Dios mío." Tears stream down her face. "I've never been so humiliated and embarrassed in all my life. I heard details about you being with another girl. Can you understand how disturbed and devastated I feel?"

"I'm so sorry. They shouldn't have read them to you or in front of the class. That's not right." Reading those texts should be against the law. Who does that? They wanted to purposely ruin my life. I can't do the same and destroy Marlena's life. I won't.

My mom loved Marlena from the first day they met. She sensed Marlena was "decent." When Marlena told my mother she'd like to elope with her boyfriend because her parents wouldn't allow her to be with him, my mom reassured her, "Be patient and stay being the good girl you are. Eventually, I'm sure your parents will open their hearts to him." Mami had no idea Marlena was talking about me. I don't feel too good about having fooled her, but what else could I do?

I stand by the bed and look down at my two-tone shoes. No way will I fight back. She'll slap the brain juice right out of my head.

She picks up her loose hair, twists it into a bun at the back of her head, and sticks bobby pins deep into it. "I was going to surprise you with a used, sturdy car today for having made such good grades this year. I wanted to drive you to the dealership after school and let you pick it. I'll be putting the loan money right back into the bank if you don't tell me who the girl is. Which of your school friends is it—Soli, Olivia, Aracelys or CC?"

Damn. I really need a car.

I keep quiet. Marlena goes to La Caridad del Cobre High. What a lucky break that my mother and Torturous Teachers still believe it's someone from my school. Mami might never figure out who the "Evil Culprit" is.

There's a huge silence. Abruptly, we hear Pedri's school bus leaving him in front of the house. My mother walks into the living room. Pedri opens the door and runs to her for a hug. "Go to your room and stay until I'm done with your sister."

He obeys.

She barges in. "So you're still not talking, eh? That despicable girl gets to finish high school in your school, and you get thrown out?"

Her heels clickety-clack something loud in my ears as she paces the room, back and forth, back and forth. My head feels like it's about to combust and crack open.

"Until you tell me who you've been having sex with in my house, you won't be allowed to leave here, bring friends over, talk on your cell, text or tweet anyone or use your iPad or laptop." Her voice rises in a frightening tone. "I just got married with Jaime. Tomorrow we begin our honeymoon, the first vacation I've had in six years, and you do this to me now? He better never find out. I've just started my life again after your father died. Don't you dare ruin my chances of a happy life with him."

She snatches my cell from my book bag and tries to find out the number of the girl who sent the texts. Marlena's digits and info is set on private. She erases all my e-mails and storms off to the kitchen with phone in hand.

Pedri runs to me. "What happened, Shyly? Why is Mami so mad?"

I sit him on my lap and hold him tightly against me. I need to feel his love around me. "Little Punk, they threw me out of school." I hug him closer, tighter, as I gulp hard and try not to cry.

He examines my eyes while holding onto the back of my neck with both hands. "Were you bad?"

I kiss the tip of his tiny marble nose, press my forehead against his, and look into his green bubble-gum colored eyes. "Nope. They threw me out because I won't snitch on a friend. Don't worry about it, okay?" I brush his golden curls away from his forehead with my fingers and squeeze my cheek to his. He's all mushy and marshmallowy.

Pedri smiles, showing his tiny teeth and one missing front tooth. "Okay."

My mom calls him and he rushes off.

I go to my room, shut the door behind me, and throw myself on the bed. I hear my mother in the kitchen, slamming cabinet doors, and banging pots and pans. It's safe to make a quick call to Marlena.

She answers, "¿Oigo?"

I whisper everything that happened, in detail, without stopping for a single breath. "Oh, no! I should have never texted you something so private."

"It's not your fault. I was the idiot reading the texts in class. I should have known better.

"Some guys only see me as sex object now. My mother is treating me like a criminal. Most of my good friends are never going talk to me again because I lied. But worst of all, Mami read what we do in living color. I'm nauseous."

"Oh, Scrunchy." She sighs loudly. "That's horrible. What are we going to do?"

"Don't worry. No one found out about you, and no one ever will."

"Texting you in private mode is the smartest thing I've ever done. Can you imagine? I'm relieved no one knows it's me. This way, we can still see each other and work it through."

I pull off my blouse, ball it up, and throw it against a wall. It's suffocating me. My friends' and Fart Face's sickening remarks are still stuck to it.

"Everything's going wrong. I should have stayed in bed today, or better yet, I should've skipped school and have gone to meet with you. I doubt things will ever get back to normal again."

"You're out of that school already. Just transfer to a different one where people don't know you."

"But I love my friends, and I want them to trust me again." I massage my head. My temples are throbbing something fierce. "The guys will just visualize me nude. That's disturbing. Those texts were private and the most beautiful thing, ever; they weren't disgusting, like they want me to believe. I wish no one had read them. I love you so much. Nobody will separate us regardless of what's happened."

An abrupt, loud scream comes through the receiver. "Shai! Who's the degenerate you love so much on the other end of this line, eh? Speak, degenerada. Speak!"

3—Exchanges

Tazer has finished off her *pastelito* and gulps down some Malta. "I can tell you've got a lot on your mind. You haven't said a word. Hey," she licks her lips, "my dad's getting some estimates on landscapes, but he says they're too expensive. Can your boss give him a ballpark figure?"

"For sure." I give Neruda the last bite of my pastry. She attacks it and swallows it in one gulp and licks my fingers clean. "Where's your cell?"

"I never bring it to the beach. I've lost two of them here."

I pluck a piece of paper and pen out of my bag and write Marco's phone number. I hand it to her. "Have your father call Marco. He's sort of like family. I'm sure he'll give him a great price." It would be ideal if I could say, "Marco's my uncle-in-law!" But I keep my trap shut.

She stuffs the number in her surfer shorts pocket. "Thanks." She swings her head sideways, trying to get her long bangs out of her eyes. "I need a serious haircut."

I ask for the piece of paper back and write Soli's work number on it. "My friend is the wildest haircutter in Miami." And it's true. Soli's a beast when it comes to 'do's. She's so popular she's got lines of people waiting for her at the shop every Friday after school, Saturday mornings and all summer long. I lift the ends of my long hair. "Don't go by me. I just let her trim the tips."

She stuffs the paper inside her pocket. "Your hair is gorgeous." I look away. Her statement makes my cheeks feel hot. She notices and changes the topic. "You sure know lots of peeps. I'll give her a call."

It's true. I know thousands of people *and* their grandmothers!

She points to a fancy hotel with a large flashing pink neon sign. "That's a gay club. They throw outrageous parties there, out by the pool, with live *merengue* and *salsa* bands. Want to come with me this Saturday night? We'll celebrate the beginning of summer vacation. It'll be a blast."

I feel like she's opening a gate for me, but I can't go through it. I've got way too many challenges to solve.

I shouldn't have come to a gay beach. That's "queer" of me (pun intended). Here I am, terrified of more people finding out about me. I was thrown out of school *and* my house for texts from another girl and what do I do? I come to a gay beach for the first time in my life. I'm just the most brilliant kid on the block, a typical genie-ass!

"I can't, really. I have a boyfriend, and he hates me going out without him." I continue to lie for me and for Marlena. What else can I do? Hang out with a butch dyke who looks like a hot guy and have people start asking me if *I'm* homo. Marlena would never forgive me, and I'd only get into deeper trouble.

I need to stay focused on my mom's and Marlena's feelings and never get swept away by wanting a different life for myself.

"No problem," Tazer says with an easygoing smile.

I stare out past a couple of girls, holding hands. I wish that could be Marlena and me. I look to two other girls taking off their bike gear and helmets, undressing down to their bathing suits. They're so lucky to be able to be free to express their love in public.

Tazer squints. "I love this beach. I've never seen you here."

"It's my first time. I came by mistake."

"Oh." Tazer's bangs fall across her face, obscuring her surprised look.

Suddenly, I realize I came looking for a place to belong. I wish I could tell her I felt a need to come and see girls together for strength. It's refreshing to find everyone on this beach looking so joyous.

"Do your parents know you come here?" I'm curious.

"My mom died giving birth to me."

I lower my eyes. "I'm so sorry."

"It's all right. It happened seventeen years ago."

"How about your dad?"

"Pipo's never home. He doesn't know a thing about me and never asks. He doesn't even know I'm genderqueer."

"How long have you been trans?"

"Ever since I can remember, I've seen myself as a b-o-i into girls."

"Have you transitioned?" He looks so much like a guy that I wonder . . .

"No. I'm scared of the health consequences of operations and hormone shots. When you first saw me, did you think I was a girl or a guy?"

"A typical guy, but with a leftover tinge of a girl I'm sure will disappear as you get older. I guess you look like a b-o-i."

His smile widens and gleams something amazing.

The beach fills up with kids bringing in blasting music. The guys show off their muscles to other boys while playing Frisbee. Girls take off their tight, expensive jeans and shoes. They have on makeup and shiny gold jewelry. You'd think they were going out to a club.

Tazer glances at his watch. "Hey, my friend Tokyo's been waiting for me. He's having a barbecue at his apartment. We get together *y descargamos* on congas, write lyrics, and eat *puerco asado* till midnight. Just like we did in Cuba." He stands and scrubs sand off his long legs full of light blond peach fuzz. "Want to come along? I know you have a boyfriend, but we can be friends, right?"

"Of course." I lie. "But I can't go now. Maybe some other time." I don't want to tell him I need a place to live. He's too handsome. I can't accept invitations from a guy who might be trying to rescue me and take me home. That wouldn't be fair to Marlena and would be detrimental to me.

He writes his digits on a napkin. "Call me sometime. Maybe we can go watch a Cuban film."

We kiss each other's cheeks goodbye, and I watch him walk away. When he's out of sight, I tear his digits into pieces and stuff it inside my bag.

4—Falling Sky

I sit on the towel and cuddle Neruda in my arms. "Don't worry. You're coming with me no matter where I go."

She tilts her head to the right and barks, *guauuu!* Neruda always understands what I'm saying. Ever since I got her from the pound, I've been bringing her to the beach. Not this one, of course! On Sunday mornings, I normally spend time with Marlena, her aunt, uncle, cousins and my little brother at El Farito Beach in Key Biscayne. Just for fun, I dress Neruda up in all sorts of garments, like tutus and pink sunglasses or in a bikini. She usually looks like a drag queen, really, and it kills my mom with laughter each and every time. I already miss hearing her laugh.

I pack up and walk toward the road. I stop in front of a pay phone, stick some change inside and dial Marlena's number. Her grandfather answers and says in Spanish, "Marlenita and the family went to pick up her boyfriend Rick at the airport."

My eyebrows shoot up. What a great surprise. Why couldn't

Marlena have told me? I guess she didn't want to spoil our time together. As her grandpa speaks about how wonderful Rick and his family are, flashbacks cram my mind:

"How dare you talk to that girl behind my back after everything you've just put me through. Tell me once and for all, Shai Sofía, who were you just talking to? I need to go and speak with her parents. They must know what you two are up to. I shouldn't have to carry this cross alone while that girl gets away with everything. She's the one who wrote the texts and you get in trouble?"

I grab my favorite red tank—the one I wear to sleep—from under my pillow, and slide it on. I sit on my bed with my head lowered. I hear you never look into a barking, rabid dog's eyes or it'll get more vicious and could attack and rip you apart.

My mother breathes fast and heavy. "My friends' daughters are all normal. It's humiliating to be the only person I know whose child was thrown out of private school . . ."—she clears her throat—"because of explicit texts with another girl. That will go down in your records for life."

"Let's forget about it, Mami, please." I can't lift my head to look at her. I wish I hadn't called Marlena till my mother was asleep, in bed with Jaime. I'm empty-headed, brainless, idiotic, stupid!

She points in the direction of the front door. "If you won't tell me, then leave."

"Mami, no. Please," I beg.

"Go! Get out of here until you decide to let me know who the guilty party is. Your teachers need to know who she is and forgive you. I want you back in that school and her thrown out."

I stay quiet.

"If you don't tell me who the girl is right now, leave. Go. Get out!"

Like a crazed animal she tears my clothes and shoes from my closet, and throws them on my bed. My laptop gets stashed in my closet. She opens all the drawers and piles my underwear, CDs, MP3 player, Kindle, some ancient vinyl records, and shoulder bag, on top of my art things.

"I've begged enough for you to tell me who the deviant is. I don't want you living in this household until you come clean."

"Mami, por favor, por favor." *I walk around after her. She stuffs all my things in my shoulder bag, and in a huge garbage bag, and throws them out the front door.*

"Go!" *she says with tears in her eyes.* "See if your secret lover's parents take you in." *Her veins swell and pop out of her throat.* "Have them *pay all your bills, love you, and care for you, as I have."*

Pedri, hearing all the commotion through the open windows, runs to me from the swings in the backyard. "Shyly, what happened?"

Mami screeches out an explanation about my being disobedient. "Your sister knows what she must do in order to come back." *She wipes her tears with the back of her arm.*

"Don't throw Shyly away, Mami, please." *He clings to me.* "Don't go, Shyly," *he bawls.*

"Mami, I promise." *I fall on my knees.* "I'll never talk to any of my friends again."

"I'll tell Jaime I let you stay at a friend's house in Ft. Lauderdale for the summer. Don't forget to take your dog." *She goes to the laundry room where Neruda has her bed and wakes her up. She practically throws her to me.*

Pedri hugs me hard and runs to his room sobbing.

My mom pushes me out of the front door. I stumble and almost fall. "I'm sorry, Shai, but I can't continue loving you if you stay with that girl." *She calms down a little.* "I love you with all my heart. I'm doing this for your own good. When you've changed, and you're honest with me about who she is, come back."

She slams the door in my face.

A bunch of sparrows fly overhead. There's a weird brown ring around the clouds. I think the sky is going to fall. I feel an odd sensation in my chest, as if I have a hole in there the size of Cuba.

"Shai, are you there?"

"Yeah. Sorry."

"I thought you had hung up and I was talking to myself."

Marlena's grandfather and I get along great. He's interested in politics and reading Spanish newspapers to us so we never lose our mother-tongue and stay up on what's happening in Latin America.

We chat a little longer in Spanish about world events. "Communism is evil, Shai. Thank *good*ness it hasn't cast its spell around the world, taking everything down with it, including people's morale, their desire to be somebody, and hopes and dreams for a better world. Communism equals death of the soul, it makes folks limp through life . . ."

When he's done, we say our goodbyes. I feel as if a train just hit me. Not because of his usual talks, which I like. But because on top of everything I've been through, I can't get to Marlena.

Why did Rick have to come today, of all days?

Rick is an eighteen-year-old Marlena met at her uncle Marco's house two years ago. He lives in Puerto Rico all year round with his dad. He visits his mom and Marlena whenever he can take off a week or two from work, and on holidays. Marlena has to act like she's into him so her family doesn't get suspicious. That stings. Her uncle Marco, Marlena's father, Rick's father and grandfather are close friends. They want Marlena and Rick to get married one day. Just my luck!

If I want to stay with Marlena, I pretty much have to accept the Rick situation. I could easily rant against her having him as a boyfriend, but that will only destroy our bond. There's no way Rick can compare to the powerful feelings she and I have for one another. Alternating people like that, though, always shuttling between two perspectives, is something I'm glad is in my past. In some strange way, I'm thankful I don't have to go on lying anymore about *my* "boyfriend."

I walk to the mailbox a few blocks away, grab a pen and paper from inside my shoulder bag, and write Pedri a note:

Hi, Little Punk. I love you more than all the raindrops that have ever fallen on earth. Don't worry about me. I'll be okay. I want you to be a little man and behave. Don't get into trouble. I miss you SO much, Pedri. I'll call you every day.

Ten kissies on the tip of your nose.

I love you, love you, love you!

Your big sis,

Shyly.

It sucks to not have my cell anymore.

I run to the nearest drugstore and buy envelopes and stamps, something I've never done in all my life. I kiss the envelope and throw the letter in the mailbox.

I bolt into a jog with Neruda on a leash. Fast red cars zoom around like flying candy. Billboards selling perfume, silicone breasts and jewelry are everywhere.

We run a few minutes in the blazing heat, away from traffic. Every step I take, I take in the direction of nowhere. It's excessively hot. My legs feel like taffy, but I keep running as fast as I can.

I've run into someone's backyard. I look up and find myself in front of a massive San Lázaro statue encased in an altar. He's standing with a golden cane and a few dogs licking his wounds. The cane turns an aqua blue. I shut my eyes. When I open them wide, San Lázaro is walking across the yard, talking to himself. I dash after him.

"Please, please, San Lázaro, you've got to help me!"

He stops abruptly and turns to face me. I bump into him and fall to the ground. He stretches out his hand. I grab it as he pulls me up with the strength of fifty men. His eyes meet mine.

"*Muchachita.*" A man's voice speaks to me in Spanish. I shut my eyes and open them many times until the blurring subsides. In front of me is a wrinkled old man with a cane. I look to my right and San Lázaro is still encased in his shrine. "You must have fainted from the heat." He helps me up. "It's 102 degrees out. Let's go inside where there's air-conditioning."

He takes me indoors and gives me an icy-cold Ironbeer soda to drink.

I feel like an intruder in this tiny place that smells of banana custard and *cafecitos*. It reminds me of my cozy home, except mine was vibrant and lively. I can definitely see myself opening up to the *viejito* who might have the wisdom to help me solve my problems.

He asks me what happened. As I sit on his couch, I can't hold in my pain. "My mother doesn't love me anymore. She kicked me out of the house."

"Oh, my goodness." He taps my shoulder with his hand. "That is terrible news. Mothers can be so emotional sometimes."

He becomes a passive listener, which I appreciate. He's showing real interest. I wish I could tell him about Marlena, but I just can't.

I wipe my tears with my forearm. "It hurts so much." All the emotions I've been feeling surface.

He takes a seat next to me. "It must be very painful. I'm so sorry," he says with kind eyes. "Just sit here calmly. I'll put on some soothing music. You'll feel better right away. My wife is about to get home from the grocery store. Calm down and you'll see how everything will soon feel better. Once you've got a clear head, call your mother and ask her to come and pick you up. By then, she should be missing you and wanting you back." He goes to the CD player and out comes mellow, soothing Cuban *son* tunes. He sits back on the sofa with his eyes closed. "Just listen and relax. Your pup can sit beside you. This is what my wife and I do when we have problems to solve."

He is very sweet. Neruda climbs on my lap and I hold her tight.

I close my eyes and let the soothing music help me think . . .

Up until today, summer used to be my favorite time of year. I guess it could be worse. Neruda and I aren't stuck being homeless in the winter. In a few months I'll need to wear layers upon layers of clothes, heavy down jackets and wool socks. I'll have to bundle Neruda up too. I don't think we'll survive living outdoors and sleeping in a cardboard box. I better find a place to stay right away. I can't go to Abuela's house. Mami will never want me to tell her what happened. She's too old and sick and I can't bring her problems. Normally, I love being human, but not today. I mean, what are we? A brain attached to a body and a bundle of nerves and feelings? We shouldn't have been made with emotions. Feelings screw everything up. Our brain structure seems to have developed in a way that sometimes makes humans act out of hate and greed. Many scientists think we come from animals.

I doubt that.

Animals wouldn't choose to do something to someone that'll destroy their life. They don't usually throw away their children. Most moms separate when kids have what it takes to venture out and survive on their own. Animals don't have the need to buy things, demolish land, build tall buildings, use and save money, kill for money, read, ostracize, gossip, hate . . .

"Right, Neruda?" *I whisper to her and pet her back.*

If I'd been a female orangutan in love with another female, my mom would be happily picking fleas off my back right now.

"I'm glad you're not one of us, Neruda."

I open one eye and look at the little old man. He's fallen asleep with his mouth open. I should be leaving this house soon. I'm imposing on him. I might need to take another bus, but where will I go?

I feel so lost without my cell.

I sink deeper into the sofa, thinking about how Soli's the only person who knows that Marlena and I are, you know . . . in love. She caught us kissing one day in Marlena's room. We thought Soli was in the bathroom, but she barged in on us unexpectedly and said, "Sweeet! I knew it all the time!" *Marlena freaked, but we all got to talk, and Soli promised she'd never tell a single soul. And she hasn't.*

The *viejito's* loud snore shakes my thoughts out of my head.

I look around and fix my eyes on picture frames of him and his wife gardening, looking happy.

My mind wanders. I think about what happened after my mom threw me out of the house:

"Get in! Fast!" *Marlena grabs my arm and pulls me indoors.* "My family's in Key West. They won't be back till later tonight." *She presses her lips against mine.* "I love you so much. I wish I could say happy anniversary and, miraculously, everything goes back to normal so we could have the beautiful time we planned." *She hurriedly takes Neruda out into the fenced backyard with a bowl of water.*

We rush into her strawberry-smelling office-turned-bedroom. For six months she's been living in Miami Beach with her tío *Marco,* tía *Hilda, and three cousins. Luckily, she talked her father into letting her stay with her uncle till she finished high school, while the rest of the family moved back to Puerto Rico.*

She gently kisses my entire face. "She doesn't know it was me, right? You didn't tell her, did you?"

I fling onto her bouncy bed and softly pull her to me. "Of course not." I lie on top of her and fill her neck with kisses. "I'd never do that that to you. I love you."

She tosses her hair away from her face and lowers her deep-set eyes. "You're my life." She plants a moist kiss on my lips. "Tell me everything."

"She kicked me out. I stashed my things behind the front yard bush and got here by bus." I recount the entire story, in full detail. "I can't go back home unless I give her the name of the 'Evil Culprit.'"

"No way?!" Her eyes pierce mine. "You'll never, ever say it's me. Right? She'll tell my uncle. He'll call my parents in Puerto Rico. My entire extended family will find out." She's talking a mile a minute. "They'll force me to move back. It'll be hell for us. I won't ever be allowed to see you again."

"Chill, Mar. They'd have to slice my tongue off before I'd tell on you."

She rolls me over and lightly sits on my thighs. I love that she's meaty and curvaceous. Her ample hips feel good on me. "I wish you could stay here, but everyone will wonder what's going on."

"I know." I can barely muster the energy to speak.

Marlena leans into me and kisses my earlobe. I love her warm familiar breath. "What will you do? Where will you go? You'll still work part-time with Tío Marco, right? I have to see you every day."

Before I can answer, she rushes to her desk, takes out a wad of bills from one of the cabinets, and hands it to me. "Three hundred and twelve dollars."

I give them back. "No. I've got some money." I won't take what she's been saving to buy a car. I'm not going to tell her I would have had my own Jeep today. I don't want her to feel guilty.

She insists I take it all and stuffs it into my skirt pocket. "Return it if you don't use it."

"Maybe I'll go to Little Havana Hotel."

"You can't afford that. Your money will run out right away." She kisses my forehead. "I hate your mom for kicking you out. I've never *seen you so sad. Go to Soli's. She'll take you in. Just remember you're in my heart. No one will ever tear us apart."*

Marlena's the second oldest of three kids and the one responsible for having taken care of her baby sister. Her maturity is part of why I admire her so much. She means what she says, says what she means, and she'd rather have her eyes poked with needles than lie. I know I can trust her, and I appreciate that.

I wrap my arms around her and we roll around in bed. She smells delicious, like watermelon candy.

I run my fingers through her hair. "I can't stay at Soli's. She lives in that tiny duplex. Her bedroom is the size of an ant."

"You know Soli will give you a kidney if you need it."

The thought of Soli and I being close since first grade lifts my spirits a little. But still, I can't be a burden on her and her mom.

"Your beautiful green eyes look so sad, Scrunchy. Now that it's summer, come over every day, and weekends after work, as if nothing's happened. I'll have my uncle drop me off at Soli's the days you can't visit." I can tell she's worried sick, but trying to make me feel better. She holds my hands in hers. "Just make sure Soli never mentions to anyone I wrote those texts."

I brush my lips against her eyelids, kiss the freckle on her earlobe and whisper to her, "Is this my freckle?"

She half-closes her eyes. "Yours and only yours." Her voice is soft and melodious.

I kiss her forehead, the tip of her nose, down to her mushy lips. I kiss every cell of her body, from her toes, up to her neck, until I find her mouth.

Time clicks by . . . We're wrapped around each other under the covers, enveloped in a cocoon of warmth.

She slips off a silver ring and slides it on my ring finger. "Happy anniversary. I've had it on all day for you. It'll help keep you safe." The tiny green emerald set in the center looks like a loving eye watching over me.

"I got you a ring too but left it at home."

"It's okay. Don't worry about it."

A car noisily parks in the driveway. Her older brother, Arturo—the

Inquisitor—is visiting from Puerto Rico for the summer.

"Shit!" We bolt out of bed and get dressed fast. I don't feel like talking to him. He asks way too many personal questions.

I plop the wad of bills on her desk when she's not looking, and rush to the backyard for Neruda. Marlena follows.

I open the back fence. Neruda leaps all over me as if she hasn't seen me in a century. "I'll call you from a pay phone."

"Go to Soli's, please. Call me from her place as soon as you get there. I love you with all my heart," she murmurs. "You're everything to me. I don't want anything to ever happen to you."

I don't tell her I'm not going to Soli's. "I love you more." I wrap my arms around her and breathe in her delicious scent. I need to take it with me for strength.

The soft Cuban music stops abruptly.

"Excuse me sir," I say twice until he stirs. "I don't mean to wake you up." I've got to make a phone call but I won't do it behind his back.

He straightens his spine up against the couch. "Oh, excuse me, *muchachita*, for being such a terrible host."

"Can my puppy get some water, and may I please use your phone?"

He opens his eyes wide. "Why, of course. Goodness, I fell asleep. When you get old, these things happen." He yawns and pats his shirt and pant pockets. "Come right into the kitchen and use our house phone. I'm not sure where I misplaced my cellular."

I sip my soda as he gives Neruda water in a bowl. Then I call Soli and tell her I need a place to crash. Soli doesn't wait for me to finish my explanation.

"Stay put. I'll be there in three seconds!"

That's one thing about Soli: she's never let me down.

5—Tongue Tango

Soli honks. I kiss the *viejito* goodbye, thank him, and climb into her primitive, freshly painted, red VW bug.

"Woah!" I open the door and plop on the passenger seat with Neruda.

Soli has undergone a wild makeover. A silver ring is stuck to one nostril of her thick nose. Pitch-black tiny dreadlocks—which she dyed blond at the tips—stand on their ends, as if they just had an electric shock. Her cherry lipstick, orange minidress, and raspberry sandals are so bright, I think I might need to put on sunglasses.

She sticks out a pierced swollen tongue. "I'm celebrating our last day of school. I'm divine, aren't I?"

I cover my eyes. "Celestial." I get weak at the knees and beg her, "Never show me again and hide it from your mom."

Soli's always trying new things. Recently, she got a boy's lip tattooed behind her ear. This bothers her mom who believes empty spaces on one's skin should be sacred. Soli would rip off an arm and hand it to a kid in desperate need of one. She's the first to help me get a group together on our birthdays to clean trash off the beaches. Last Thanksgiving, we gathered friends to cook at a homeless shelter that helped feed the needy. I love that she supports me in everything I do.

She slaps my cheek. "Sure. Like, I'm going to hide my tongue from Mima." She blasts some trance music, puts her foot to the pedal and *off* we go!

In addition to her being smart, strong-willed and the horniest kid in this city, Soli's ability to stay optimistic about the world at large is astounding. She's earned a reputation among friends as the wildest, most fun-loving girl in our school. Yesterday, when we got our yearbooks, hers was instantly filled with memories of pranks Soli's pulled, like the day she met with Mrs. Superior-Sicko and told her she needed to take the year off to sail around the world, alone. "It's already been done by a teen, but I'd like to beat her world's record." For days, MSS tried hard to talk her out of it. When she was about to call Soli's mother, Soli agreed it wasn't a safe idea.

Soli's a thrill seeker and adventurer. We both love water sports and got hooked on sailing and kayaking—we do it during school holidays (her feisty aunt charters catamarans off of Key Largo). She talks about saving enough money to go sky diving, getting her pilot's license to fly a jet, and crazy things like that. Her love of acting in school plays has landed her many lead roles. Most of our mutual friends think she's destined to become an actor.

I doubt she'll ever do that, though. She'd like to one day buy a house for her mom and knows she needs steady, reliable work for it to happen. That's why the wackiest kid around will be going to university for a master's in psychology.

"What a screwed-up day, Shyly." (She's called me Shyly since first grade and has spelled it with a y ever since, and it's the reason Pedri spells it that way too). "Fart Face didn't want to let us leave till we told her who wrote the texts. She thinks it's me." She laughs. "I told her, 'It's not me, but if I knew who it was, no way would I ever tell *you*, or any teacher in this *disgusting* school.' I picked up my book bag and flew out the door." She momentarily glances my way. "What they did was wrong. Things like that ruin people's reputations. As if any of us in the whole class were virginal. If she'd read my private texts to my exes, she'd have collapsed from a seizure. Fart Face could have taken you aside and spoken to you in private. She should have never, ever, read those texts to your mom."

I lean over and smack her a kiss on the cheek. "You're the greatest friend *ever.*" There's nothing like support when you need someone you trust by your side.

"I don't care what they say, Shyly. I'm not going back there next year anyways. I'm transferring to Miami High. You're coming with me."

"Nope. I'm quitting school."

Without a mother to look over my shoulder, I can do whatever I want, read and study what inspires me, and live my life as I please. If my mom doesn't want me, then she'll be in for a surprise if she ever decides to speak to me again. For sure, I won't be the same person she left behind.

"What about your dream of getting a scholarship and studying art and architecture in Paris and teaching at Miami Dade College or U of M?"

"I can study and learn on my own, here. Let's change the subject."

I've always dreamed big. Even though I knew I'd never end up in France for lack of funds, what artist wouldn't want to live where art and culture were born? Paris, a city bursting with cafés where ancient, dead authors and artists like Camus, Picasso, Gertrude Stein, Alice B. Toklas and Sartre once roamed, inspires me. I've spent lots of time daydreaming about walking past the same table where Camus once sat.

I know I'm not destined to sit where past literary geniuses, existential thinkers and the intellectual elite once did, but it never hurt to wish.

In *The Sun Also Rises*, Hemingway wrote, "No matter what

café in Montparnasse you ask a taxi driver to bring you to from the right bank of the river, they always take you to the Rotande." I've always imagined walking hand in hand with Marlena through Paris, living together in a tiny attic somewhere, painting and making love at all hours of the day and night. I'd sell my paintings, and she could do whatever she wanted.

Now I know for sure I'll never make it to Paris. I can easily immerse myself in studying at home. This is the United States. The place we came to run away from communism. Everything is at our fingertips, readily accessible if we search for it.

Soli and I talk about the Incident. I tell her every single detail that happened after Fart Face dragged me out of class.

She wags her head from side to side. "Those teachers are out of control. They need a good roll in the sizzling sack." Abruptly, she surprises me. "I told Mima about you and Marlena being together."

"What?" I spring up on my seat. "Are you *insane*? You know Marlena thinks people will believe she's a sicko who goes around checking out girls' boobs."

Poor Marlena. The shadow of homophobia with its pointy fangs and massive claws follows her everywhere. I'm scared too, and always have been. But she feels terror. She's actually told me if anyone finds out, she'll kill herself. Marlena's obsessed with wanting people to think she's straight.

"That's insane."

"Not really. Look at the way CC and Olivia acted."

I throw her a steely look. "You shouldn't have told on us, especially on a day like today. Marlena can't find out."

Leave it to Soli to tell her mom about me after what I've just been through. And besides, just because I'm in love with Marlena doesn't mean I'm ever going to label myself a lesbo. I prefer wandering across the world (or at least my corner of it) without a stamp on my forehead. At this point I won't put my personal life out there for everyone to keep gossiping about.

I tremble inside to think Soli will start telling other people and it'll soon reach Marlena's and my mom's ears. "Chill." She twirls a teeny dreadlock around her index finger. "I told Mima the day I caught you guys doing the Tongue Tango, almost a year ago."

"Holy pube!" I cover my face with my hands. "Your mother's known *all* this time?"

Soli's mom is the sweetest, kindest lady you'll ever meet. Honestly, she's like a living saint. Just last year she had fifteen strangers who came from Cuba living in her teeny rental duplex. She fed them, found them jobs under the table cleaning houses, and cheap efficiencies for them to live in. I guess I shouldn't be too worried about her knowing. I'm sure she won't spread the word.

Unlike Viva, most older Miami Cubans are religious and conservative. Some embrace gay guys but find girls together disgusting. Some gay Latino boys are more open about their sexuality. They're praised as "fabulous" and "funny." Some right-wing Latinos are so whacked. They think lesbians are a perverted breed out to destroy common decency.

I know my culture has come a long way, but the homophobes need to read everyday stories about girls who like girls. That way, we'll be seen as "normal."

"Yup, Shylypop. You know Mima's amazing because of her belief in metaphysics. She's known forever and has never treated you or Marlena bad, and she's never told anybody about it." She lifts her pencil-thin right eyebrow. "She loves you like hell even if you *are* a homo."

"I'm not homo, turkey. Labels are so constricting. I don't want a target on my back. I'm just in love with Marlena."

Soli's talking about my being lezzie, and I keep telling her I'm not gay; I'm just me.

The thing is I don't know *any*thing about living a lesbian life. Soli thinks my loving Marlena stamps me as one. Like I said, I want to be free to be myself without being branded, especially at this crucial time in my life. I'm not a cow. I'm a human being.

"Sure. You're not a lesbo, and I'm not an Afrrrrrro Cubanita."

I smile simply because she thinks she knows it all. And what the hell. Maybe she does. But then again, she might be wrong. I jam up the radio, squeeze Neruda to me and stare at the cars rushing by us. She swerves in and out of lanes, passing cars as smoothly as if she were gliding down a water slide.

I lower the music. "You think Olivia, CC and Aracelys will forgive me for lying?" These were my good friends at school, since I can remember. I dread the response.

"They were the *worst*. You know how dramatic Olivia and CC are. The drama queens said they'd rather lick scum off toilets than be your friend again. They're pissed you fooled them. If they don't get over it, they were never your friends."

My heart is feeling something heavy.

"Don't stress, Shyly. You've got *me* and all my friends. Who cares about those stupid thugs, anyway."

Soli never hung with CC, Olivia or Aracelys. I'd spend time in recess either with them or with Soli and her friends. They didn't dislike one another; it's just that they had nothing in common. CC, Olivia and Aracelys are into impressing others with the schools they plan to attend, like Yale and Harvard. The truth is the only thing their parents can afford is a community college. To Soli, those three are transparent, self-indulgent, ego-centered snobs. To me, they're just giving the world glimpses of what they'd really like to do if they had the money.

On the other hand, CC and Olivia dislike Soli because she says it like it is and spends far too much time with me.

Soli asks me to tell her every gory detail about what happened with my mom. I let it spill.

"Your mom's a nutsack." She slaps my cheek. "You'll be all right, Shylypop. You're staying with us. Don't you worry. Mima and I adore you."

I love Soli to death and back to resurrection, too. I guess I'm lucky to have a great friend I'm tight with.

As she drives and we bop our heads to the music, I think about some of the wacky things Soli and I have done. Like the time she motivated a bunch of school friends to spy on our science teacher, a renowned celibate, Ms. Asunción (better known as: Ms. Ass) with a remote control robot we'd given her as a present—Soli bought it at a spy store, and it had a teeny hidden microphone installed deep inside its head. We, and the rest of our mutual friends (the ones we both like), were thrilled to hear Ms. Ass talk about us in the staff room. We felt she was far too stunning to be celibate. The entire school thought she and Ms. Mariela Lagos were lovers. Sadly, we never found out anything scandalous.

I bet next year CC and Olivia will tell Ms. Ass what we did. Luckily, I won't be there to get in trouble. Unfortunately, I'll miss our good-humored tricks no one found out about because we were such exemplary students.

Soli dumps me in her front yard and yells to her mom, "Mima, Shyly's in bad shape!"

Viva comes to me, picks me up by the waist, and swings me around. "Shylita!" Her eyes light up so much, it makes her pastel pink polyester housedress look even brighter. She doesn't make me feel ashamed or embarrassed, like Mami, Fart Face and my "ex" friends made me feel. So I try to act normal and give her a bunch of *besitos* on her cheek.

Soli lets Neruda loose from the front seat. She runs full speed to me, as if I were a steak on the loose.

"Later, gators!" Soli waves goodbye. She booked just two people for haircuts today and is leaving for work early. She works cutting hair at Heads Up, where she meets more guys than most people have hair on their head.

Don't let Soli's stories of one day wanting to climb snow-capped mountains and teaming up with me to turn black burbling oceans from capsized oil into crispy clean waters veer you from her true nature. Her biggest passion? Boys.

I carry Neruda in my arms so she doesn't run after Soli's car. I sing to her, "Nerudini Miniweeni wore a size three bikini. I took the poet to the beach, now she thinks she's a genie." In case you're wondering, I have two sides to me: a deep thinker and a ditzy blonde.

She licks my face as if I were a snow cone.

"Nerudi is full of sand, Shylita. You need to take her a bath."
Viva pushes my hair away from my face. "Soli tell me what happen." Her tiny slanted eyes show concern. "I is so sorry, *mijita*.
Your mami and those teachers has a lot to learn in this life. Your
mami will come around. She just be in shock. You and Nerudi is
welcome to stay here until she lets you back. And if she no let you
back home, you stay here forever."

I let out a long sigh of relief that must have been stuck in
my spleen.

You can fool yourself into believing people you care about
will always love you, no matter what. It isn't until they take action
and prove it, one way or the other, that you'll truly know for sure.

"But you must keep in touch with your mami and tell her
where you is living. Keep tings organized and take care of Nerudi
so she no ruin nothing. She cannot do *caca* or *pipi* in the duplex.
Okay?"

I kiss her café-colored cheeks. "Thanks, Vivalini. I'll organize every day. And don't worry. I've trained Nerudi to not poop
or pee indoors."

If she's so kind to help me, I'll make sure I'll be at my best
behavior and help her as much as I can, too.

I place my little mud-ball on the ground and she runs after
a lizard.

Viva starts in about how I need to register at another school
right away and finish my education.

"I'd rather pierce my eyeballs and get a tattoo of Sai Mu on
my chin than go back to school." Sai Mu is a swami guru with
an Afro she's in love with, but she won't admit it. She drools
when she looks at his pictures, which, by the way, are in a collage
framed and hung on one of her bedroom walls. I try to be funny,
just to get out the pain that's stuck inside me.

"*Ay*, Shylita." She lets out a sweet laugh, like a lullaby.

I dash through the doors and pass Viva's altar to Sai Mu surrounded by mangos, bananas, tangerines, stones and leaves. The
duplex smells fruity fresh and it livens my spirits.

Viva scoops up my little fleabag and follows me indoors. I

leave a text for Soli: *pick up my things from behind the cherry bush after work.*

6—La Gringa

Viva left to clean a house—what she does for a living—as I was scrubbing Neruda clean. Finally, I'm showering.

I've been blocking thoughts from my brain while soaping myself and humming songs my dad sang to me as a kid. He'd make his voice go deep and strong, then high and soft. He'd sing:

Shylita, my chiquitica
is the cutest mariposita . . .

Every day when he arrived from work I'd hide behind the front door and "boo" him as he walked inside. He'd place a hand to his heart, turn his head left, then right, and say in a quavering voice, "Bring back my daughter, spirit. I can't live without her." I'd appear before him and fling my arms around him. He'd pick me up and swing me around. "She's alive!" he'd scream and eat me up in little kisses. There was nothing like curling up in my dad's arms and feeling loved, safe and protected.

I miss my dad. If he were alive today, he'd have put those teachers in their place. Papi would have never allowed my mom to kick me to the curb.

I hear loud bangs and turn off the shower. *Boonga-boom-boom!* I can tell it's Soli banging on the front door. She's got a key. I know she's knocking just to bother me.

I've stayed to sleep here many nights. The first time she knocked that way I thought she needed my help. I dashed to open the door with my heart in my mouth. She cracked up at my expression. Her ways don't fool me anymore; I'm onto all of them.

Neruda rushes to the door and barks up a storm.

"I'm coming! I'm coming!" I dry up in Soli's room and scramble around in my bag for my jean shorts and green, hol-ey, sleeveless T. I slip on my sandals, jump over piles of Soli's clothes, get to the living room, and swing the door open.

Soli bolts through it. I try my best to crack a smile. "Wasss up, Hootchi Momma?"

"*You're* up, Shylypop! And I won't let you get bummed!" She picks me up, throws me over her shoulder, drops me on the flow-ered peach and orange couch, and holds my wrists down.

I struggle to get out from under her. "Get *off* me!" She's got me pinned down good and has started to tickle my stomach. Twisting and turning, I howl, "Stop!"

"See, I win every time, ha!" she smiles triumphantly. She takes my face with both hands, presses her lips to my forehead, and kisses me with her usual loud, *Muuua!* "Eat your Wheaties for breakfast and spinach for dinner, you big wussy. You ain't nothin' but a wimpy fembo."

Soli and I have always loved goofing off. Introspective as I may be, I've always been an extrovert, like her.

But Soli doesn't get that right now I need silence and peace, something I've never craved. The day-to-day rowdiness that comprised our happy lives seems like something of the past. I just can't get into the playful banter we always had going. I don't want to push her away, but I'm in no mood to fool around. Still,

I'll do my best to make her feel I'm okay.

I unexpectedly pinch her left boob and she lets out a ballistic laugh. I push her off me and rake my dripping wet hair back with all ten fingers. I pass the arched entrance into the bright orange kitchen filled with spider plants and hanging copper pots.

A gringa-looking girl with shoulder-length strawberry-colored hair, green eyes, and long arms and legs follows Soli into the kitchen. "Shyly, this is Rynn. She's a lezzie." She turns to the girl. "Rynn, this is Shai, but you can call her any nickname you want. She has dozens." That's true. It all started the day CC proclaimed, "No one without a nickname will be accepted into our Honorable Ho's Club. Nicknames for everybody!" The club was started by Aracelys. She wanted to befriend girls who wouldn't lie or gossip (what a crazy idea, since that's what girls normally thrive on). That day, everyone had a different nickname for me. They had no clue I was the only one in our group who'd withheld information that kept them from getting a real glimpse into my true life, or I might not have been considered an "honorable" enough member to join.

I guess I can see why they're so pissed. But then again, how praiseworthy and respectable is it to shun a friend simply because she likes girls? Well, maybe it's because I lied, but a fib can be easily forgiven. I have an inkling it's all about my sexual preferences.

I couldn't help lying. I didn't mean any harm. Even if Marlena hadn't been so terrified of my telling anyone about her, I probably wouldn't have told my friends about me, either. Who cares how I spend my private time, anyway? So *what* if I invented a boyfriend in Spain who expressed his undying love for me by Skype and e-mails? They should forgive me and get that I was scared to tell them about me for fear of losing them. I knew enough about them to know they were always making fun of dykes and making grotesque faces and remarks if they thought a girl liked them.

"Hey." We kiss each other hello. Rynn stands up against a wall with arms folded over her chest. She barely moves and reminds me of a lamppost.

I have a gut feeling Soli's bringing her here so I can start having lezzie friends to chill with. Rynn is really attractive. I have trouble looking straight into her eyes.

I pour ground Café Bustelo into the coffeemaker and before I can ask her about herself, Soli begins:

"Shyly's a trip. She loves to paint. She can't live without e-books, nerdy romantic music, and she turns old men's golfing polyester checkered pants into shorts and bandanas. She's Green and visits homeless and sick kids at shelters. She's going to change the world and is antichemicals, against pollution, hates pesticides and she rarely eats meat," she tells La Gringa, as if she gave a royal raccoon's whisker.

"I eat everything, but I'd rather spare some animals' lives when possible," I tell Rynn and turn to Soli. "How would *you* like it if people roasted *you* and had *you* for dinner?"

"I wouldn't mind. I'm sure you've grilled Marlena up good and taken a few bites out of her."

When Soli and I are with a bunch of new Facebook friends, or just someone I've never met, she makes me the center of attention. The first few times, I didn't know where to hide. Eventually, though, when I realized everyone got a kick out of it, I ran with it. Now, she's starting with her mischief. She's never talked openly about Marlena and me to anyone. I guess what happened today gives her the license to do so. She knows word's already spread all over Miami about my lascivious acts and she feels free to loosen her tongue and say what she wishes.

"Shyly's thinking of becoming a nun."

"Really?" La Gringa has question marks in her eyes.

"Yup." I try to keep on a serious face and ask if they want fruit but they don't. I grab a plum from the fridge and bite into it with a snap. "Ninety-nine percent of nuns proclaim the right to withhold information about their sexuality. In fact, most nuns lead underground romantic lives. Right now, if we were to peek into a convent bedroom, we'd see them embracing and getting down, way down. It's a party every night at the convent. I'm headed there tonight. Want to come?"

La Gringa chuckles.

The plum is so sour I make a face and throw it back in the fridge.

I prepare *café-con-leches*. The smell of freshly brewed per-colated espresso fills the duplex. Soli takes a sip and adds more espresso to her cup. "Dark is better." She's talking about her clove-colored skin.

Rynn's face beams brighter than a flashlight. I can tell she's fallen for Soli. Too bad Soli's not into girls. Rynn seems like a great catch.

We're interrupted by a sky filled with rioting hawks in flight, and we gaze up through the bay windows in awe. They leave our sight and I catch a glimpse of mandarin and lemon trees basking in the sun. Why is there so much chaos in this world when life could always be this beautiful?

They sit on the living room floor as I grab one of my archaic CDs from my shoulder bag on the couch. I put on my favorite song, *ever:* "Girl from Ipanema," by Astrud Gilberto and Stan Getz.

I go to the fridge, take out a box of *churros*, and throw it on the coffee table. I always feel at home when I'm here. In some ways, I feel as if Soli is my sister and Viva my second mom.

Soli rips open the box. "¡Grrrr . . . *qué rico!*" She sticks a *churro* in her mouth and nudges La Gringa in her skinny ribs as she crunches away. "I told you she'd put on geeky, three-hun-dred-year-old music, didn't I?"

Rynn grins and her adorable, slightly buck teeth stick out.

"Where did you and Soli meet?" Her eyes dart around, checking out the wall-to-wall plastic framed paintings of saints, colorful goddess figurines, tall plastic banana plants, the mural I drew two years ago of the ocean and plastic pink chandeliered lamps (Soli's mom decorated the place).

We answer at the same time, "La Virgencita de Guadalupe Elementary, the worst Catholic grammar school in the history of the universe!" Soli slaps her right thigh, and lifts an eyebrow.

I dunk a *churro* in my *café-con-leche*, stick it in my mouth, and munch on it. "We met in first grade. Her mom cleaned the school, and she got free tuition. Soli was the only black kid in school. She was really shy to ask others to play with her. I befriended her. We played at recess and had a blast."

I remember all the fun times Soli and I had in elementary school, and the trouble we'd get into simply because of our rebellious nature and fast-paced brains. We were the two in class who always raised our hands first, with such enthusiasm we nearly pulled a muscle and practically fell off our seats. "I know! I know the answer! Pick me!" we'd say in unison. We'd spend all day studying together at Soli's house after school (the bus dropped us off here, and then my mom picked me up after she got home from work) and so we were confident we knew all the answers.

Then there were the times I disagreed with teachers when they weren't prepared. If I got told to go to the back of the room for disrupting the class (informing educators their research was way off), Soli joined me on her own accord. "I agree with Shyly." At the end of the day, teachers took a liking to us and never really punished us or gave us detentions. How could they? We always handed work in on time and were too eager to learn, please and get good grades.

She smiles proudly as she texts a few of her boy toys. "Shyly's my closest friend."

"It's good you had Shai for a friend." La Gringa sips her *café-con-leche* slowly, as if scared of finding a goldfish in it.

Soli dives in. "Shyly just got thrown out of school *and* her house." She explains the reason my mother kicked me out. My stomach starts to burn something terrible. Rynn listens calmly.

I feel vulnerable as Soli talks about my texts in vivid detail. I don't want to think about what happened anymore. I avert my eyes to the windows, gaze up, and see the aqua sky floating by as if it were an ocean of clouds.

Rynn doesn't even bat an eyelash. "No big deal. Those texts were sweet. You should see the ones my ex and I sent each other." She turns to Soli. "Shai's uncomfortable. She's looking away from us. Let's talk about something else."

I'm impressed by her sensitivity.

The conversation twirls to the fact Rynn is single. She likes to date many girls without getting attached so one day she can find the right one. "I've never been in love," she says. She's got a lot in common with Soli.

Rynn spins the subject around and speaks about the ultra-chic haircut she wants Soli to give her. I'm in my own world, thinking about my day, when Rynn touches my shoulder and my thoughts dissolve and shift to her. She wants to tell us a "story." Soli and I prick up our ears.

"Last year on spring break my mom came to visit us from Oregon. After their divorce, she and my dad still get along. We went to Kingdom COMEedy, a teen street drag show with my drag queen brother Joaquin. Our mom dressed him up and he performed as 'Tatiana Titi.'"

Soli and I burst out laughing.

"Tatiana Titi and her gag partner, Temper Tantrum, dressed to kill. They wore outrageously colorful feathered outfits and tall, thick wigs. They performed the funniest comedy act you've ever seen. The crowds were in stitches, until Tatiana Titi changed her tacky clothes and transformed into Joy, an elegant girl." She looks away from us, then down to the floor. "The audience became dead silent when Joy sang a love song whose lyrics she wrote." She pauses a moment, then goes on. "She got the biggest stand-ing ovation. Then, out of nowhere, Reina appears from the back of the stage. She hugged her so hard and told the audience she wanted Tatiana Titi to be on her next *Drag Me Down* TV show!"

"Yeah, Bitches!" Soli and I honk. That's our favorite pro-gram, the only one we never miss.

La Gringa clears her voice. "Joy started doing serious under-ground drag shows when she was twelve. That's how she made her money." She throws out a sweet smile then looks down at her long skinny fingers with the saddest eyes I've ever seen. "I'm so relieved she's got a chance for a better life now."

I put my hand on her shoulder. "Yeah. I hope she wins. We'll be rooting for her."

A deep silence fills the room. Suddenly, Soli and I realize Joy was leading a really hard life and now has her first chance for a future.

Rynn abruptly changes the subject. "What high school will you be transferring to?"

"I'm quitting school forever." I take a hot slurp of *café-con-leche*; it goes down smooth. "And you?"

"After my parents divorced, I told my dad if he didn't transfer me to Delphi High, I'd go live with my mom in Oregon."

We talk more about her dating life till Soli spins the focus back on me. "I can't believe what Fart Face did to you." She takes a few slurps of *café-con-leche*, then bites into a *churro*, and the sugar crystals shower the floor. Neruda licks the floor clean.

"That's so horrific." Rynn's a great support, which is amazing.

"If teachers at your school had found texts like mine, wouldn't they have kicked you out, too?"

"No way. Our principal is trans. Your instructor's behavior, then expelling you, would never be permitted in my school. In fact, I think it's against the law. That's a cause for hiring a pro bono attorney. That teacher and principal need to be fired."

She's right. But then I'd need to tattle on my mother. She'd get in serious trouble for throwing a minor out of the house. When loving parents who make one wrong move are involved, it's hard to know what to do.

"I can't snitch on my mom. I need to walk away and forget about it," I tell her. "Your school sounds incredible."

"It's an expensive private school for intellectually gifted and non-ignorant genius kids." She goofs off and throws me a suave smile. "Like *moi*."

Soli says, "Shyly's wicked-smart. A straight-A student. I make A's and B's, but her grades never waver. Wish she could afford to sue their ugly asses first, then go to Delphi. If I were wealthy, I'd pay for her tuition there."

Rynn's expression turns droopy. "If I had money to use as I wanted, I'd help you out, too."

I really like this girl. She's a person with a heart. I want to open up to her, but feel a little shy about it.

Rynn wipes her line-of-a-lip with a napkin. "Delphi is a great school. It's because you were at a Cuban private school that you were treated that way. Conservative teachers suck so bad."

She clears her voice. "My parents are the best, though. They're totally open-minded. My uncle is an ignorant Republican, like all the right-wing assholes here. He hates gays, blacks, environmentalists and shit like that." She shakes her head. "He's twisted. And to top it off, he lives with us because he lost his job. I can't wait till tomorrow. I'm heading to Oregon for summer vacation to be with my mom. I'm like my parents. My uncle, your mom and your teachers are ignorant fools. You're a million steps above them all."

Soli changes the conversation. She always does just when things start getting intense. She hates talking politics, or anything serious, for too long. She says, "It cramps my style, Shylypop."

She starts advising me. "Today, all the hoodrats who made fun of you or did you wrong need to be erased from your mind. Don't you *dare* give them the time of day again."

I start leafing through pages of a magazine, catching every word she's saying, without seeming sad.

Right before the Incident, Soli and I had been spending some of our spare time at the beach, swimming, rollerblading and things like that. We never had the need to give each other guidance or vent about problems. We were too busy having fun.

I want to reach out and hold Soli and Rynn's hands and tell them I really appreciate their support. But something stops me. I suddenly feel gloomy beyond my control and don't want to start sobbing.

Soli does a three-sixty. "Hey, tell Rynn how I used to wear pigtails in elementary school."

I pull my little tick-machine to me and squeeze the furry ball into my arms. Soli's trying to entertain me. She knows I'm going through hell and wants to make me laugh. I don't want her to feel bad. So I start:

"She always had three pigtails, two on the sides, and one on top of her head. She looked like she was sprouting trees."

"Hey!" she slaps my knee. "I was *way* ahead of my time."

"Absolutely!" I pinch the tip of her nose. Neruda barks at her in agreement. "Her mom starched and ironed her dresses every morning. Her uniform was stiff as a board."

Soli tosses her head back, and lets out a melodious laugh. Her eyes light up. "Remember how Mrs. Agria used to grab your cheeks and pinch them hard when you were sketching instead of paying attention in class? Remember the day Mrs. Guantes cut your shaggy hair in class, and gave you short bangs because, she said, 'I can't see your eyes under there. You do have those round things inside sockets, don't you?'"

"What a whacko!" Memories fly around me.

She faces Rynn. "In third grade, this girl, Olga, once yelled to me, 'Black Bootie Bitch!' Shyly screamed to her, 'Look who's talking. You're white like dirty sour milk, at least *she* looks like yummy chocolate!'" Soli goes on. "Another time Olga screamed to me, 'Hey, Charcoal!' Shyly said to me, 'Don't pay attention to her.' She pulled me by the hand, took me to the far corner of the playground, and started making jokes. She made me laugh with her wacky sense of humor." It was hard for me to see the way that one girl had it out for Soli. I'm glad I was there to protect her.

I look to the colorful friendship wristband I gave her for her birthday and remember she and I were the only kids in our class without fathers. Her dad died of a heart attack a month after mine passed away. Soli was as inconsolable as I'd been about Papi's death. We were there for each other to console one another. That was the only time I've ever seen her weep uncontrollably. Every year, around the time our fathers died, Soli, her mom and I do candle rituals and dedicate the day to our dads. We spend it remembering them and doing things they loved, like horseback riding, eating their favorite foods, playing catch (they both liked baseball) and things like that.

Having grieved together bonded us in a way that's indescribable, and that's why our friendship is indestructible.

I rub the wristband she gave me for my birthday, and we

throw each other a smile.

One thing about Soli is that things never get to her unless they're huge (like the death of her father). She's not sensitive like me. Look at all the horror that kid put her through, but as long as she had me, she didn't care. And she's not neurotic about it, either. Nothing fazes her. Everything that happened to me today will be stuck in my heart—like a sharp knife that gets twisted in there—for*ever*. Soli says she's never even cried about all the horrific names Olga called her. Things just slide off her chest easily. And that's a large chest, let me tell you!

I wish I could be like Soli. I don't know why I'm so thin-skinned. It's a curse, no doubt.

Viva comes indoors and spreads kisses. "¡Eh, *familia*!"

"Rynn," I jut my nose over to Viva, "this is Viviana Celina de la Risa Catalina del Carmen Cabrera Prieto de Santillanos." Viva giggles and her chubby belly ripples. I can tell she loves that I've memorized her entire birth name. A little thing like that is a bold statement that matters to her, it says loud and clear that I care. To Viva, a gift like this is far better than anything material I could possibly give her.

She plops on the couch and fixes the little mercurochrome-colored bun on top of her head with bobby pins. When she finds out I haven't yet called my mother, she reprimands me, "Shylita, call your mami *now*. Tell her you is staying with me."

Viva and my mom don't get along too well. Let me rephrase that. Mami doesn't respect Viva too much. She thinks Viva doesn't know how to rear children. She disapproves of Soli doing whatever she wishes and says, "Allowing a girl to roam the world on her own and go in and out of the house as she pleases, isn't a sane way to raise a child. That woman is missing some screws. How can she not place rules for Soli to follow? I can understand if Soli were a boy."

Isn't life ironic. I don't see Viva kicking her daughter to the curb anytime soon. They have a beautiful relationship based on love and more love.

"Yeah, Shyly, get it over and done with."

I hate having to do this but I must. I'd rather be in denial and focus on the times I'd look up at my mom, naïve, questioning and she regarded me with tenderness. If I'd go to her consumed with grief about a parakeet or hamster that had died, she'd hold me and reassure me, "Everything's going to be okay. Go ahead. Cry. Crying is good." The following day, she'd come home with a baby pet.

How can a mother change so drastically on you?

Soli throws me her cell. I drag my feet as I pace up and down the living room. I feel my heart in the pit of my stomach as I press my mom's digits. I know I have to call her or Viva won't let me stay.

"¿*Hola?*" she answers in a stern voice.

"Hi, Mami." I shake inside; it feels like a marble is stuck in my throat.

She growls, "Hi, Mami? Hi, Mami?" She repeats it, as if I didn't hear her the first time. "How will a 'Hi, Mami,' ever take away what you've done to our family name? You've disgraced us." I gulp knives and razor blades and bombs that explode in my stomach.

"Mami, please relax." I sit next to Viva on the couch and lay my head on her lap. She gently smoothes the hair away from my face.

"Re*lax* when your own daughter gets thrown out of school for obscene texts and lies about having slept with that degenerate in my house? Is the *degenerada* Soli? Is it?"

"No, Mami. It's not Soli. I swear on Papi's grave." She knows I only swear over my father's dead body to say the truth. I close my eyes. "Mami, I'm in really bad shape. Don't make things worse." I feel like I'll die of a heart attack if she keeps this up. We've never really fought. Of course, we've had your typical arguments, but she's been the type of fun mom all my friends wished they had.

"If Jaime finds out, I'll kill you!"

I go on with a trembling voice. "Viva will let me stay at her place if you don't want me anymore." This is a hint, to see if she still loves me and wants me back. I mean, if I were a mother, I'd want my child back no matter what.

"How could I want you after everything you've put me through? The humiliation! All my friends will find out about this. You've ruined my life, and you'll be a bad influence on your little brother. Can you imagine if he'd found and read those texts?"

The cell is on speakerphone. Everyone's hearing everything.

"I've replaced the locks. You're never stepping foot in here again unless you tell me her name. That girl's parents need to know what she did and how her actions have destroyed our lives. Go ahead, stay with those immoral people who enable you to not be honest with your own mother. Live it up. You'll have no rules now, and no one to set limits or tell you what's right or wrong. Have a fun life." She clicks the cell off.

I feel my throat tightening. Tears want to burst out of my eyes but I won't let them. I need to keep it together.

"*Uy*, Shylita." Viva helps me sit up. She lifts my chin with her index finger. "Your mami loves you *mijita*. She is just scaring you into changing."

"Shyly, don't worry. Your mom's just overreacting because she's shocked and hurt. All this time she thought you were straight and her close friend. Give her some time. In the meantime . . . you're about to start your full-time job and you've got us."

Rynn jumps in. "Your mother's the one with the problem, Shai, not you."

Why doesn't it feel as if my mom destroyed our relationship? Why does it seem like it's all my fault?

People in good relationships take them for granted, as if you knew your loving family will always be there for you no matter what. No one ever teaches you that there are threats to your life that can instantly destroy everything that was once precious.

Something feels broken inside me. I'm so damned lost.

Soli tells Viva about how there are millions of homeless kids and some commit suicide after their parents kick them out of the house. Viva's eyes show concern. "We love you *mucho, mucho,* Shylita. Tings will be better. You will see." She smoothes her hand on my face. "I is going to buy you a bike in a little while, after I take a bath. No need to get yours at your mami's. And soon, I will buy you a cell phone."

Viva takes a *merenguito* from her dress pocket and hands it to me.

I don't want anyone to worry about me, or think that maybe I'll be ending my life, so I act goofy. "Yummy! White plastic sugar!" I lift it in the air. "*Merenguitos,* nothing can be better for a quick diabetic coma!"

Neruda takes a flying leap and almost grabs the *merenguito* from my hand. The right side of Viva's lips lifts as she giggles. She holds my hand like only a mother can. She kisses my right cheek and Soli kisses my left cheek. I think that maybe, just maybe, I'll live through all this.

7—Landscapes

Rick stayed in Miami two weeks. Marlena and I were bummed. She had to see him every day. The good thing was that she snuck calls and texts to me every second she wasn't with him. And, we talked every night via video phone before going to sleep. Yesterday, Rick the Dick left. Woooo hoooo!

Last night, after an early no MSG Chinese takeout dinner, while listening to blasting music, I helped Soli weed her closet of clothes she'd outgrown. I learned something about Soli: she kept Sunday dresses she wore as a kid in a box, tucked away in a corner of her closet. She said, "They remind me of happy times when Pipo took me to parks and museums."

Her floor ended up littered with piles of clothes she'd grown out of. I ended up adopting jeans, minidresses, sneakers, sandals, vibrant colored blouses, shorts and winter jackets.

Viva came by shuffling her feet in a silly dance, carrying a bag full of clothes she spilled at my feet. "They no fit me no more." She pulled out a pair of flowered, gabardine slacks. "I has them since Cuba." She plucked a checkered polyester blouse and eyed it against my chest. "This color be beautiful on you, Shylita."

I loved everything nerdy and geeky. Instantly, I fell for the retro bell-bottoms, garish colored blouses and polyester pants she made me try on. I couldn't wipe the smile off my face.

Before I went to sleep I called my mom again, to see if she'd changed her mind. She hadn't.

This morning I woke up at four a.m., sighing. I did yoga on top of the rollout sofa-bed to ward off the feeling of doom settling inside me.

At five, after a breakfast of almond cereal, milk and berries, with a boiled egg for protein, I quietly rushed out the door on my tall handlebar bike Viva bought me.

I raced through traffic with a warm breeze blowing in my face, contemplating my dubious future. I practiced talking to my mom in my head in a soft tone. "I'm just a child. Don't you care what happens to me? Remember what you used to say about Viva's rearing habits? If I didn't have Soli, I'd be sleeping in the streets. What kind of a mom does that make *you*? Please take me back."

Nothing came out right. I always seemed to blame her.

I couldn't knock the thoughts and feelings of desperately wanting to go back home out of my head until now.

I've just arrived at the site where I'm about to start a full-time job with a crew I've never met.

Tazer's dad hired Marco's company. We'll be working on the front yard landscape of his three-story villa.

Tazer is nowhere in sight. I park my bike and see the crew waiting for me. Everyone looks about seventeen to twenty-one. I glance up at the sun and it disappears behind a dark cloud. I don't blame it. I feel like hiding too.

Angel, Marco's partner, tells me in Spanish, "I want you to keep an eye on the gang until I get back with more trees and mulch. I don't know these people well. Marco just hired them. I trust you to not let them slack off."

"No problem." I couldn't care less about anything right

now. He could've said, "Your job today is to pour truckloads of venomous rattlesnakes on the plants for fertilization and lie on them," and I would have answered, "*¡Fantastico!*"

Before he marches, he explains what needs to be done, which sounds like, *Blih, blue-blah, bloh, blih-bleh*.

I look at his unshaven round face and nod as he's talking. I know my job by heart.

Angel tells everyone that texting, talking on the cell, or listening to our iPods or MP3s isn't allowed. "There are dozens waiting in line for your job. Kids spend their lives tweeting and hearing music and getting nothing done. If that's what you want, then leave now and I'll get replacements." We'd need to hand him our cells, iPods and MP3s every morning upon our arrival. He said Marco's niece, *moi*, is in charge until he arrives. I leave a smile from ear to ear on my face, that hurts to keep plastered on, till he leaves. I guess Marco and Angel want to lie about me being Marco's niece so they won't laze off.

Landscaping bosses always leave new workers feeling unsettled, restless and desperate to make plans behind their backs, like bringing extra cell phones. They don't understand that an incentive, mixed with encouraging words, and trust, will motivate employees into wanting to follow rules and go the extra mile from the get-go.

As soon as Angel bounces, a short, scrawny guy who looks my age, with flaming carrot-colored hair, shining green eyes, a puffy lower lip and a grease stain on his left cheek says in a husky voice, "*Hola*. I'm Che," as if he were the prince of the world. He slaps me a high-five that makes my hand sting. "I'm named after the revolutionary. My father is Argentinean and my mother, Cuban. They were both crazy about him. I'm not, but it's too late to change my name."

"Hey." I throw him a smile.

He's got a tattoo of two nude girls on his left arm. Their breasts are hanging out all over the place. Just what I need so early in the morning: a freshly peeled look at life.

In the crew there's an olive-skinned girl with a sweet, dazed look in her made-up doey eyes that makes her look sleepy. She's got straight, dark hair with tiny, heart-shaped, painted peach lips. A pinkish skin discoloration takes up the entire right side of her face. She's wearing large gold earring hoops and tons of gold bracelets. You'd never think she'd be the type to get her hands dirty in a job like this.

She throws a shining smile my way. "Hi, I'm Camila."

"*Hola.*" I kiss her cheek. She smells tangy, like orange zest. Every time I get a whiff of a citrus scent, it brings me right to Marlena, a tangerine aficionada.

I turn to the next person.

An attractive, short, snowy white stocky girl, wearing a sleeveless purple tank—as little as a bathing suit top—showing hard muscles and soft mannerisms, gives me the biggest smile of all with two adorable crooked front teeth. Her hair is buzzed, which makes her tiny ears stick way out in a funny way. I guess you could call her androgynous.

A dimple the size of a dime pops out when, with sparkling crystal blue eyes, she says, "Hey, what's cookin'? I'm Jaylene Morenson." Her cheeks flush, as if she dabbed on rouge when we weren't looking. She shakes my hand.

"Hi." I smile.

So far there's an andro, a macho sicko guy and a drowsy girl in my crew.

I've worked part-time long enough to know that eventually someone will bring forth madness. Like Gauge—a guy in my old crew—who believed he was an alien from another planet. He filled our ears with stories of his people's "heroic intentions" to land here and show us how to rule over ourselves. He'd say things like, "In my dimension, we don't posses the urge to kill, experience greed, or the need to manipulate. I'm here getting my PhD in evolutionary paleobiology. As a professor, I'll teach humans about us, so one day you're ready for our arrival. You keep beaming signals into space about silly snack foods. You should be broadcasting the need for help with your unsolvable social problems, like death, poverty, war, drugs and bullying."

Gauge talked about how "perplexed" he felt living among humans and our strange mating habits and rituals. I wasn't disturbed or amused by any of it. I figured he'd been reading far too many dystopian novels, until, of course, he told Marco, "I need to leave early to get to a doctor's appointment." The following week he came back with stitches, saying, "The doctor inserted an iron metal rod inside my esophagus so my people in my dimension can follow me more carefully."

Because of Gauge, I knew to expect the unexpected.

Che smacks his gum and stares Jaylene up and down, up and down, with elevator eyes. I can tell something weird is brewing in his swollen, cocky brain.

A tall, husky, ruddy guy dressed in a crumpled-up blue T, worn jeans and a bright red nose, speaks up. "*¡Hola!* I'm George Prios." His hands are calloused, and he's got an intense look in his coffee-ground eyes, as if he's ready to jump into work. He smacks the arm of the burly guy next to him. "This is my big brother, Rey. He speaks just a wee bit of English."

"*¿Qué pasa, calabaza?*" Rey's large copper-penny eyes smile. "At home they call me El Tigre." He's wearing all white, has got thick moppy honey-colored hair and a bushy, dark beard. He's stocky and does remind me of a tiger. He extends his hands for a strong handshake.

The crew now consists of the andro, a snoring girl, a wacked-out sicko perv, the roaring tiger and his intense workaholic brother. We're missing the homophobic nun to wipe the smile off the lesbian, a coffee distributor guy to wake up the snoozer, and a priest (or rabbi) to "cure" the perv.

A shipment of trees, plants and flowers was delivered yesterday. Marco's weekend crew placed them according to the design. I look around me. Everything's a huge pile of trees, like a messy jungle.

I adore trees. They lift my spirits with their green brilliance that helps choke back pollution so we can breathe cleaner air. I feel lighthearted, as if I've just hiked up a mountain and with every step, I've let my troubles slip away.

Jaylene rubs the nubs on her head while everyone just stands around, as if waiting for instructions. I know they know what to do; they're probably just testing me.

I remind them, "My uncle Marco wants us to push the plants back and dig holes *exactly* where the plants were."

"*¡Bárbaro!*" Che grabs a shovel and gets to digging right away. He's working next to me, showing off his scrawny, popped-out muscles. It's strange to look at the girls on his arm. Every time a muscle moves, they squirm around. Maybe he gets more action from watching the tattoo than in real life.

I dig a hole that's three feet in diameter and depth, and stick a small bottle palm in it. I love the way the tree looks pregnant. I shovel the earth back into the hole and plant a bed of purple flowers around it.

I remember the day my mom told my dad she was expecting over the phone.

"We're going to have another baby!" Six months later, my dad came home from working in New Jersey as a horse trainer (he was always away six months out of the year). When the doctor said my mother needed constant rest or she'd lose Pedri, he prepared dinners every night for the three of us after he arrived exhausted from work. "I don't want your mom to move a muscle," he'd say. On weekends, instead of our usual movie night, he'd rent DVDs. The three of us watched films cuddled on the couch. He was always spreading kisses, giving my mom foot massages, scrubbing, laundering and doing chores while whistling around the house.

The night my mom's water broke, my father ran out the door, climbed into his car, and started the engine without us—and with his pjs on! We brought him back indoors and helped him pick clothes to wear. His hands were shaking so much he could barely drive to the hospital.

I stayed in the waiting room with my grandmother. My dad came out shouting, "It's a boy!"

Che nudges my ribs and releases the memory out of my head. He points to El Tigre. "For a whole year, that guy asked

Cuban authorities to allow him to come visit his family here to no avail. They kept denying him because they considered him an 'antisocialist blogger.' He came in a *balsa* in shark-infested waters, in secret, without telling a soul. And that dumbo-eared girl with the guy's haircut," he juts his nose in Jaylene's direction, "she's into girls, guys and anything that moves."

"So what if she's try-sexual?"

"Oh. You're one of those, too?"

"I was joking."

"Well, if you're not careful, Shai, she'll soon be after your tail."

My heart beats fast. The palms of my hands get sweaty and I wipe them on my overalls. I stand on the shovel and jump on it a few times to loosen the earth under me. It won't take this nosy guy too long to figure out my life. There's no way I'll even hint at having once been known to friends as a free-spirit, artist, free-thinking environmentalist who transformed into a special-ized lying piece of shit nobody wants.

"She won't get *my* tail, that's for sure." The last thing I need is for Marlena's uncle to find out about Marlena and me. He'll realize what's been going on under his nose whenever I sleep over at his place. I'm positive he'll tell Marlena's family and we don't need more drama and heartache.

I've got to make sure to keep my relationship intact and sacred.

He whispers loudly so Jaylene, across from us, hears. "Don't be fooled. Those girls will haunt you till they catch you . . ."

I interrupt and catch him off guard. "Oh, so you're saying they're as bad as some guys?"

He stares at me for a moment, then says, "That's not what I meant. Just be careful with bi's." He sniffs the air. "I can smell them a mile away. They prey on beautiful girls like you. When they capture you, they leave you for a guy. After they've used the fellow up, they'll leave him for another female. It's a vicious circle."

I want to roll my eyes at the empathy, utmost care and

consideration he has for people who aren't like him. I'll keep chucking whatever he says out my imaginary window and go on working. I hate that I'm stuck with a judgmental guy. Where's the morbidly endearing Gauge when I need him? The truth is that sometimes Gauge broke my heart. When everyone shunned him, laughed at him, or told him to shut up, I wanted to pull up a chair next to him and ask him to tell me more stories. But Che, no way. I know he already expects a lot of comments from me, and for me to take his side, as he judges everyone.

I don't respond.

He points toward Jaylene. "I can turn any *invertida* around. Once *tortilleras* and bi girls have a taste of me, they *never* go back." He smirks. "They just need a *real* man."

This must be the stupidest guy on the planet. "I doubt that. She'd probably prefer a dildo to do the job." I feel like telling him he could stick his shovel where the sun doesn't shine, but I don't.

I can already hear him spewing one tangent after another, rambling away his misogynistic thoughts about lezzies and bi girls. If he knew I was closely connected at the heart to that subject, I wonder what he'd say. Having to deal with this type of idiot isn't going to be fun. I wish I had a stronger personality and the courage to ask him to zip it.

Jaylene overhears and comes over to us. She wraps her hands around the shovel handle. "A *real* man?" She bores holes into his pupils. I love the way she stands up to him.

He grins and spits on the ground. "Yeah. You're just too scared to try me." He smiles. "I told you I'd give you the best time you've ever had. I'll shave so smooth you'll think you're with a girl."

"Just because I like both genders, and am up with the queer movement, doesn't mean I'm insane. Your type doesn't do it for me, Crud." She says it loud enough so everyone hears. Everybody looks up and stops working.

"You tell him," George speaks up and turns to Che. "I've got a few girls I can introduce you to if you're having a hard time meeting females."

Before Che responds, I say, "Hey guys, my uncle's coming back soon." Surprisingly, they get back to digging. I keep digging, trying to mind my own business, but Jaylene stays put.

"You know what they say, don't you?" she asks Che. He shrugs. "Well, I won't give you the pleasure of finding out." She leans over and whispers into my ear. "They say imbecilic macho ignoramuses like him have small shriveled up worms. They have to prove their masculinity by talking shit. You think any girl into girls would ever go for *him*?"

I want to laugh, but I don't. I need respect in this job. I've got to play it wise and safe and befriend everyone. On the other hand, I admire people like Jaylene and would like to get to know her better. She doesn't wear a façade and will probably expect the same from me. I don't think I should undo this mask any time soon, though.

"Oh, so you like me, eh?" Che tells her. "You're giving me so much attention."

"If you were the only life-sustaining force on Earth, I wouldn't date you, an obvious misogynist maggot."

He lets out a chest full of anger. "At least I don't try to hide my true lust behind bisexual political theories. You'll hook up with anybody. Admit it and we'll move on."

I realize these two have a history of which I don't want to know about. "Guys," I interrupt. "Come on." They shovel in silence.

Jaylene is the first to finish the biggest hole of all. Without asking for help, she picks up a small, heavy date palm tree and places it in the hole she dug. She throws in the rest of the soil and pats the earth down. She plants white lance-like flowers in a circular way around the tree and goes for the hose. She knows her stuff.

Che is having a hard time with some coral rock. He's hitting the rocks extremely hard with the shovel, with a lot of force, trying to break them loose. "*Oye*," he looks up to me as he wipes sweat off his brow. "She's just acting tough because deep down she's into me. I took her to the movies once. She didn't text me back. I know she's playing hard to get. I bet if I ask her out again, she'll hook up with me."

That's all Jaylene needs, a worm after her butt. "Ask her and see." I stick the shovel in a crack on the earth and whack my foot hard against it, thinking it's Che. I'm cracking open his skull to plant colorful flowers in there. He needs something pretty to shake up his messed-up head.

"Those bi's will screw anybody. That's all I wanted from her. Come to think of it, I won't ask her out again. I'm glad nothing happened between us. You better stay away from her if you don't want AIDS. Who knows what STDs people like her are carrying." He continues to shovel.

I've never met such an idiot in all my life. I'm going to have a lot to deal with in this crew.

8—A Tazer Seed

Morning passes quickly and before you know it, Tazer gets home. Angel is off with Jaylene to the tree warehouse nursery. Tazer comes by with *croquetas de pollo* and cold pineapple juice for everyone.

"*¡Gracias!*" The crew throws down their shovels and runs to the snacks.

We walk away from them and stand under a tall, bushy, Gumbo Limbo tree. He's looking really handsome in khaki pants and sandals and a dark forest green tank top that shows long lean muscles.

"*Oye, chica*, you look sweeeeeet. Long time." He smacks me a kiss on my cheek.

"Hey. Good to see you again." In a strange way, I'm excited to see him. I just hope he won't bring me problems with Marco.

It's tempting for me to befriend Tazer and people like Jaylene, but it's not easy to cross the boundary I've kept myself behind and step into other territories right now. All I need is to lose Marlena because of one simple slip. My friendship needs were so fulfilled until the Incident. I don't like feeling isolated when I have a string of new people I can befriend, right in front of my face. I know Marco will find it strange if I talk too much to Tazer, but not if I stick with Che.

"Look what I found while digging." I stick my hand in my pocket and bring out a smooth turquoise-colored stone. It's got thin black streaks around it. I'm saving it for Pedri. I love to give natural things like rocks, leaves and hand-picked dried flowers. They mean something special, and you can save them forever.

He scrutinizes it as he rubs his fingers over its smooth surface. "The markings are so artistic, as if someone drew them. I love it. Thanks."

Oops. He thinks I'm giving it to him. That's okay. I'll find another one for my little brother.

Tazer's thick dark eyebrows and sparkling eyes are stunning. His skin is smooth as a mango peel. It's too bad he dyes his hair with chemicals. Maybe I can get him to change his mind about growing back his natural color.

"You look striking in boots." His smile radiates.

"And you look handsome in pants."

He lets out a smooth, boyish laugh.

"Hey, where's your dad?" Angel needed to show him the backyard design I drew with Marco's help last week, when I didn't realize we were at Tazer's house. Marco points to the trees and plants from a book, and I draw them in. It's a piece of guava.

My favorite part of my job, though, is to be allowed to sketch in some elements of surprise, unexpected moss paths, wild bushes or anything I'm moved to draw, really. My strength lies in being able to see an empty lot and know how to make it beautiful simply by following my gut feelings. I need to keep proving to Marco I no longer need photos of trees to know how to design.

When I was little, I was always engrossed in playing a computer game my father gave me for my birthday. As soon as he realized I was in love with painting jungles and forests, he got it for me. I'd place a kid (myself) in a forest. I sketched myself surrounded by toucans, wild animals and all sorts of colorful plants from my imagination. I befriended the tigers and rode the elephants. In the end, it became one big animated story I shared with my family. My mom said it was the only thing that kept me still for hours when my father was away in New Jersey, working.

"My dad, well . . ." Tazer stares at his long fingers, "I practically live alone with our maid, Sulima. My father's a workaholic. He's only here when he's got an appointment. He's juggling two girlfriends and he's always flying them places."

I'm always surprised at how unpredictable people's experiences can be compared to what they look like. I'd have never thought someone so joyous would have a dad who doesn't care. You'd think folks with parents who neglect them would be in a corner, weeping all day long. I guess anyone could say the same thing about me, now that I belong to that special tribe of "orphans" with parents.

I'm glad he feels comfortable telling me intimate things. I guess he can see I'm a trustworthy person.

"Now that my father's rich, on weekends he flies them all over the place—one at a time, that is—especially to the Caribbean. If he didn't send me pics of him on my cell, I might not know what he looks like. Luckily, he texts and calls me once or twice a day."

His words remain floating in midair. He tries to smile, but I can see right through him. I *to*tally get it. I wish my mom would start sending me pictures of her and Pedri.

I can't relate to a noncaring dad, even if I barely ever saw him. He was the greatest father who's ever lived. I yearned daily for the moment to see him arrive from New Jersey and carry me in his arms. My father read me comics when I was sick and took good care of me when my mother wasn't around. He loved me more than life itself. But now he's gone, and all I have are pictures and memories.

Tazer's father should wake up and realize that in one second, everything can end, and he's wasting his time by not embracing his only son. I ask him a lot of questions because I'd like to get to know him better.

I learn that in middle grade, he was a star soccer player at his school's co-ed soccer team and won many trophies. His greatest dream was to one day be on the U.S. Men's National Soccer Team.

"In high school, they only had co-ed and exclusively girls or boys' teams. I was only allowed to play on the girls' team, which I refused." He made a fuss and became an activist, fighting for kids like him to be allowed on the boys' team to no avail. "I almost moved to New York to join the New York Boys' Soccer Team, where a genderqueer friend played," he said. At school, he became a bit of a rebel and made many friends. To this day, he says he's friends with his elementary school "buds." Back then he couldn't face moving away to New York and leaving them behind.

Tazer is so charming. I could see him being extremely popular.

We move farther away from the crew and stand under another Gumbo Limbo tree full of oval-shaped dark green leaves.

"Too bad you didn't get to play on the boys' team, but I'm glad you stayed or I'd have never met you." I feel my ears turning red and look away from him. I'm saying what I feel and hope that Marlena won't be upset. I can't help but want to tell him something nice since he opened up to me. I can always let Marco know I was speaking business with Tazer. I bite my thumbnail. "Do you ever miss not having a mom?" I lean my back against the cool-feeling copper-red bark, stuff the *croquetica* in my mouth, and wash it down with a sip of delicious pineapple juice.

"Not really. I don't miss what I don't know and have never had. But I still long for my family in Cuba." His smile reassures me. "What's terrific is that I have no one on my back telling me what to do. I've got a lot of different types of friends, and I'm always out and about. Like tonight. I'm staying over at Teal's apartment. She's twenty-four, her body is filled with tattoos, and she's filmed a documentary on Cuban lesbian exiles. Teal's having a viewing party for select friends. They're all older than me. Some are even my dad's age."

I lift my eyebrows in disbelief.

"We're critiquing the film for her to help her make it better. When they leave, she and I will be up all night editing the piece. I'm sure my father would disapprove. But hey, if he started getting into my business now I'd just move away. I love him tons, but it's too late to have him meddle in my life."

He changes the topic. "How's it going with your boyfriend?"

The more we talk, the more I like him. He's smart, rugged, yet tender all at once. He's got a softness about him and a strong sensual voice that matches his tall, slender and lean muscular body. He's generous and sensitive in a sweet boyish way. I can tell he's a fun, deep, smart and good person with a great heart. Something strong within me wants to be his friend. I wonder how I can work it out so all parties involved are happy and tongues won't start wagging.

I cover the glare of the sun leaking through the branches with the palm of my hand. "Great," I say. "I love him to death." I'm talking about Marlena, of course!

"Grand. I didn't tell you when we met at the beach, but I'd just been dumped after a silly argument about food. I refused to eat pizza. She wouldn't bend. Dori climbed into her car and screeched away. That night, I went to her place and there she was with a husky baseball player guy." He scrapes pieces of peeling bark from the tree with the stone I "gave" him. "The guy came to the front door and shook my hand when she introduced me as her ex."

"Woah. That must have burned."

"It stung. Especially when she started telling him personal things like, 'Tazer's a girl underneath it all.'"

I wish I could tell him he looks like a hot sexy guy, and he'll soon find someone worthy of him, but I don't dare. He might think I'm making a move on him.

Tazer puts a hand on my shoulder. "Let's forget about me and my woes. Are things okay with your mom?"

I'm caught off guard. "Well . . . uhh . . . well . . . let me put it to you this way . . ." I jump in and tell him about a "dyke's" texts to me, without mentioning her name. I explain the way I was treated afterward and how my mother threw me out of the house. It just pours out of me. But I lie. "The lesbian wrote in explicit detail what she'd do to me under the covers if I dated her, but I'm not into that." I go on and on.

His eyes widen. "Hell. The teacher read it to the class?"

"Yeah. It was horrifying." I look away from him then smack into his eyes. I don't want him to know about Marlena and me. I'm almost sure this information will be safe with him, but I doubt Marlena will allow it. I don't blame her. I mean, Marco knows the guy and his dad now.

"I wish you'd told me at the beach your mom had just kicked you out." He looks at me with a sparkly puppy-dog face, the type Neruda puts on when I pet her belly.

I look down at my working boots. "It wasn't the right time. I was dealing with too much."

"I get it." He bites the skin off his thumb. "We have a lot in common. We can do what we like with our lives without parents hounding us. We're free to be ourselves without needing to follow rules. That can only be a great thing."

"I don't know, Tazer. I'd rather have my mom and brother back."

"Freedom comes with a price. I guess you can get lonely without a family who cares," he admits. "On the other hand, you'll make decisions on your own. You'll mature quickly and have a thrilling life while you're at it. Oh, and the best part is that we never need to come home if we don't want to." His smile makes his eyes glow.

"I still have a curfew. I'm living with my best friend and her mom. She's easy but there are rules."

"If things get too strict over there, you can move here. I'm serious. My dad will never, ever know. This is pretty much my own place."

"Thanks."

There's a certainty in Tazer's voice, a tone bordering on "everything in life is grand and will work out just fine" that's energizing. I relish his self-assuredness and love his enthusiasm.

His smile broadens. "Now that we're getting to be friends, I'm stoked you're being honest and sharing with me."

Yeah, I'm more honest than a pathological liar.

This sucks. What the hell am I doing? Here I am with a fantastic person I could talk to truthfully about my life and what do I do? Tell him lies to keep protecting my girlfriend and me. I probably shouldn't have said anything at all.

A soft breeze comes our way. He pushes his long bangs away from his face. We stand, just feeling the gust on our faces.

"Breezes like these could make anyone a believer," he says.

It's true. On such a hot, muggy day this wind makes me feel like we're floating on an ocean wave.

I sip the sweet drink and it goes down soft as rainfall. "A believer in what? In a god?" I don't know exactly what he means.

He crosses his beautiful arms over his flat chest and leans his broad shoulders on the tree. "I'm certain I'm one with everything and everyone that exists and existed, and together, we make God." I know many people who believe the same thing, but that's not me.

We talk about our philosophies. I let him know that in fourth grade, I stopped believing in a god up there with a little wand after my buddy Ray died of a complication from Chronic Fatigue Syndrome and Multiple Chemical Sensitivities. I prayed so hard that year. I even went to church on Sundays. The day Ray passed, I started thinking about poverty, war, illnesses, rapists, pedophiles and how unjust the world was. That's when I began critically reflecting on everything I'd been taught that suddenly made no sense. My parents and teachers didn't know how to answer my questions. My dad kept saying, "God is a mystery and we don't know why he chose to take Ray." Our teachers said idiotic things like, "It was God's will Ray died," or "Everything happens for a reason," a cliché I've learned to hate.

"If there's a little girl right now being stabbed in the heart by a kidnapper, suffering as she bleeds to death *for a reason*, and a teen somewhere having the time of his life traveling the world after inheriting a billion dollars, then this is a truly insane world."

"I agree," he states.

"That's why I can't be part of things that are evil. No way could I be one with Hitler, murderers and criminals."

"So what do *you* believe in?"

"In myself and in something I call Sacred Nature. Feeling one with nature soothes me. She feeds all of us. That's why I must take care of her and keep her sacred. When I'm in nature, I feel connected, like I belong. It's as if I know where I come from, and where I'm going."

"Nice." He cracks a big juicy smile.

I talk to him about how jails are filled with murderers and serial killers with faith in god. "If I were to create my own religion, it would be called True Environmentalism, you know, the type where people actually practice what they preach. There are plenty of my ex-school friends' parents who called themselves Green yet spray their lawns and dogs with pesticides, wash clothes with chemicals instead of nontoxics, and use chemicals for everything."

"I get you."

"I also believe in love from my little brother, my best friend, her mom and Neruda. They'd never hurt me, or anyone else.

"I don't think I'll ever trust anyone again except for the four I mentioned. I no longer believe in people. They can turn on you from one second to the next. And nature . . . well, it's always had its natural catastrophes before people polluted the earth, but now it's letting us know it's suffering greatly by expressing its pain with more severe hurricanes, earthquakes, tsunamis and tornadoes. It's trying to save itself from the extreme pollution folks keep making that has everyone getting sick. I see it like this: if you're allergic to smoke and someone locks you in a room full of cigarette, cigar and pipe smoke, you'd whirl around the room like an insane maniac, too, trying to find a window to leap out of."

I change the subject. "You don't use pesticides here, right?"

"Nope. I'd never do that."

I open up to him a little. "My dad died of kidney disease

caused by pesticide poisoning a year after my little brother Pedri was born. He was a horse trainer, and he used to spray the horse corrals with that junk to keep bugs away. The doctor said pesticides seeped into his bloodstream and fried his kidneys." In Cuba, my dad was an engineer and a pilot, but since he didn't know a word of English, he ended up working at his hobby (he adored horses).

"That's awful. I'm sorry."

I lower my head. "Thanks. I was thinking . . . you've got so much land that, after the landscape's installed, maybe I can come over and we'll plant an organic veggie garden together. Then, we can watch foreign films. Just please don't tell anybody here or Marco about it. It's a long story." I can't believe these words just slipped out of my mouth so easily without considering Marlena first. I need to do what feels right for me. I don't want to upset her, but she must understand that I need friends right now, especially because she has a boyfriend on the side and won't let go of Rick.

"For sure!" He gives me a knuckle-to-knuckle punch.

I notice Angel parking and Jaylene climbing out of the truck and heading off to work.

"Hey, it was fun talking with you but I've got to go," I tell Tazer. "Do you have a CD player?"

He raises his voice to the crew. "It's retro boom box time! Get ready for beats!" He runs off and comes back with a huge, ancient ghetto blaster and blasts some tunes.

"¡Música!" the crew trumpets.

Jaylene makes up some *cha-cha-cha* steps on the spot and wiggles her butt. "Cuban power!" She twirls once, twice; *uno, dos, tres*, then goes back to digging.

"Jaylene's definitely gay," Tazer assures me.

"She says she's bi and calls herself 'queer.'"

"She's too butch and political to be my type. I like feminine girls."

I look around me. The rows of palms we've planted remind me of the Cuban countryside, of women on stilts with windblown hair. Soon the emptiness in Tazer's land will be transformed into paradise. Maybe that will happen to me too. While I work, I'll scoop out every bit of love I had for my old friends who shunned me, and plant a Tazer seed in my heart. Who knows? Maybe it'll grow into a magnificent friendship tree. I don't know. Just maybe.

9—Yours and Only Yours

For the past two months, it's been a blast living at Soli's. I'm sleeping on the living room pullout couch and it's super comfy. Of course I miss my mom and brother, and think about them 24/7, but that's another story.

Soli, Marlena and I go to the movies with Soli's friends, and whoever she's dating, on some weekend nights. Afterward, we hit the beach boardwalk. Surprisingly, Marlena has allowed us to walk with our arms around each other as Soli and her straight friends do. I'd like to stray with her to spots where no one can see us kissing, but Marlena always thinks there's impending danger. "That's reckless. What if they catch us?" she'll say.

"Who'll find us half a mile away hidden by shrubs?"

No matter how much I try to talk her into it, she won't budge.

I still go on Facebook every day even if it still kills me to know CC, Olivia and a few other friends I've known forever X'd me out. A lot of my elementary school friends are there, some from high school. They're into very different things than I am and we barely get together.

I help Viva clean, wash clothes, organize and cook. I've taught her to play chess. She's become addicted to the game. Every time we're together and have spare time, she wants to play. Usually, I allow her to eat my queen, simply because it thrills her. She had thought it was a game for intellectuals and scholars and had been scared of it. She's gotten so good I'm going to need to stop giving her chances!

Just for fun, and to behave like eccentrics we've seen in foreign films, I've had Viva pose for wacky portraits wearing outrageous hats, large sunglasses, miniskirts and knee-high boots we get at the thrift shop for pennies, while listening to loud opera for inspiration. She's such a sport. That's one of the reasons I love her so much. We sell the paintings at Little Havana's Cultural Friday Art Festivals for big bucks. I try to give her half the money, and also pay rent and food, but she won't accept it. She makes me save it in the bank so I can buy myself a car. My mother still won't let me come back unless I spill the *frijoles*, but at least I get to talk to Pedri every day. He sneaks calls to me when she's taking a bath.

Marlena hasn't been keen on my befriending anyone gay or trans, especially Jaylene or Tazer. She's jealous and thinks everyone's into me. When she isn't happy, it leaks into our relationship. I still want to keep things smooth. That's why I keep making up excuses. I started telling Jaylene and Tazer I couldn't chill with them and their friends because I was spending time with my "boyfriend." Luckily, after we stopped working at Tazer's house, I've never seen them again and we've quit texting. I don't feel good about lying, but Marlena has nothing to worry about now.

Some days after work, I throw my bike in the back of Marco's truck and we head on over to his house—he always invites me to eat. I rinse off with a hose before diving into his Olympic-sized pool with Marlena. We compete to see who swims the fastest. I usually win, but then end up allowing her to beat me by doing a slow version of the butterfly stroke. After dinner, and a few real-ity shows we watch with the whole family, we head to bed. When everyone's sleeping, Marlena and I explore, traveling slowly through specific points of destinations. We have a beautiful time under the sheets.

There's terrible news, though.

Last week, Marlena's brother left early to go back to Puerto Rico because of an emergency with his girlfriend. As soon as he arrived, her parents called. They said she wouldn't be finishing high school in Miami, as they'd promised her. They missed her too much. Her mom had already enrolled her in "Academia Escolar" a private, highly expensive high school. Now she has to return to Puerto Rico right away to start classes in a few weeks.

We just finished an exquisite brunch with Marlena's fam-ily: ham steaks with pineapple chunks dripping in their natural juices, fluffy plantain omelet, Cuban bread drenched in dripping butter and glasses of guava nectar.

We sigh in unison when the taxi man honks.

Marlena's *tío* Marco, *tía* Hilda, *abuelita*, and little cousins help Marlena and me carry her bags into the taxi. We kiss every-one goodbye and climb into the backseat.

From now on I know what to expect. I'll be stuck in a dense fog between the Island of Missing Her and the coast of Hell. Marlena's departure is hurtful in a way that only secret lovers can understand. Her family will miss her, but never as much as I will. I've tasted all of her, kissed her starting at sunset, all the way up to dawn, while her two moons lit up our nights. I'll miss her warm body stretched out next to mine so much, but I can't show it so she doesn't get too sad.

A bearded Cuban guy with a hairy chest and bushy arms remarks, "*No hablo inglés.*" He doesn't speak English, and that's great with us. He puffs on his big fat cigar even if there's a sign that says: NO SMOKING. Disgusting smoke ringlets float up to the ceiling.

We roll down our windows and I throw my head out for fresh air. I look past the expressway, toward the shoreline filled with neon apartments. Marlena's uncle's house is getting smaller and smaller in the distance, and my heart sinks.

I look at Marlena and my trying to hide my feelings goes out the window. "I can't believe you're leaving. It's so damned depressing. What will I do without seeing you every day?"

"Don't worry. After my eighteenth birthday I'll come here for work. I promise." She whispers, "Nothing will ever separate us."

I shake my head. "That's six hundred years from now. Can you imagine not kissing or making love for that long?"

"*Uy*, Scrunchy. It's a year and seven months from now." She averts her eyes from me and stares out the window. Marlena's not the expressive sort who likes to reveal her feelings and opinions to anyone but me. But right now, her cool, distant and introspective demeanor feels as if she's pushing me away. I mean, it's the last time we'll see each other in ages. I've got to get her to stay close.

I scoot down to where Hairy Taxi Guy can't see me and whisper to her, "Okay, okay. I'll wait for you till my teeth fall out and I turn into a wrinkled prune."

A bunch of guys pass us in a Jeep blasting disco music. They're holding hands and having a blast, like they just don't care.

Hairy Taxi Guy throws them a bird. "*¡Maricónes de mierda!*" He tries to repeat it in English, "Focking fags full of sheet!"

I slouch down with my knees up on the back of the passenger seat. "What a prince."

Marlena looks into the rearview mirror to make sure Hairy Taxi Guy isn't looking at us or trying to understand our conversation.

Finally, she opens up.

"It's so much easier when no one knows about you, Scrunchy. Our sexuality shouldn't be in people's faces anyways. I love it that our relationship is secret. It makes us more passionate about trying to find time to be with the other. When you don't sleep over, we have to hide just to kiss." She smiles. "Hiding makes everything extra special. What we've got is so beautiful. I wouldn't change it for the world. I bet people in relationships like ours last forever."

I look at her incredulously. "You wouldn't want to ever hold my hand in public like everyone does?"

"Nope. I know if you could you'd change me just like *that*." She snaps her fingers and her bracelets *clink-clank* all the way down to her elbow. "Can't you see how it makes us so much more desperate to be together?"

"I think we'd be that way no matter what."

Marlena is somewhat of a tortured soul. She wishes she could be free of feeling terrified about anyone finding out about us. "In my next life," she once told me, "I want to come back with an all gay family. I'd like to live in an all homo world without a single straight person in it."

Recently I let her know I had an urge to become politically active against bullying. She freaked and said, "All we need is for you to draw attention to us by becoming one of those crazy raving separatist lesbians."

She lifts her hair up from her neck, lets it loose, and down comes a cascade of curls. I take a good look at her and my world spins. Unless I visit her, I won't see her beautiful face for almost two years.

I grab my sketchbook from my shoulder bag. "I'm going to sketch you one last time. I won't be able to do it again till *la luna* drops from the sky."

She throws me a smile that is so warm and tender. I wish I could stick it in my pocket so I could keep it forever. "Great." Her eyeballs roll over to Hairy Taxi Guy, then to me. "But just act normal." I knock off my sandals, remove my seat belt, lean my back against the door, and put my feet on her plump thighs. Now I have a reason to stare at her without Hairy Taxi Guy thinking I'm a weirdo homo.

I outline her profile with my charcoal pencil: her sunken eyes, a nose that broke when she fell off trying to ride a bike, the delicate shape of her lips, her round chin, elegant neck and a big

puff of hair. I fill in details: her cheekbones pop out, her hair becomes wild tumbling locks, her thick eyebrows and long spidery
lashes come alive in smudges of wavy browns. I even catch the
way she's looking away, so Hairy Taxi Guy doesn't get any ideas.

A deadly silence falls over me as wind funnels in through
the windows.

As I take my colored pencils and color everything in, words
flash in front of me. They crash deep into me like wild waves,
inspiring me to add the final touches:

Luminous. Anxious. Dire. Tender. Lush. Breasts. Plump.
Caresses. Humid. Radiant. Melancholy. Languorous. Tears.
Shoulders. DON'T GO! Desolate. Drenched. Collapsing. Arms.
Emerging. Soaring. Moist. Mouth. Breath. Sea. Dripping. Coiling.
Nibbling. Wet. Bewildered. Liquid. Breathless. Sliding. Moist.
Panic. Sobs. Thistles. STAY HERE WITH ME! Trembling.
Desperation. Soaking. Laughter. Hungry. Soft. Succulent.

I've drawn pure beauty.

I pat her thigh with my foot. She looks my way and I show
her the sketch. She throws me a sweet grin and goes back to being her pensive self.

I guess Skype, texting and e-mailing will have to do for a
long while. I'm buying a video phone with a large screen today.
Looking at each other's faces will give us the strength to over-
come anything, especially Rick's distractions.

Traffic is thrashing by. Cars are zooming from lane to lane,
swerving fast in front of us.

I cross my arms over my chest and eye Marlena suspiciously.
"I'm sure you're wrong about what you said yesterday and I *can*
come visit you."

Last night, while lying in each other's arms (Marlena's aunt
thinks I sleep on the pullout sofa in Marlena's room) Marlena
said, "There's no way you can come visit me. My parents will
figure it out." Those words startled me.

No one had ever been allowed to sleep over at Marlena's
house when she lived with her parents, except me. Her family and
I got along well. Our moms were always talking and exchanging

magazines and recipes.

Her sweet dad was threatened whenever a boy who wasn't Rick called her. He'd put on a fake, rugged voice to announce a lie while she spoke to the guy: "Rick is on his way here, Marlena. You don't want your boyfriend waiting outside for you too long, do you?"

I, of course, was thrilled—her father staved off boys interested in dating my girlfriend!

She leans against the car door and sticks her elbow out through the window. I think she's hiding something from me. Lately, since her brother Arturo left, it's as if she's keeping a major secret inside her, but she won't talk about what's bothering her, no matter how much I ask.

Minutes pass and she doesn't say a word. It's so quiet you could hear a mosquito pee.

"It'll be weird if you visit me in Puerto Rico. I have fifty-two cousins. They won't leave us alone a second. We won't have a minute of privacy." She sighs. "I don't want to talk about it now; it's too stressful."

It's insane she's opting to not see me for those lame reasons. I try to let it slide. I know she's in as much turmoil as me and I don't want to make things worse.

A song comes on about Juana Palangana—Bedpan Juana—who looks like a banana. I can't bear seeing my Marlena so sad. I try to make her laugh and rotate my hips in my seat, snap my fingers, and make beatbox drum sounds with my mouth, *Gún-dún-dún-gún!*

She cracks a loving expression. "Hey." I jut my chin in the direction of her fingers and whisper lightly, "Are those *my* fingers?"

She wiggles them, throws me a shining grin, and whispers as low as if we were in church, "They're all yours."

"If they're *all* mine, then I want them to stay *here* with me. Don't take them back to Puerto Rico, please."

She looks down at her delicate hands with a wilted expression.

I know what she's feeling. I get that she doesn't want to leave, but she has to. I guess my bugging her to stay is like rubbing vinegar on a cut. But still, I hate that she hasn't found a single way for us to see each other. And she didn't fight to stay, either, like she did last time and won.

We're inching our way through Little Havana's Calle Ocho's Parque de Dominó, where tons of men and a woman are playing dominoes and drinking *cafecitos*. The sugary smells of *guarapo* and *mamey* shakes seep into the taxi.

"The Castro family, those bastards!" a round-bellied man screams to a shriveled up *viejito*. The little old man looks like a heap of leather under a sombrero. Loud domino sounds slap around the tables.

Now I say something on my mind I left for the last minute. I despise talking about things that bother me right away. I let them simmer till they're just about to explode inside me.

"Mar, please don't keep dating Rick. You know he's in love with you."

I'd never go out with a guy or another girl while involved with Marlena. I feel upset knowing he's back in Puerto Rico, waiting for her to arrive, and I don't count.

Her look turns so intense it practically throws me off my seat. "I'll have to date him. If I don't, my family will become suspicious." I see anguish in her face. "You know I love you and only you. I'll be with you forever. There's nothing to worry about."

As if I shouldn't be concerned about Rick the Dick being desperate to get into Marlena's pants. She's not into guys *at all*. If you ask me, she's playing with fire.

She keeps talking about why she has to see the damned guy. It's not upsetting because she's faking it with him. Part of why it bothers me so much is because no one considers our feelings, as if she and I don't have a right to be together. Rick gets to have her in public. I don't.

"Well, have a blast with Rick. Maybe I'll go out with Syrio, a friend of Soli's who thinks I'm fascinating *and* scorching."

"Really?" I guess I caught her attention.

On occasions, like when Rick was visiting her, I was known to improvise. I felt compelled to tell her that unless she dumped him, I'd date this one or that one. She'd say, "Don't! If you do, that's the end of us. You know I'm only seeing him so people will never find out about us. I'm doing it for us, so we can be together. I'm pretending to be into him. Please don't mess things up for us. I love you with all my heart." I stopped giving her anxiety or risking losing her for good.

"Yeah," I tell her now. "He's a long-haired guitarist who wants to become a zoologist. He writes his own lyrics and is planning on traveling the world during summers doing odd jobs. And even though he's straight, he volunteers for homeless gay kids." She knows that would be my type of person.

She coughs and clears her throat. "Well, that's nice."

"Nice?" This isn't the response I want from the girl of my dreams who never wanted me to risk our relationship by starting to date other people.

She whispers something barely audible. "Go out with him. Make him your boyfriend so your mom will let you back home." She sounds like a different person. "Try being his girlfriend; it's not a big deal. It's so easy. Your mother will think you like him, and she'll stop giving you a hard time."

I'm biting my thumbnail. Marlena has always taken a strong dislike to guys I've thought were handsome or whom she wrongly thought liked me.

Out of nowhere, she sighs deeply and changes the topic. "There's something I haven't told you."

"That you're coming back soon, and we'll live together forever?"

Her face contorts into a sorrowful expression and her eyes become watery. "I wish."

"What then?" I sit up straight and face her.

"My brother found my journal. That's why he left early. He took it with him to Puerto Rico."

"What?" I feel my heart pounding in my chest. "Why didn't you tell me?"

"I wasn't about to spoil our last days together. I didn't want you to worry like I was worrying. You've been through enough."

Marlena's diary is far worse than any text she's ever written me about our times together. In her journal, she writes her most intense feelings, desires and poetry about us in our most intimate moments.

I look out the window at the whirling gray streets, wondering if this craziness will ever stop. "Arturo swore he wouldn't tell anyone if I quit seeing you."

I feel a glimmer of hope in my heart. "You lied and promised, right?"

"Yes, but he texted me this morning that he's changed his mind. He'll tell my parents, but no one else." She closes her eyes as if in prayer. "I tried calling him back but he wouldn't answer the phone. I've texted him dozens of times but he won't respond."

"How can we make him stop?" She should have learned from what happened with me. One thing I've gathered from all this is that private texts and e-mails must be written in code.

"It's not in our control."

"I hope he never tells your uncle Marco."

"Don't worry. He won't. Arturo said the more people know, the more my name will be smeared. He says he'll kill me if I get a bad reputation and Rick finds out."

"He better not touch you."

I feel scared for Marlena. Arturo is a big, argumentative guy known for verbal outbursts. He's so intimidating and irritating that I find ways to leave when he's around.

"There's nothing we can do. We've lost. I wish I'd never written those texts or anything about you in my journal."

"We haven't been beaten if we still love each other. You never think outside the box. What's wrong with you? We can find a billion ways to stay together."

She speaks in a sad, low tone. "It's impossible. We're doomed. We'll never be able to see each other again. Arturo said my mom is going to stop paying for my cell phone. He said I won't be allowed Skype or a video phone."

"We've got e-mails, IMs, chat, Facebook—"

"Arturo is changing our home phone number. He's making

my parents stop paying for my e-mail service too; he's gone crazy. We won't be able to contact each other anymore."

"You can use your friends' laptops."

"No way. I won't risk them finding out about us."

I shut my eyes really hard and rub them. "You can e-mail me from the library or text me from a friend's cell." There are so many quick solutions. "We can IM every day. I'll save money and buy you a BlackBerry, iPad, iPhone, whatever you want, and pay for the monthly fees from here."

She takes a big gulp and whispers so low I must force myself to listen. "They'll search me and find it. I can't deal with this. It's too hard. I'm not strong like you."

"Don't talk like that." I stare out the window, at the fluffy clouds. They always soothe me, but it's not working right now. I glance back at her. "Listen, just lie and promise your parents you'll never communicate with me for as long as you live." I rub my face with my hand. "I know they're really religious. Tell them their favorite guy, Jesus, was all about loving people like prostitutes and sinners. Let them know if Jesus pardoned Mary Magdalene, they can forgive you."

It's strange how some people follow a series of myths in the Bible, written by men over two thousand years ago, that weakens them and makes them followers instead of free thinkers.

"Oh, Shai." Her seriousness makes my stomach ache. "Arturo read me parts of my diary where I talk about how much I love kissing your entire naked body . . . and the way you . . . we . . ." she doesn't finish her sentence and takes a deep breath. "He said he's going to read every detail to my parents. Can you believe it?"

"What a sicko." Memories of Fart Face reading my texts to the class crash into me. It's a double-whammy of burdens stitched together making a senseless string of more troubles for us to become untangled from.

"Everything's changed. Nothing will ever be the same. I'm sorry I didn't tell you about the diary sooner." She looks gently into my eyes. "How can we stay together with them knowing and without things getting worse?"

"Just stay. Don't go back." I rub my temples. I'm getting a huge headache. "Don't board that plane. We'll figure out a place for you to live."

"I can't do that. Arturo will come find me." I see sadness etched across her face. "I'm trapped." She wrings her hands. "I know my mom will hound me twenty-four hours a day now. She's neurotic about anything gay."

Ignorance sucks. Parents are so inept sometimes. They should be worried about their children's well-being, not intimidating them or hating them for being who they are. I'd like to put up a colossal sign outside their home stating, *LOVE not H8*.

I look away from her. How could she not want to find ways to ever see or talk to me again? What's gotten into her?

"You're breaking it off?"

"I don't want to, but what else can we do?" Her voice is meek. I know she doesn't mean what she's saying. She's just terrified.

"We'll figure something out."

"Okay," she says, but she doesn't sound convinced.

I feel sorry for Marlena. I know what awaits her is hell. If anything, we should be upset with her brother and my teachers. Don't we live in the United States, the land of the free? Aren't there laws about privacy to protect us? Just because we're teens, can't mean we don't have civil rights.

I look out the window and remember last night. We scanned her uncle's neighborhood from the roof one last time. The wind howled as we sat with legs crossed, holding hands in silence. We kissed and kissed and kissed. I'll never be able to do that with her again.

We get to the airport, inch up the ramp, and park. "*Gracias.*" Marlena pays Hairy Taxi Guy. We dart into the airport, push through the crowds, and before you know it, it's almost time.

I see a sign on a bathroom door that says "Fresh Paint. Do Not Enter." We walk in, lock the door behind us, and rush into a mandarin-smelling stall. "I love you with all my heart and soul." She caresses my hair and face with the gentlest touch in the world. "I'll miss you so much. I'll die without you."

"I love you with all that I am." I hold her face in my hands and fill it with soft kisses. "I can't wait till you come back."

Her voice cracks. "I don't think I'll be coming back. I'm serious. You've got to believe me. I won't be able to handle being with you here. It'll be too stressful." She breaks down into sobs.

I lift her chin with my index finger and kiss her tears. "Please, don't ever say that."

She squeezes her cheek gently against mine. "I'm so sorry. I'm so very, very sorry, Scrunchy."

I gently glide my hands against her dark velvety face. "We'll work it out, Mar. Our love is powerful; it's for eternity." I kiss her cherry mouth, then her closed eyelids. "Don't ever say we'll never see each other again."

She kisses my entire face. "You're right. We'll find a way. I'll miss you so much."

I squeeze her in my arms. "You'll be all right. I went through it. We'll be together forever, no matter what." I wait for a response.

Instead, she checks her watch. "Hurry! It's time!"

We rush toward the screening area.

We sink into a sad silence, hugging hard, holding onto each other.

She lets go of me and walks stoically through the metal detectors. Tears streaming down her face, she turns to wave to me one last time and calls, "Take good care of yourself."

It sounds as if we're never going to see each other again.

I mouth, "You too."

10—Pink Petunias

Since Marlena left, whenever I have free time, I work on learning art design, photography, sculpting and film/documentary. A girl on Facebook who attends Yale sends me her homework, and all her old books, in exchange for a Renaissance style portrait I did of her. On my own, I'm learning the history of art and see slideshows of all the masters' work. I'm also learning architecture, with information I get from one of Soli's clients who goes to the University of Miami's School of Architecture—I exchanged a portrait of his dog for the info. I'm fascinated with Gaudi's wild-style Spanish architecture and Cuba's mix of Colonial, Art Deco and Modernism. I also love Miami Beach's Art Deco and spend as much time as possible sitting across Ocean Drive under palm trees for shade, painting the buildings from across the way.

No matter how busy I keep myself, not a day goes by that I don't think of Marlena.

It's midnight, March 26th and Marlena's seventeenth birthday. Soli and Viva are asleep. I steal into the dark back porch with Neruda at my heels. I sit on Viva's rocking chair and rock back and forth, back and forth, squeezing Neruda to me. I hear clapping thunder, and watch thin veils of rain covering the trees.

Days have been longer without my Marlena. She left seven months and four days ago. At first, she wrote me long snail mail love letters dripping in beautiful words every day with pictures of her attached. She wrote about playing tennis, swimming at the ocean with a bunch of new straight friends.

As time went on, her letters stayed passionate and sounded like this:

"My old friends found out. I can't believe how fast word spreads. I've made new friends. I don't think they know or I'm sure they'd shun me too. I wish you could live here. It's even more fun than Miami. The only setback is not being with you.

"I dissolve into tears sometimes, from being unable to communicate with you the way we did. At nights, I close my eyes and visualize you next to me. I allow myself the illusion that our bodies are touching . . .

"I found my old ballet shoes in a box. I'm sending them to you with a pair of shorts and the tight jeans you loved me to wear. You said they smelled like me, and you loved how they looked on me, remember?

"The other day, my mom almost caught me at the post office, getting my mail from you at the PO box address you bought me. Thanks for sending me money to pay for it. It's weird to write with a pen. I'm so used to e-mailing or texting. This is hell. I have a new laptop but I can only use it for school work. This punishment is really cruel. I can't wait for our bodies to meet again, skin-to-skin, and to kiss your sweet mouth till forever . . ."

She managed to sneak collect calls three times a week. As things got smoother, she made her family believe I was history *and* a grave mistake. Her cell phone, Skype and online services were restored. Her e-mails, IMs, texts and pictures poured in. These are some of her texts (I've never deleted them):

still hard 2 live w/out u in my life. missing u. a soft kiss on the lips. help! dying to c u!!! love u!!! miss ur kisses!!! my promise still holds: day i turn 18, going back 2 u. how many days till then? applied 4 scholarship at U of M. woot woot! te quiero mucho! *get your own*

apartment right b4 i arrive. i'll live in a dorm so my family can visit.
will come c u every day 2 study at ur place. i'll spend sultry nights w
u w/out anyone knowing. sweet kisses . . . i'll always love u. fantasized
bout u today, yesterday, tomorrow and every day! miss ur touch . . . miss
u more than ever. going crazy w/out u. don't like Rick's kisses. nubs.
wait 4 me. don't date anybody else. all this will b over soon and we'll b
in each other's arms.

i know it's hard to wait, but ur the only 1 4 me. I'm the only 1 4 u.

Eventually, she started calling me late every night via Skype,
and when no one was home. We'd be together and have the time
of our lives. Virtual lovemaking is nowhere near skin-to-skin
contact, but we figured out a way to enhance our experience:
we sent each other clothes. We'd each put on the other's garb
(including underwear). I'd get to at least smell her distinct, sweet
scent surrounding me.

All was back to normal.

I was expecting Marlena to move to Miami next year. She
seemed to have gathered enough courage to tell her parents she'd
applied to U of M and if not accepted, she'd be attending FIU.
There was hope for us. Even though we'd never live together, we
were staying a couple.

Then last month, the calls, e-mails, photos, Skype visits,
texts and IMs abruptly stopped. I've tried every possible way to
contact her, to no avail. I know she's still alive and well, because
Marco mentions her often. I've been working hard, and chilling with friends I met on Facebook or with Viva and Neruda on
weekday nights and holidays. Early weekend mornings, around
five a.m., I pack a picnic and ride my bike to Key Biscayne beach.
I sometimes like being alone. There, I walk, swim, sketch, read
e-books and write poetry till after sunset.

Soli and I kick it on weekend nights. I got her, whatever guy
she's dating, and Facebook friends who want to tag along, into
seeing foreign films and hanging at Bohemian Café on poetry
nights. Unfortunately, going out in a group makes me yearn for
Marlena even more.

I miss her face, her gestures, her voice, and everything about her. Now mild breezes bring the smell of the damp, green night into the porch, but my stomach is twisting as if I'd eaten a jar of habanero peppers.

I rock back and forth, back and forth, thinking, like I've done every day since Marlena left. Sometimes, life doesn't make sense. Just when you believe everything is a bed of pink petunias, a cat comes and poops on it.

I didn't get to sleep till late last night. I'm riding my bike home from work through woodsy Coconut Grove, with a cool salty breeze filling my lungs.

I can't stop remembering what happened today:

Beep-Beep! "*You guys stay working. Shai is coming with me!*" *Marco commands in his usual Spanish. I throw down my shovel and climb into his sneaker-smelling blue Dodge Ram pickup truck. "We're going to the nursery warehouse to pick up more trees."*

He speeds off.

"I've got some great news. My brother called from Puerto Rico to tell me Marlena got engaged to Rick yesterday!" His eyes sparkle. "I just spoke with my niece. She sounds happy as a fiesta!" *He scratches his barrel belly and sings, "Here comes the bride, here comes the bride . . ."*

I gulp hard, turn to look at him, and put on a smiley face. "Incredible."

What the hell? Engaged at seventeen? Did Marlena get pregnant? I bet that's the reason she stopped contacting me. I'm sure she thinks I'll push her away. I won't. She should know better than that.

I pedal as fast as I can. A sudden pain fills my chest. Disillusionment engulfs me. My body feels heavy and weak. But I must keep going.

Marlena doesn't like guys that way. Did she feel she had to have sex with Rick? My beautiful Marlena is being dragged into something she doesn't want to do. A vision of her face when we used to be together appears before me. Her eyes flutter. Her moans rise up and down and swim into me, gently . . .

I'm snapped out of my thoughts by a red Beemer honking at me. "Get off the f*cking road with that f*cking bike! ¡Comemierda!"

"I love you too!" I scream, and swerve over to the sidewalk before he runs me over.

I can't keep going at this speed. I slow down, out of breath, and pedal effortlessly. Riding my bike is part of me, just as painting is something I was born to do. The word Ride flashes before me. Marlena, unlike most girls I know, wasn't born with an innate desire to ride a guy as soon as her hormones kicked in.

Once, Soli got her a sex toy just for laughs and told her, "So you and Shai can experiment." That night, when we were alone, Marlena became insulted. She told me in a stern voice, "I'm *never* going to let you use this on me. It's unnatural." When I asked if she'd use it on *me*, to see what it felt like, she threw that silicone, flexible thing across her room so hard it dented a wall. She later shoved it in a bag, and returned it to Soli in case I had any ideas about using it on myself.

So much for experimentation.

Girls are what Marlena's into and absolutely nothing that even remotely resembles a guy. She doesn't even like hot dogs! I've asked her if a man had ever done her wrong but she said, "No. I was just born loving girls, loving only you, that is."

I get back to thinking at least her family never told Marco on us, but that's not the way I wanted to hear about my girlfriend again, thank you very much. I hope she's not really marrying Rick the Dick.

If she's not pregnant, I anticipate she's getting engaged so her family gets off her back. That she hasn't been able to contact me tells me she might be going through difficult times. If she finally calls me, I can't get pissed or judge her. That will only make her distant. I'm going to need to stay calm, allow her to talk, and be as understanding as possible.

I zip onto US 1 and pass a truck burping black fumes. "Thanks for spreading lung cancer!" I yell to the driver while holding my nose and pointing at the guck polluting the air.

When are people going to get they're destroying the planet that sustains us and in turn, making humans sick? Vehicles should be made electric and of recycled rubber so if you crash, you won't get killed.

I zip onto Little Havana, gulping down my disappointment about Marlena and Rick, wiping tears with my shoulders. I let the smells of cut grass and coconut milk soothe me before I get home. I don't want to bring Neruda or Viva down and must act joyful.

I park my bike and fling the door open. My furry chicken-pot-pie leaps onto me. "How's my little miniscloopi, the cutest macarooni in the world, eh?" I scoop her up and fill her with smoocheroonies. She licks my eyelids and nose.

Viva stops brushing the ceiling with a sopping wet broom full of the nontoxic cleaners I bought her. She kisses my cheek. *"Hola, mijita."* She produces a pink tissue from inside her bra and dusts the drooping crystals on her plastic chandelier. "How is *la mariposita* today?"

"I is so fine I shine," I goof, trying hard to hide my feelings. "Don't forget that spot." I point to another corner of the ceiling. "Who knows *what* bacteria is growing there." Viva is a psycho cleaner.

"Ay, Shylita." She laughs sweet as guava cream.

I check my iPhone for the hundredth time to see if I missed Marlena's text or call. No such luck. I check my e-mails to see if Marlena wrote. Nope.

I plop on the sofa to call Pedri as Viva leaves to buy Neruda Milk-Bones at the corner *mercado.* On her way home, she'll stop at her best friend Adela's apartment for a *cafecito* and long talks about her guru, Sai Mu, astrology, and "spiritual" things.

I call Pedri like I do every day after work. I don't give three flying *fricasés* if my mom keeps answering and hanging up on me. All this makes me feel so sad and lonely, really. It's unclear why a mother won't take her child back, especially when they always got along so well and there was so much love between them. The pain about her behavior is so hard that most of the time I'm working on forcing myself to not think about it.

People don't understand that you can't just abandon a child and go on with your life without harsh consequences. We're growing farther and farther apart. One day, maybe I won't want to love my mom anymore because it'll hurt too much. Maybe she'll want me back when I'm older but it'll be too late. Her new husband is more part of her life than I am. How can that be? How can I be worthless to my mom?

It's difficult to stay in denial 24/7 when you're not allowed to speak to the little love of your life.

Pedri answers. "Little Punk!"

"Shyly!" I imagine him throwing his arms around my waist and squishing his tiny head against my stomach.

He sniffles into the receiver. "Pedri, what's wrong?"

"I miss you." It's getting harder and harder to live without my little brother. I want so much to hold Pedri in my arms and comfort him; it's unbearably painful to not be able to do so.

I wipe tears from my eyes. "Me too. I miss you so much I could die."

"Why don't you sneak into the house at night to come see me?"

"Mami changed the locks a loooooong time ago. I don't have the new set of keys, or I'd be there every day. But no matter what, I'll always love you." I shut my eyes. "Hey, close your eyes and think that I'm hugging you." I envision myself squeezing him to me. "I love you more than anything or anyone in this world. Can you feel that?"

"Yeah!" I can feel his smile radiating around me.

I sit on the couch and imagine him on my lap, the way he always put his head on the curve of my neck and sucked his thumb. I miss his coconut cookie smell that reminds me of home.

"Did you get the letter and pictures I sent you this week?" He told me Mami has been in the habit of throwing out my mail.

"Yesterday, Mami ripped up and threw away the cartoon book you made me. I cried the *whooole* day. I didn't eat or nothing last night. She promised she'll give me everything you send me from now on. I'm saving your old letters and pictures inside last year's lunchbox." I always send him tons of funny pics of Neruda, Soli, Viva and me, since he doesn't have a cell and Mami won't allow him online yet.

"Don't worry, Little Punk. I'll make you a new book; it'll be even funnier! And I'm sending you my favorite painting of Neruda with bananas flying around her."

He gives out a sweet belly laugh. "That's funny, Shyly. I can't wait. I'll put it up in my room. She's so cute. I miss her, too."

"I know." It's so unfair what our mother is doing to us.

"I can't see Neruda anymore neither. That's not fair. I didn't do nothing wrong." And neither did I, I think.

I hear Mami and Jaime talking. I speak fast into the receiver. "Call me later, when she's taking a bath. I love you more than the clouds and the tallest trees, and all the flowers on earth."

"I love you too, Shyly. More than all the puppies and kitties and ponies in the world."

Click! We hang up fast so Mami doesn't catch him on the phone with me.

Mami will have to cut off my fingers to stop me from calling Pedri. She'd have to chop my legs off to keep me from visiting him at school during some of my lunch breaks from work. It should be against the law for my mom to be doing this to us. It's hard to know I don't have rights, but my mother does. She makes choices for me that are wrong.

Just as I'm headed to go online, my cell rings.

"¿Oigo?"

"This is a collect call from Puerto Rico. Will you accept?"

"Yes!"

"Hello?" Marlena's voice sounds distant, far away.

"Mar!" I get up and walk around, then plunk back on the sofa and exhale a great sigh of relief. "It's so good to hear your voice." Words pour out fast in different directions. "Are you okay? It's been so long. Marco told me about your engagement. Why did you stop calling me? What happened?" I'm jittery and out of breath. "How are you? You're not really marrying Rick, are you?"

"Hi, Shai. I'm fine." She doesn't call me Scrunchy. Her voice sounds odd, not the tone of someone excited to talk to me. "I became really busy and haven't been able to sneak another call till now."

"How are things at home? What's happened since we last spoke?" I can't stop from asking questions. "Marco talks about you all the time. Are you being forced to marry Rick? It must be so difficult." I don't mention the pregnancy.

"No. I'm not being obligated to do anything. Everything's great at home because I've changed."

"Changed?" I drop my head and look down at my feet. She doesn't sound like my old Marlena; she's someone I don't recognize. "You mean you've changed because you're acting like you're in love with Rick, but you're not going through with the marriage, right?" I want to hear with all my heart she still loves me, she's coming back to live in Miami as we'd planned, she's not marrying Rick, no matter what, and she's not with child.

"No. I mean I'm really different now, Shai. I'm not the same person. What we were doing was wrong." She speaks in a dead tone, as if she were talking about dust on her counter, as if our two years and eight months together—not counting last month—didn't mean a thing. "I don't want to be that way anymore."

"That way? What have they done to you?"

A flashback of Marlena standing by the window of her room the first time she told me she thought she was warped because she loved a girl, hits me hard. We'd been together over a year and it was the day after Thanksgiving. She and I had just finished a meal of leftovers with her parents. They were alarmed about news of a gay serial killer, bullying and stabbing effeminate boys to death in broad daylight. The criminal was on the loose. I will never forget what Marlena's mom said:

"I don't blame that man. I'd take a shotgun to *all* gay kids." She turned to Marlena and her siblings and said, "I'd rather have a serial killer for a son or daughter than for any of you to be homosexual."

She continues after an awkward silence.

"Don't make it difficult for Rick and me. We're getting married next Sunday. My entire family made a collection and are flying us off to our honeymoon in France. My wedding will be catered with French cuisine." I turned her on to French foods, and I always told her my dreams of eloping with her to Paris. What a stab in the heart. I even learned a bunch of French words with a CD. I taught them to her so we could speak French to each other and no one would understand us. It all sounds so cruel.

"Next Sunday?" Ouch! "Are you pregnant? Tell me the truth."

"Of course not. I just want to get on with my life and get out of my house."

As she speaks, a flash of one of our last dinners together at a French restaurant shakes me. Her uncle and aunt were celebrating their twentieth anniversary. I can still see Marlena biting into a slice of *tarte au citrus* and savoring it as the sun entered through the window and filtered through her hair. All I could think about was how beautiful she was and how much I wanted to kiss her. While everyone spoke, I imagined that one day we'd celebrate our twentieth with friends and family, too, somewhere in France.

How could I have been so wrong?

"Is *this* what you're calling me for, to kick me in the stomach?"

She lets out a strange moan. "I called to let you know I've moved on with my life. I can't be like that with you anymore."

I must be the stupidest person alive. All this waiting, for what? I'm such a damned fool.

I grab Neruda and place her on my lap for comfort. "But being like *that* was the happiest time of our lives."

"But it's not right." Someone took my Marlena and replaced her with a robot.

"You're sounding wacko, like my mom and Fart Face and the kids that called me names." I sigh. "I don't know what's gotten into you. It's your crazy family's fault. You're letting them force you into believing what we did was wrong."

"No, Shai." She pauses a second, then goes on. "I don't want to feel so different anymore. Hiding is too stressful. I'd like to belong with my family and friends and be free to be me. I need to feel good about myself, and I won't if I'm with another girl. What we had was just a phase for me."

Marlena has slipped away from me.

"A phase?" I sit on the floor, grab my sketchpad and a pen from the coffee table, and start doodling. "We've known each other for so long and were together almost three years. You *know* our love was real and beautiful. You *know* you loved me with all your heart." I throw the sketchpad and pen on the floor. "You told me you only talked about boys when we met because I liked them and you didn't want me to think you were weird."

She clears her throat and steers into another direction. "All I can say is that I'm committed to Rick. I've decided to accept his proposal."

"You're so young. This news is so twisted. Did you fall in love with him? I can understand *that*."

She won't answer my question directly. "I want to marry Rick." She talks in a dry tone, without much feeling, like some-one depressed. "He comes over and we have dinner together every night with my family. We hang out and watch movies. We also go to the beach on Sundays, together, as a family, with his parents and mine. We get along great."

"But are you into him like you were with me? You couldn't keep your hands off me, remember? In fact, you kissed me first! You're the most lesbian girl I've ever met, and I'm meeting tons of them." I need to see if she has any jealousy left in her.

"I'm trying to fall in love with Rick. I think eventually I will. He's good to me, good for me, and my family loves him." She stays away from the lesbian remark.

"So you suddenly stopped loving me, wanting to kiss me and be with me; wanting me right there next to you to sleep with at nights like you said, right?" I close my eyes and wait for the answer. Once I know, I can move on.

There's a long silence. She covers the receiver, and I think I hear her sniffling.

"I still care about you," she says carefully, in a quavering voice. "You were my closest friend."

"Friend?!"

"Yes. We had a lot of fun, and we went through a great deal together." She sniffles and sighs really deeply. "I can never go back to the way we were."

I look outside the backyard windows. Light purple streaks melt into yellows and reds. But at least they sink in vivid colors.

How can the two people I loved and trusted the most have lost track of everything that's really important in life? I need to stop caring. It's useless to keep convincing myself that family, friends and girlfriends will be loyal and care about you till the end. Everybody's out for themselves first. No one really gives a shit. I hope Soli doesn't turn on me too. She, Viva and my little brother are my only hope for humanity.

She coughs and clears her voice. "I need to hang up. Rick is about to get to my house, and I've been out too long. We need to work on our invitations. I don't want anyone getting any ideas."

I massage my temples, they're throbbing with pain. "Can you call me some other time so we can finish this conversation?" It's hard to believe Marlena has let go of me so easily. But if my own mother can do it, why did I expect more from her? I've got to admit, though, it's hard to believe that at seventeen, she's getting married. That kills.

"I can't. Don't you understand? It's over. I pray you have a good life. I hope you find a boyfriend who adores you as much as Rick loves me. Accept this and let go. I'll pray for you so you too can change and lead a more normal life."

"I don't need prayers and I *hate* being normal."

I'm startled by Soli's loud banging on the front door and her shrieky singing as she walks in: "Food time! Food time! I brought food for all of us, Shyly, so you don't have to cook tonight." She places a large garlic-smelling bag on the kitchen table.

"Betrayer," I say into the receiver with gritted teeth. I throw my cell against a wall, and dash into the bathroom with Neruda after me. I slam the door behind me, swing it open a few times, and shut it so hard I think I've broken it.

"What happened?" Soli comes to the bathroom door.

I tell her everything. "Marlena kept me hanging. She's such an asshole! I hate her so much."

I punch the door over and over again till my knuckles bleed. Why did I believe her? Why am I such an imbecile?

I drop to my knees. A hard pain fills my bones. I curl into a ball on the cool terrazzo floor. *Nothing matters. I hope the sky closes in on me.*

Soli knocks lightly on the door. "Open up, Shyly."

Neruda jumps on me to lick the blood off my knuckles and comfort me. I place her next to me and spoon her.

Soli pleads in a calm tone, "Please, Shyly, come out."

My body shakes with pain. I stick my head in the toilet and throw up neon-yellow bile—the color Mami would've loved me to paint the bathroom walls.

I wash my face, splash cold water on myself, brush my teeth, and open the door.

She grabs me forcefully and pulls me against her. "I *know* it's hard."

Tears burst out of me.

Memories of my mom and Marlena get all tangled up into one. They're both traitors.

Soli throws the piles of clothes off her bed and we climb onto it. I cuddle up into her arms under her patched quilt. She smells like caramel candy, like she used to when we were little. "You're my best friend, Soli. I love you so much. Please don't ever leave me."

"I'll never leave you, Shyly. We're friends for life."

11—X'd Out

There must be an epidemic of betrayal going around, casting a dark tinge around everything and everyone I come in contact with.

I don't know how to detach from the bitter feelings and sadness that comes from losing people you belonged with. My mom, Marlena, and friends can't all be wrong, can they? They say it takes two, but I'm not sure where my fault lies. What did I ever do to *them*? It's definitely my stupidity to have trusted and believed that family, friends and girlfriends would stay around forever, simply because they loved you.

I won't be a beggar, though, pleading for them to take me back. I'm going to change and put all that behind me.

Today is the Betrayer's wedding. I'm sure they'll be serving Marlena's favorite appetizer, something we discovered at a food and art festival on our way to our first picnic on the beach: *foie gras*. We dared each other to try something new and didn't know it was duck liver or we might not have eaten it. Regardless, it was delicious (and too expensive!). I hope Rick gorges on it, gets sick and barfs all over Marlena while they're doing it.

Soli and I tore up Marlena's snail mail letters and burned them. I cut up the clothes she'd sent me and threw them in the trash. I feel like such a fool. I should have been dating other people while she was with Rick. I asked Soli to take me to a gay club. I'm determined to forget Marlena if it's the last thing I do.

Soli and Diego, her newest boy toy, brought me to Papaya's, a mixed club. The funny thing about Papaya's is that most tourists who come here don't get that it means you know, the girl's part. That's what Cubans call it.

There's a famous Cuban saying that comes to mind now because some conservatives use it as an antigay slur, "*Dime con quién andas y te diré quién eres/*Tell me who you hang around with and I'll tell you who you are."

We got in thanks to Diego, better known as DJ-Smooth, a part-time DJ and Poetry Slam poet here, who fixed us up with false IDs.

Tazer called Soli for a haircut, and she invited him to come. Soli's been buzzing and dying Tazer's hair for months now. I stayed completely under the radar because of Marlena, and sent my hellos. Now that Marlena is out of the picture, I'd like to become friends with Tazer—if he'll have me, that is.

Papaya's is filled with gays, straights, bi's, trans, drag queens and kings, but mostly with feminine-looking gay Cuban girls who don't label themselves. They all look straight, wear makeup, fancy shoes, perfume and gold jewelry. I think I want my next girlfriend to be a gringa; they're drama free, very cute and extremely smart. It would be fun to meet an out-of-state girl who doesn't know anything about Cuban culture. I'll introduce her to all our fun sayings, food and craziness.

I'll take her to my grandma's apartment in Calle Ocho, where excitable Cubans scream and gesticulate heavily, all at once, to make a point. I guess I miss Mami's way, how she, like every Cuban mom, yelled at the top of her lungs to call me for dinner when I was actually a few feet from her, in the living room, watching TV. I wonder what my new *Americana* girlfriend will think if we walk around and a group of girls, talking about this and that, just break into dancing mambo without any type of music whatsoever. I'll tell her stories about my dad's tiny, ancient convertible. On some Saturdays, we'd pack the four-passenger car with him, my mom, me, two cousins and my large grandmother who'd complain in Spanish, "Let's go pick up your aunts and uncles. We can still squeeze a few more people in here!"

Yeah. That's what I'll do. A gringa will be fun to impress with all our insanity. I'll make her laugh with stories about how when I got sick, my mom rubbed "vi-vaporru" on my chest and inside my nostrils and I was better by the next morning. She'll ask what that was and I'll let her know, Vicks VapoRub, of course! She'd need to get used to drinking *cafecitos*, because every Cuban is addicted to espressos. Since I was in diapers, we had *cafecitos* before going to sleep and upon waking up in the mornings, and it's why we're all always so happy and lively. I don't know. Maybe an American girl won't be into me because of my wacky culture. We'll see.

I look different from everyone else, as if I don't belong. I threw on my tight white hip-hugger corduroy pants and a white silky top that shows my belly button. I slid on my square-toed brown ankle boots and smudged a little organic mandarin lipgloss on my lips.

I'm twirling around a group of drag queens. T-girls start shuffling their feet around me, clapping with hands up in the air, singing, "Shake it! Break it!" We dance nonstop for well over an hour. I'm all sweaty so I stop for a breather and kiss the girls goodbye.

There's something about drag queens that draws me to them. In one way, they break my heart because I'm sure they've been through a lot. On the other hand, they're mostly brilliant and hilarious and don't take themselves seriously. But still . . .

Soli and Diego are in a dark corner, arms around each other, making out. She looks weird in Diego's baggy jeans and floppy shirt, my work hiking boots, and a nose ring that sticks out like a sore wart. She's trying hard to look butch, just for fun, but it doesn't work.

Soli leaves Diego and comes to me in long strides, smiling, arching her right eyebrow.

"Shylypop," she fiddles with her nose ring, "dancing with queens is a blast, but why aren't you asking a girl to dance?"

I point to my left foot. "It hurts. Do you have a problem with *that*?" I don't know why I'm shy around girls, especially ones I like. Asking a girl I don't know to dance is hard. No. Actually, it's painful. If she says "no" I won't know what to do with myself.

At twelve, thirteen, and the beginning of fourteen—the age most boys start looking at girls—guys I liked didn't pay attention to me. I was bony, had buck teeth, braces and bangs down to the tip of my nose to cover zits on my forehead. Luckily, right before I met Marlena, I gained weight and lost my pimples and braces. After my transformation, boys began to pay attention to me. Still, rejection isn't fun.

Soli stands with her hands on her waist, looking down at me, pressing hard on my foot with hers. "*This* foot?"

"*¡Pendeja!*" I pinch her butt and she leaps in the air.

She steps aside and tosses her head in the direction of a group of girls. "You should be all gung-ho about dancing with girls. You're not a coward." She doesn't allow me to respond and dives back in. "Ask a girl to dance."

She'd make a good dominatrix.

"Later." Looking away from her, I place my feet on top of the little glass table with my hands clasped over my stomach.

I'm not attracted to girls who wear makeup and perfume. I wish they had mixed clubs where girls came in jeans and talked about fun things like music, art, international politics, lit and languages. But I forgot when I asked Soli to bring me to a gay bar that finding a down-to-earth club in Miami would be like searching for a dry spot in the middle of the ocean.

She snorts in reply, "I'll ask someone to dance with you."

I straighten my spine and stare her up and down, with attitude. "I just want to listen to music for a while. Do you mind?"

"You've got to forget Marlena. The only way you'll erase her from your mind is by being with another girl, right away." She hoists up her pants with both hands and fiddles with her nose ring. You'd think Soli had bull balls for lunch; she's being so overpowering.

"I *have* forgotten her. She's *her*story." I wag my head from left to right. "Stop mentioning her, Turd-Ball. What's *wrong* with you? And her name is Betr*a*yer." All I need is for Soli to keep rubbing Marlena in my face. Why doesn't she just leave me alone and let me be?

She pulls a chair next to me and sits. "The damned Betrayer, okay?" She waves Diego over. He's talking with some guys.

"Listen. As soon as we arrived, memories of how Marlena and I used to dance when we were alone shook me hard." I soften up. "She didn't know how to move. Can you believe it? I taught her. Marlena is the only girl I've ever danced slow with, Soli. Dancing slow with her while we kissed, was the most beautiful feeling I've ever experienced in my life."

She slaps her cheek and raises both eyebrows. "Well, if *that* isn't the sweetest thing I've ever heard. You're a hopeless case."

"And you? You're as sensitive as a potato chip." My mouth feels dry. I take a sip of ice-cold virgin piña colada and it gives me the shivers. I look into her eyes. "Don't be so mean." I'm forced to forget instantly, like Soli and everyone else in the world does, when they break up. I wish I weren't such a dork. Soli's right. I'm so damn sensitive.

"Shyly, you've got to ask a girl on a date, tonight, before we leave. You *have* to start seeing other girls immediately." She gulps her sombrero drink and crunches on a couple of ice cubes. "Take it from me. I know how it goes."

I move my legs off the table, place my feet on the chair, and bring my arms around my knees. "Right. Take it from *you*: The queen of *perfect* relationships. You've left more guys than there are people in China." I clasp my hands. "Look, bringing me here was a huge mistake. It's making me realize I was just in love with Marlena and I can't fall in love with another girl. I know she was it for me."

I think being with girls is just going to be one painful hassle after another. Classic fairy tales we were forced to read as kids in school should have provided us with info about what to expect if you fall for a person of the same sex. Little Red Riding Lezzie would be a teen attacked by a homophobe—the Big Bad Wolf!—on her way to visit her ailing beloved girlfriend. The Three Little Pigs were living a gay, merry life until their house got blown down by a bully. Don't stray from the straight path and only talk to straight strangers of the opposite sex is what they fed us.

No one prepared us for this.

"You've *to*tally lost it." Soli starts rolling her eyes this way and that way.

She's never had a love-of-her-life, so she doesn't know what I'm going through. I wish she understood so she'd leave me alone.

Instantly, I realize what will make her lay off my case.

"You're probably right. I'm telling Tazer the truth about Marlena and asking him to introduce me to his lesbian girl-friends." I hope this makes Soli shut her trap. "Maybe my heart will beat out of control like it's having an orgasm when I meet one of his friends." I smile big.

"Way to go, Shyly! I can't *wait* till Tazer gets here." She's all jumpy and happy like a kid at a party.

"Hold up. Don't go blabbing about my personal life to Tazer till I'm ready to tell him. Okay?"

Her smile falls away. She yells to Diego again. "Git your sweet A over here, boy!" It's his day off from DJ'ing and he wants to chill with his boys. He's a good one for her to control. Diego's got a soft spot for Soli, and that spot sure isn't his ding-dong! I know they won't last. She can dominate him, easily.

Diego strolls over with a lesbo vacation pamphlet in his hands, drops with a *plop* on the chair next to Soli's, and leafs through it. Soli says he's the silent type addicted to reading any-thing he can find.

Soli plunks on his lap. "Hey, check it out!" She grabs the

pamphlet from his hands. "A lesbian cruise ship! For you and any girl in here, Shyly." She jams it into my face.

I swat it away. "Shut up, al*ready.*"

Diego wraps both muscular arms around Soli's waist and kisses her earlobe. "Let 'er be, bird." She shrugs her shoulders and leans back into Diego's strong body.

"Go ask *her* to dance before Tazer arrives. You've got to try out a bunch of other girls before he introduces you to one." She told Diego about Marlena and me. He didn't give a flying porcupine.

Soli is pointing to a dark voluptuous girl sitting alone. She has hair like mine: multicolored streaks from the sun, straight, and down to the middle of her back. Soli knows I like feminine girls with meat on their bones. Although I'm slender due to paternal genes, I'm not interested in anyone who talks all day about low-carb diets and is obsessed with losing weight. Instead, I get a kick out of girls who *love* to chow down, like that they're bulky, and who eat voraciously with gusto.

Diego gently kisses the back of her neck. "Chill, Soli. You're crimpin' my nerves." He smiles and winks at me. I smile back. I like Diego; we get each other. Soli leans back, stretches her arms above her head, finds the tips of his hair, and plays with them. Diego's and Soli's cheeks meet as she rests the back of her head on the curve of his neck.

A tall, thin guy, with a slight hook nose, mildly acne-scarred cheek, and long, black wavy hair, wearing tight jeans with an open vest, comes over to us. "Hey, what's shaking?" He greets Soli with a kiss. Soli tells us he's a straight haircutter whose name is Francisco but everyone calls him London. He explains, "In eighth grade I was chosen as one of two kids who got a free trip to England. After I came back, everyone had nicknamed me London and it stuck." He's into music and politics, works with her, and comes here with his bi girl cousin on weekends to dance. They talk awhile as he takes a swig of a strawberry colored drink. He asks all of us, "It's a luscious lez, want one?"

Soli jumps in. "Diego and I are all set." She juts her nose in my direction. "Shai's the one who needs a luscious lez, but she only drinks stuff like lemonade." I know what she's trying to say, but I hope he doesn't catch on.

Before I can say, "No thanks," he calls the waitress over. "One lemonade, please." His smile radiates. "So, what's happening in *this* corner of the world?" he asks me. I feel myself blushing. I place my feet on the floor and smile shyly.

Soli tugs at her nose ring and scrunches up her nose. "She's a nerd. Look at her." They scrutinize me. "She's scared of lesbians in gay clubs."

Soli grabs my hand and Mr. Luscious Lez grabs my other hand, and they pull me to the dance floor. Diego goes to talk with the DJ. The waitress finds us and hands me the lemonade. She tells London, "It's on the house." He thanks her. I take a swig and it tastes damn good. Dancing next to me, Soli whispers into my ear, "He's amazing to work with. He's cool with everyone being gay."

"Maybe I'll go out with him." I'm open for experimentation, now that the Betrayer doesn't give a royal toad's turd about me.

"You come to a club filled with beautiful girls and you want to be with a *guy*?" Soli stares me up and down. "What's *wrong* with you?"

"*You're* what's wrong with me. You want me to forget Betrayer, right? Well?" I just want to be left alone to do what I want without Soli in my face.

I take another swig and before you know it, the glass is empty. Mr. Luscious Lez takes my glass and places it on the bar. He comes back with arms up in the air, twirling around me. I dance really close to him and we start a body-to-body slide-and-grind.

"I didn't know Soli had such beautiful friends," he says over the thump-thumping music.

I grab the very ends of my hair. He closes his dreamy dark eyes, and I brush his closed lids softly with my hair.

The acne scar on his right cheek pops out when he grins. "You're not gay, right?"

I move away from him and twirl around him twice. I think

about it for a minute, then say, "Right." I guess it's just a matter of semantics. If he had asked, "You've never been in love with a girl, right?" then *that* would be a different story. I'm not lying, so I don't feel bad.

"Cool."

Soli's suddenly in my face, poking fun at a sixties-style dance a friend's grandmother taught us, acting as if she were swimming, holding her nose, wiggling down as if going underwater. She doesn't let me get into dancing with London. I whisper sharply into her ear, "I know what you're doing. Get out of my face so I can get to know him better."

She dances way up closer to me. I gently push her away. "Snap, Soli, you're such a major pain."

I take London's hand and start doing super wild go-go dances from a seventies rerun I learned. The girls create a circle around us and clap loudly. I'm moving really sexy, causing a commotion, feeling pretty damned popular.

London's eyes say it all. After the crowd disperses, we dance three straight songs.

He plants a kiss on my forehead. "I'll be right back."

Soli twirls around me until he brings me another lemonade.

He hands me the drink. "For the prettiest and sexiest mover around." He takes me by surprise and smacks me a kiss on my lips. Suddenly our mouths lock. He makes out with me more intensely, and I swiftly remove my face from his. Kissing him isn't delicious; it feels nothing like it did with Marlena. I made out with two other guys before Marlena, but no one compares to her. I miss our deep, smooth, sensual kissing more than ever, but I say zip and just smile.

I gulp the lemonade down fast, to wipe the taste of his kiss off my mouth. I want to just be friends. I'm over the experiment.

Now everything around me is whirling in slow motion. I can't seem to stay on my feet. Soli grabs the glass from my hands and holds me up. "What's wrong with you? You can't be drunk." She sniffs the glass. "There's no alcohol in here." She hands the glass to London. "Is this *really* lemonade?"

He lifts his broad eyebrows, and it makes his nose and scar seem fascinating. "I hope so. Jon Espada is bartending tonight. He's giving me free drinks."

Soli's eyes widen. "Jon? You *know* he's hard core into Ecstasy." She looks toward a husky, muscular guy who's grinning. She turns to London. "You asshole! We should have a choice whether we want to do X or not."

London explains, "But I didn't know he was spiking the drinks."

"I'm *not* high," I say, while acting as if waves are jerking up my right side, popping to my left, in slow motion. Things around me seem to be swirling fast. I'm one with everyone here. I love everybody and I know they love me. What a great life.

I explode in jittery muscle moves and intricate foot shuffling that has me stumbling around. Soli catches me. "Let's go back outside." She pushes London aside. "Get out of my way!"

"But Soli, I'm serious. I didn't know."

"Move, idiot. I don't want to see your face *ever* again."

London holds his hands up in the air with the glass in hand, as if a cop had a gun to his head. "Okay. Okay." He walks away.

Soli grabs my hand and pulls me to the table. The girls next to us are talking loudly about wanting to become doctors and lawyers. I lean over to Soli and whisper, "I miss Marlena sooo much."

She's telling me she wants me to hook up with one of the *Cubanitas* when I look up and see a familiar face. "Hey, hey, hey, Tazer Spacer, long time no see. How's it shakin'?" My knees are wobbly, but I act normal. "What choo doing here?"

"Hey, *chica*, great to see you again. Soli asked me to come." He smacks a kiss on the top of my head and leaves a fresh mint scent around me. Suddenly, my lips tingle, and I have an urge to kiss him.

"You're adorable!" I look him over once, then twice. Tazer really is beyond handsome.

He hugs Soli and shakes Diego's hand as he's introduced. I try to stand and feel woozy. My arms feel like Jell-O and I plunk down on the seat. "What's the scoop, Taze? You in a Daze?" My words come out funny.

Tazer wraps his arms around me for a powerful hug. He fixes his suspenders and punches Soli in the shoulder. "She's slamming cute."

I stare at him. He looks stylish with baggy dark brown pants, a tight chocolate-colored shirt, and brown and white two-tone fifties-style shoes. I can't take my eyes off his suspenders.

Tazer talks about how he's excited that his dad hired Marco again to do more landscaping. "Marco came over last week for another estimate. We'll be able to see each other every day for a few weeks, Shai." The conversation spins around to the club. "I love this place; it's got the best music in town. And lots of hot babes, too."

Diego beams. "I'm one of the part-time DJ's and hold Poetry Night here on Tuesdays at eight. Come check us out."

"Definitely." I stare at Tazer's pinstriped bangs as they talk about music, lyrics, poems and scripts. The lines are turning blurry on me.

Tazer snaps his fingers in front of my face. "You look weird. What's up?"

Soli explains, "Some *i*gnorant I work with let his friend put an X or two in her lemonade without telling us about it first." The sides of her mouth droop. "She's really stoned out of her mind."

"No way I'm stoned!" I trumpet and everyone's eyes zoom in on me.

"Where's the guy?" Tazer barks.

"Forget it," Diego scolds. "Pick a fight here, and your ass'll be in the slammer."

"I'm not a fighter. I was just going to put him straight."

"Come on." I grab Tazer's hand. "Let's dance!" I pull him with me to the dance floor.

Tazer undulates around me with fists in the air. He's a creative dancer with slick body moves. I dare him with elaborate upper body movements. He follows with feet shuffling.

I grab his arm. "Let's go to the ocean, *now*." I feel all sparkly inside. Feels damn gooooood to not have to worry about fears or my mom's homophobia!

"Now?"

"Yeah, so we can swim with the sharks." I trip over someone and almost fall.

Tazer picks me up in his strong arms and carries me to our table. I hold on to him by his neck as he sits. I end up on his lap. Out of nowhere, tears pour out of me and I can't hold them back.

"What's wrong?"

"The Betrayer . . . my ex, Mar . . . Mar . . . Mario, the love of my life. The Betrayer is getting married today." I'm wetting his neck with my tears.

"I'm so sorry, Shai. It'll be okay." He gently caresses my hair.

"Help me forget, please . . ."

He holds me tightly and out of nowhere, his touch makes me quiver all over, as if every cell of my body is exploding.

"I promise. I will. I'll help you, Shai. Don't worry."

Soli and Diego come back and see me curled up on Tazer's lap.

"She'll be fine," Soli says. "The X will wear off soon. She's just getting over someone."

"Betrayer. Betrayer . . ." I repeat.

"She needs to get out of this loud smoky place," Tazer insists. "I'm driving her home."

He helps me stand up. Soli takes me by one arm and Tazer by the other. Diego walks next to us, reciting a poem supposed to make me feel better: "Livin' in Shakespeare's fool paradise, a state of happiness based on false hope . . ."

I kiss Soli's shoulder. "You're my best friend. I love you more than all the leaves in the world and all the grains of sand."

She pushes my hair back away from my forehead. "Me too, Shyly. You'll be all right."

Tazer kisses Soli and shakes Diego's hand goodbye and they go back into the club.

My stomach feels as if I swallowed a puddle of slime. Rick is having sex with Marlena now. He's touching all the sacred places that used to belong only to me. She used to say we'd be together forever. "Forever is such a lie," I say out loud.

I plop in the passenger seat and just when Tazer starts the engine, I throw my head out the window and puke chunks of dinner. "I miss my little bro. Take me to see Pedri. Take me now."

"It's too late, Shai." He gets a handkerchief from his pocket and wipes my mouth. He reaches for his shoulder bag and plucks a bottle of water and makes me drink it all.

I guzzle it down and feel better.

We're driving back. The buzz buzzing in my ears sounds like angry wasps. I slide off the ring Betrayer gave me that I haven't been able to let go of, and throw it out the window as far as I possibly can. "Screw you!" I yell into the balmy night, remembering that Marlena probably already said, "I do," to Rick the Dick.

12—Act Natural!

Yesterday was brutal. Today I had to work at Tazer's three-story villa again and act happy. Marco left for the week to go to Betrayer's wedding.

The morning was in my face like slime and I couldn't wipe it off. I started the day in a sweaty daze, ready to dig holes and stick plants inside, as hard and as fast as I could. And I did. I focused so intensely I barely spoke a word to anyone, except to Tazer for a minute during our break. He had to leave and couldn't stay talking.

I'm beginning to understand people who steal. I bet they're feeling frail and alone. They've had folks they've deeply loved and trusted turn their backs on them over and over again. They'll do anything to fill up the black hole inside them that keeps getting bigger with every betrayal.

I hope I don't become a jaded thief.

Luckily, I've promised to make myself feel better by trying to concentrate only on the good.

All day I've been melancholy and only focusing on my losses. It's not as if I didn't have a happy childhood with parents who adored me. Maybe I should start bringing forth those memories to keep my mind occupied.

Last night, I forced myself to think funny things to avoid sobbing myself to sleep. Like when the only gringo family in our entire community moved next door to us from a small town in Ohio. Just for fun, I taught them wrong Spanish. I translated English sentences with common, funny, Cuban bad words. Instead of "Good morning, how are you today?" they naively learned to say, "My butt itches bad," and silly things of that nature. Mami thought it was hilarious. Instead of making me apologize, she texted and e-mailed all her friends about it. She loved me once. She really did.

I need to remember to keep going to the great times in my life because they somehow soothe me. Sometimes, they make me sadder though, and have me missing my family even more. But it's good to recall that you were once loved.

Now, I dash indoors from work, vigorously pet Neruda and give her tons of smooches. "Skooti-Bootie, I've missed you *so* much!" She slobbers all over my face. Her tail swings fast as a windshield wiper, making her whole backside twist from side to side.

Viva runs behind me with a mop in hand. "*¡Dios mío! ¡Ave María!* Take off the muddy shoes!" I hand them to her and walk around with socks. "I is gonna give Neruda a bath. Then," she insists, "I will boil your shoes."

I walk into the bathroom, peel off my grimy clothes, throw them on the floor, and jump in the shower. "Okay!" I yell to her. "Boil my shoes, add ketchup to them and we'll have 'em for dinner. What the heck, we only live once!"

She lets out a sweet, musical laugh.

"Soli no cook today. She go to a boy's crib after work," she states from outside the bathroom door.

"Crib?" I laugh to myself. She picked up the lingo Soli and I sometimes use for fun.

She goes on. "All Soli Luna thinks about is boys, boys, boys!"

If Viva *really* knew the truth about Soli's crushes on guys, and how she's dated all of Miami, she'd have a coronary and croak. Back in Viva's time, seeing more than one boy at a time meant you were a ho, especially when men like Viva's grandfather, nicknamed Casanova, was famous for having a roving eye. Viva won't even go out with another man just so she'll keep the memory of her dead hubby alive. Soli is the modern day Casanova, and obviously inherited her sexiness from her favorite *abuelo's* genes (*que en pas descanse*/may he rest in peace).

"Don't worry! I'll cook!" I boom from a stream of water pouring over me.

I learned to cook from my mom. When I was a kid she allowed me to help her in the kitchen.

Mami would poke the stewed chicken (or whatever she was making) with her index finger and lick it to check if it was done. She'd go from picking veggies in the fridge, to the range, to checking pots and pans. She let me taste everything with a spoon and asked what the concoction needed. "Do you think we should add more salt and oregano," she'd say. After learning all the spices, I'd come out with incredible suggestions, things like, "Add cinnamon and ginger to the meat, Mami. That'll make it yummier." She'd go with whatever I said. In the end, the meals were a success, and she'd rave to my family and neighbors about my cooking. She made me feel so proud and accomplished.

Memories of her slicing onions every night while singing to a salsa CD and twirling me around while the food was simmering make me more confused. I want to stick to the positive, but, suddenly, everything has me missing her. If she loved me that much as a child, how could the one wrong thing I did have changed her opinion of me? I don't want to think about my mom any more. I'm determined to push all thoughts of her away. I'll focus on Viva, who makes me happier.

Viva's the only Cuban mother on this planet who doesn't even know how to boil milk. She burns toast, and even adds salt when what is needed is sugar. She's a total wacked-out differently-abled "chef."

I bathe and dress in tight button-down hip-hugger jeans, a thick brown belt, and a short, chartreuse, silky Brazilian top Viva ironed and hung for me on the towel rack. After getting so cruddy at work, I love to scrub till I'm squeaky clean, then dress nice, even if I'm just staying home. I've told her dozens of times not to iron my clothes, though. I hate it! But she doesn't give three cracked coconuts.

Viva's by her seven-foot statue of *La Virgencita María* lighting candles and praying, as I sauté onions and green peppers in olive oil. When they get soft, I add sliced carrots, cubed potatoes, salt, oregano, and cumin. I stir fry everything ten minutes then pour in a can of organic garbanzo beans and one of tomato paste. I throw in a few cloves of crushed garlic, and a handful of olives and raisins. The pot gets covered with a tight lid to cook while the white rice bakes.

I learned a great deal of tricks from helping Mami. Luckily, now it comes easy to me and I *love* it.

"*Boong-caboong-boong-bang*!" Soli's pounding on the front door gives us a jolt.

"Use your keys, nut case! We're not going to open!"

Neruda flies to the door and slides smack into it. Soli leaps into the living room like a wild panther in heat, smelling slightly of perfume. "Yuk!" I hold my nose. "You're a stink bomb!" I go around opening the windows. Then, I make her wash behind her neck and ears.

"Mima, Shyly, I'm in *love*, totally *enamorada*!" Soli dances around, flapping her arms, imitating a chicken, in her skintight miniskirt under a guy's white shirt. My pup howls and hops around like a bunny rabbit, wild with happiness. "I've fallen in love with Diego!" She lifts Nerudi's two front legs and twirls her around. Soli goes a little nutty once a month around the time of her period, which I call the PM Double S: Psycho Maniac Soli Syndrome.

I dice a tomato and throw it over the food, squeeze a lemon over everything, then pour a teaspoon of the juice the green olives are packed in, and stir. "Yes, Hootchi Momma. You're in love, ice no longer melts, and your butt's gone flat."

I serve the three of us. Viva brings three glasses of *jugo de melocotón* to the table, and a sliced-up avocado and onion salad. She and I sit to eat.

Soli sticks her plate in the fridge. "I'm going out to dinner. I'll save it for later."

"Soli, you no cook or eat with us no more. Please, Soli Luna, sit and eat with us, like a family."

"Listen to your mom, creep head. She just came home from cleaning *four* houses." Viva hardly ever scolds her. She pretty much has no control over Soli, but she tries. "When your mother talks to you it's as if she's talking to a Cheez Doodle. You don't give a flying banana."

Soli picks at some garbanzo beans from the pan, sticks them in her mouth, and licks her fingers clean. "Mmmm . . . I don't have time to cook, Mima. Shyly cooks delicious." She washes her hands in the sink and wipes them dry on her skirt.

"Shylita works too. She clean up, organize, cook and she help me with everyting."

I shoot Soli a steely look, which means, *You could at* least *fake your mom out.* Soli always knows what I'm thinking and vice versa. No need to talk.

She pinches Viva's cheek. "Okay, okay, Mima. Chill. I promise to cook more often." She winks at me from behind Viva. I throw her a smile as I stuff my face.

"Shylypop, I'm serious," she goes on, all bright-eyed. "I'm really in love with Diego."

I take a few tablespoons of rice, throw it in the pan, and stir it around in order to suck up every drop of *salsita*. I pile it back on my plate and gobble up some more. "Right, and I'm a celibate priest wearing nothing but a thong in outer space visiting alien sex fiends for an orgy."

Soli lets out an ear-splitting laugh.

Viva noisily scrapes sticky sauce from the pan and shoves a spoonful into her mouth. "*¡Qué rrrico, Shylita!*"

I love when people like my food. It makes me feel like they love me tons.

Soli opens the fridge and finds a leftover chicken drumstick from Pollo Tropical. "Hey, Organic Celibate Nun, I redid Tazer's bangs in blue, blond, black and red streaks, just a few minutes ago."

"Why not give him ammonia to drink? That might make his skin grow vivid patches and leak in bright colors to match his gorgeous hair."

Soli chuckles. She tackles the tough chicken fat between her front teeth and pulls at it with her thumb and index finger. "Tazer was my last appointment. He's so incredible. We're meeting at Cha-Cha's at seven thirty tonight; it's a gay Cuban organic veggie restaurant that just opened. Can you be*lieve* it?" She throws the drumstick back into the fridge and takes the fork from my hand. "Stop gorging! You're coming with us."

"I'm not going out to dinner, dingbat." I grab my fork. "Can't you see I'm eating with your mom?" I try to not act excited about my friendship with Tazer. Soli will stuff him down my throat till I'm nauseous. If anything's going to happen with Tazer, I want it to occur naturally, without Soli getting involved and spoiling everything. "And besides, I already saw Tazer today."

"Well, at least come greet Diego. He thinks you're amazing, Shyly. He wants to say hi. He's out in the car. Come on!"

"You've got Diego waiting out there all this time? You're so rude." I hope one day she finds someone who won't tolerate her ways. That'll be the day she might fall in love.

"I no teach you bad manners, Soli Luna. Tell Diegito to come eats with us. We got *mucho* food to share."

A flow of *merengue* rides the wind into the duplex from Soli's car. We stay quiet, listening to the jamming beat that moves me to go outdoors and see Diego. He's witty and an all-around great guy. I like him better than any of Soli's other boy toys.

I stick my plate in the fridge and kiss Viva's cheek. "You won't get mad, will you?"

"No *mijita*. You go and has some fun." I follow Soli outdoors. Viva holds on to Neruda so she doesn't chase us.

I run out with arms spread wide. "Diego!"

He climbs out of the car. I throw my arms around him for a hug.

"Hey little bird. What choo up to?"

"Just chillin'." I smile and use his lingo.

He rakes back his pitch-black, spiky hair. "Come kick it wit us." He's wearing a tight black T-shirt that shows a six-pack and super muscular shoulders and arms.

Before I can say a word, Soli insists with the speed of a reckless car, "Shylypop, you're coming *with* us, and that's *that*!" She pushes me into the car. "To Cha-Cha's!"

Soli drives like a red ant on speed, zooming down the expressway, swerving from lane to lane as we pop around like popcorn in our seats.

She squeezes into a tiny parking space and darts out of the car. Diego, looking psyched, bolts after her. I spring out as if someone's put a torpedo up my butt. We dash down the Miami Beach boardwalk like rock stars followed by millions of roaring fans.

Everywhere we look we see people skating, bicycling, or just walking. There are plenty of muscular pretty gay boys in sleeveless white shirts, cut-off jeans and work boots, and lots of butch and feminine girls walking and talking.

A storm is creeping our way. I feel it coming. It's getting gusty. The clouds are changing from puffy whites to sheets of dark gray and it starts to drizzle.

We hurry to avoid getting wet and wait under a tarp for the rain to stop. I see Tazer under a canvas umbrella watching a row of Afro-Cuban women dancers and drummers on a stage. He dashes to us when he spots me. He's wearing a dark green shiny basketball shirt tucked inside a pair of loose-fitting almond-colored pants and brown leather boots. On his neck hangs a crystal-beaded necklace. He looks like a debonair prince.

We spread hugs.

"You look goigious, Shai." He sounds happy as a conga beat.

"You too, Tazeroni Macaroni." He looks as masculine as Diego.

Soli slaps him a low five. "Beauteous dye job."

"Yeah, this genius haircutter restreaked it for me today. I wanted more colors. She's astounding." Tazer adjusts his small, square, purple glasses. The rain has stopped but the night is windy and our hair is flying all over the place. The ocean waves are crashing against the boardwalk and we're getting sprayed. It's a perfectly romantic night, and if I can jumpstart my heart for Tazer, everything will be perfect.

Soli insists with a mighty swing of her hand, "Let's go!"

We sit at a small table in a cozy corner under a large luminous umbrella, near the crashing waves. It's beautiful out here, but I miss Marlena's face. Why must she still be stuck in my heart? Why do I need to remember her now, before a meal? I take a deep breath and exhale.

Probably because of the times her parents took us to restaurants before they moved back to Puerto Rico. Her thin, tall dad dressed in his usual camel-colored suede jacket and black tie. Her curvy, large mom usually wore tight dresses, showing cleavage. Marlena liked a special dish when they could afford it: lobster with butter and a side salad topped with pineapple chunks, cerrano ham, shredded cheese, pine nuts and croutons. She dredged everything in blue cheese dressing. While we ate, Marlena and I played with each other's feet under the table. If we tapped each other once, it meant, "I'd rather be eating you, instead," twice spelled, "Can't wait to be with you when we get the hell out of here!"

I push the thoughts way out of my head. She's not worth even one minute of my time.

The conversation whirls around from Tazer and I meeting at the beach, to my quitting school and working full-time, to how Soli met Diego at Books & Books and the following day she cut his hair. Soli tells Tazer, "He's a motorcycle mechanic, poet extraordinaire, and part-time DJ. Look at him." Her right eyebrow arches, and her pupils dilate. "He's the most delicious guy in the world."

His smile gleams. "I'm Goddesses' gift to girls. What can I say?"

Soli's right. He's handsome, fun-loving and multitalented.

She presses her lips against his mouth and takes a bite out of his cushiony lips. "We took one look at each other and it was love at first bite." Soli's stomach rumbles and Tazer chuckles. What Tazer doesn't realize is that Soli's belly can't go long without a guy. She's starving for Diego, practically doubled over with hunger, dying to eat him up like Kentucky Fried Chicken; finger lickin' good and all that other crap.

Everyone's talking a mile a minute about this and that when our waitress walks to our table. Our eyes meet and I lower my gaze to the floor. My heart is doing a strange thing inside my chest, like a rumba.

"Hey guys, I'm Gisela." She leans forward and her loose silky white blouse dances around her dark, clove-colored skin. "All meals come with wild rice or whole wheat Cuban bread. What will you be having today?"

I want to say, "You, please," but I can't get the words out of me. My tongue might be trembling. I bet she's noticing. How embarrassing.

Soli points to number nine on the menu. "I'll take the Homo Erectus Hummus with lots of Cuban bread and a Messy Mango shake." She slides her finger up to number one. "He'll have the Faggy Frijoles with rice and a Big Banana shake." Soli takes control. Diego's *definitely* not a *machaso*. "For dessert, I'll have the *Tortillera Turrones* and he'll have the Dripping Dyko Donuts."

Tazer hands Gisela the menu. "Number thirteen. The Lower Lips Lentils with rice and a side each of Pounding Plantains, and Trans Tamales. To drink I'd like a *Mandarina* Fizz and for dessert the Genderqueer Gelatin."

I stare at my menu and don't dare look up into Gisela's sparkling, large, droopy eyes lingering on me. "Number seven. The

Flaming Fembo Frijoles with *Mariquitas*, and a small Prissy Sissy *Mamey* shake, please." I look up into her dark eyes. "Thank you." She's so delicious. Just having her near is making me hungry.

Gisela tosses her unruly, curly-wild, mahogany mane to the side and scrutinizes me in one long swoop. "The Fembos are my favorite too." My eyes dart fast around the restaurant and land back on hers. I smile, cross my hands over my chest, uncross them, and cross them again. I am such a dork!

Sometimes, when Soli thinks I like a girl, or I know she's into a guy, we play a game of inventing things about her or him.

I'd say Gisela is a goddess from a secluded island in a mythical region of paradise who's never found real love. There, girls feed each other grapes, swim in the ocean with dolphins, fish and cook on firepits under swaying coconut palms. They roam the island barefoot, happily, without a single problem. Gisela works some days at a restaurant to bring back that one girl she might fall in love with. The day she meets Shai, Gisela will train her in the ways of love. Gisela falls madly and passionately in love with Shai and promises to never even look at another girl. They live happily ever after in that other dimension having a torrid love affair that lasts forever.

Tazer asks Gisela, "What's going on around here? Why all the balloons and banners?"

Gisela smiles and her pudgy nose scrunches up. "A lesbian film producer celebrated the opening of her movie here last night. Afterward, a group of us went next door to catch the documentary based on Miami Beach's lesbian community. I love being part of the beach's lesbian scene."

When I hear Gisela, she brings me hope that the chaos inside me will subside. I yearn to feel a girl's lips against mine while soaking in the scent of her hair around me. I want to let go and move on, but how does one abandon years of beautiful memories? I'd like to be part of a bright world where I can make a difference, not one of hiding for all the wrong reasons. Gisela inspires me to lead the life I deserve.

She resembles a disheveled poet, as if she just bolted out of bed, showered, slipped on the first thing she found, and didn't fuss about her looks. Everything about her seems to gleam, including her two front slightly crooked teeth and clear braces.

Someone from another table calls her. Gisela winks at us. "I'll be right back with your food." She bolts and leaves the sweet smell of apple pie floating around us. I want to sniff the air and keep her scent inside me, but Soli will make a commotion over it.

A velvet cloud dances in my brain; I close my eyes and let this feeling flow.

"I can tell you liked her," Soli whispers loudly, and I'm slapped out of my dream state.

"Do you?" Tazer asks in a deep whisper, right into my ear.

Diego's eyes widen. "You're smokin' hot for her."

"Cut it out, guys. She'll hear you." I gently kick Soli's shin under the table. "I just think she's interesting, that's all."

I'd be so embarrassed if Gisela heard them going on like this, but in all honesty, I'm excited about meeting a lesbian. This is the first time since Marlena I'm attracted to a girl. But how could I possibly let her know I'm into her? I'm not sure how to do it with lesbians. It's nerve-wracking because they're so experienced with other girls. I just know it came easily for Marlena and me.

Tazer gently punches my arm. "You're too feminine for her. She needs a guy like me." He makes a muscle that pops out of his arm. "I've been working hard at the gym. Like it?"

Before I can answer, Soli leans over and grabs it. "*Uyyy*, almost bigger than Diego's."

Tazer cracks his knuckles. "Gisela looks a bit like my friend Clarissa, except Clarissa is thin and has short hair." His eyes brighten. "I've been heavy into drama and scriptwriting at school. Clarissa wants to be a novelist. We just finished a satirical play."

We're all ears.

"Check it out. The best scene goes like this: The mom of the girl in our lesbian script finds her in bed with another girl. Right before her mother faints, the girl screams to her lover, 'Act natural! Act natural!'"

Everyone lets out a hearty laugh.

Soli slaps Tazer's shoulder. "You're such a talented story-teller." She twirls a few dreadlocks around her index finger. "I'm surrounded by homos. What's this world coming to?" She points a finger at me. I step on her foot hard, under the table. I don't want her to out me to Tazer until I'm ready to tell him why I had to lie. I need time to figure out a way that he won't get pissed at me and walk away like my school friends did. "This one's a homo . . ."

"Sapien!" I shout and the girls from the next table look over at us. The hum of the soft background music becomes a roar. I clear my throat and smile as I shred my napkin into pieces then roll it into a ball. Soli gets the message and shuts her trap.

I must tell Tazer the whole truth when we're alone. I should have never, ever lied to him to protect Marlena, or my mom, two people who, in the end, don't care about my feelings.

The rain has stopped. Soli and Diego go outdoors a few minutes to look at the end of the drumming and dancing show. Tazer leans over the side of his chair and presses his lips against mine for a quick pop kiss. I'm trying not to act surprised.

I separate my mouth after the sweet peck and sit staring at him tentatively, not knowing what's just happened. "I like you," he says.

Soli and Diego come back indoors. I avert my eyes to see if Gisela saw the kiss. She's nowhere in sight. Everyone starts talking and I sit in perfect silence.

I never thought I'd be attracted to two people at once. I like the way Tazer's lips felt on mine. It's good to be interested in others again, even if nothing comes of it. It's great to have people into me, something I never really experienced (except for Marlena, of course!).

It all feels so new, weird, awkward, but good, too, and I don't want to push anyone away.

Someone walks in with dark wavy hair and flawless white skin who reminds me of my mom. Even Soli mentions it. We sit staring because the resemblance is so uncanny.

Before the Incident, Mami and I spent time together every single Sunday morning. We'd take Pedri and Neruda to parks all over Miami and hang out talking or skating. This gap I feel about Marlena and my mom is becoming harder to take. What a reckless use of my time to keep stewing in disappointment and hurt, though. It's not easy to let go and start a new life even when someone as fascinating as Tazer is interested in me.

The woman buys some oatmeal cookies at the counter and walks away. I give out a long, sad sigh.

I look to Tazer. Right now, I'm more attracted to Gisela than him. I don't want to hurt his feelings. What he just did with me is what I was thinking about gathering the courage to do with Gisela, if she'd go out with me, that is. But not just a pop kiss. Way deeper. What do I do now? Maybe Tazer pop kisses all the girls he's attracted to and he's not expecting anything from me? I hope so.

Gisela places our food on the table without taking her expressive eyes off mine. It feels like she's wrapping her warmth around me. "Enjoy." She smiles a smile of dripping ice cream cones as she walks to the next table.

Soli, Tazer and Diego talk up a storm. Diego recites a few original poems for Tazer to hear. Tazer doesn't seem stuck on not having gotten a reaction from me. That's a relief.

My eyes scan the restaurant. I see girls holding hands with their girlfriends. I wish I could go up to Gisela and strike up a conversation. I'd ask her to come with me on a long bike ride to the beach, then a picnic under the moonlight. I want to kiss her so badly it burns!

Tazer whispers to me while Soli and Diego take a break to kiss. "I'm jealous. I can tell Gisela likes you. That's why I kissed you: to get her attention away from you, since you're straight. I like kissing girls. Don't worry. It's nothing serious."

Whew! Just what I wanted to hear.

He goes on. "Here I am, thinking I'm *her* type, and she ends up going for *you*."

"Just because a girl looks feminine doesn't mean she has to like the opposite of her, or that two feminine-looking girls together will act like submissive wimps in bed." This slips out of me.

"And how do *you* know that?" Tazer squints.

"I've heard about it. I bet some butches and guys like you are softies in bed, and some girls who look feminine are crazy-wild passionate and assertive."

"You're right. My ex looked feminine and took total control in bed. I loved that about her."

I quickly change the subject. "I need to speak to you alone, soon." I'm dying to come clean about everything.

"Okay." He starts talking about Gisela and how he doesn't like every feminine-looking girl he meets. "She's not my type with that hair that looks like a soft ringlet Afro, and the solar energy, intellectual look. Don't get me wrong. I can get into big curvy girls with junk in their trunk, but I'm just not into the environmentalist-looking types. The braces don't do it for me, either. You're all natural, but you don't look it or flaunt it. Know what I mean?"

"Yeah." I feel relieved Tazer isn't into her and change the topic. Now *I* start talking with everyone about that and this.

We finish our meal. On our way out, I sneak a card into my pocket, with the name, phone number and address of the restaurant.

13—H8ing

I'm placing my red tall handlebar bike I painted yellow-orange flames on the frame, in Tazer's shed. I'm glad Marco isn't around. Since today's our last day working here, Tazer invited us for breakfast at six a.m. I'm here fifteen minutes early. Angel won't be here till seven.

"Hey! ¿*Qué pasa?*" Tazer kisses my cheek. "Those are mighty fine looking golfing slacks." I smile. After I wore down my jade green and black checkered, loose-fitting thrift-shop pants, I turned them into ankle-short hip-huggers.

That's another thing I learned from my mother: how to transform old clothes into a brand-new look.

"You're looking mighty spiffy yourself." He's wearing a thin silver necklace, loose-fitting blue jeans and a maroon T-shirt with large yellow letters that say "I Don't Bite." Underneath those words, in small fine print, it states, "Unless you want me to." Tazer is gorgeous to look at.

Surprisingly, the moment doesn't feel awkward.

I plant a kiss on his cheek and sing, "Tazeroni Macaroni was riding on a pony, eatin' some baloney . . ." The sides of his mouth curl up. "I can't wait to chow down. I'm starved." Suddenly, he starts looking at me with a sparkle in his eyes, and I can't stop thinking about Gisela. How unfortunate is *that*? But I'm such a chicken. I'll probably never call Gisela—I'm sure I'm not her type—*or* date Tazer.

A few bees buzz by and I quickly move out of the way.

"My nanny went through a beekeeper stage," he tells me. "For a time, we had bees all over our yard and so much honey we didn't know what to do with it. Once, I was in my little plastic pool with friends. A bee stung the tip of my nose. For two days I looked as if I'd grown a testicle on my face."

He entertains me with hilarious stories about when he was a kid. I learn he was the opposite of what he looks like now. When he turned fourteen he sprouted from being short and pudgy. His nanny dressed him as he liked: in boy pants and shirts. After he told his dad he was male, his open-minded father allowed him to have a short boy's buzzed haircut. His dad always wanted a boy anyway. We're interrupted and look toward a sleek black car coming into the half-moon driveway.

Camila's big brother drops her off and waves goodbye. We greet each other with kisses on our cheeks. I remember Tazer likes feminine girls and hope his focus stays on Camila.

Che honks, "Yo, Dudes!" and parks his rusty, dented, green pickup truck in Tazer's driveway. Everyone except Jaylene is riding in the back. The rowdy crew piles out next to us.

"Where's Jaylene?" I ask.

Che bites off his gloves and stuffs them in his blue jean shorts pocket. "That stinking jerk? I asked her out because she was giving me too much attention the other day. Some girls act like they hate you when they really want you. She blew me off and called me a 'misogynist' yet again. That was uncalled for. You're out of your mind if you think I'd let her ride in *my* truck." As if his vehicle were his teeny ding-dong! I'd rather ride on a mule to work than in *his* nasty truck! Jaylene is right. The guy seems to not respect girls too much.

Tazer dives in. "Hey, I've been rejected by many girls. So what?" He turns to look at me and his eyeballs land back on Che.

"Why can't you two see she's a man-hater?" Che says. "I don't buy that she likes guys. She's a lesbian separatist with an agenda disguising herself as bi. Don't you hear the shit she talks about males being inferior to females?"

"She says that to piss you off, not because she hates all guys," Tazer says.

"I don't buy it. She's a Nazi feminist dyke who give guys a bad name."

"Only *you* can give yourself a bad name," I tell him. "I've heard her talk about boys she's dated she really cares about and respects. It's not as if she's going to rub her gayness or politics on your truck and leave a big queer smudge." I'm surprised Che hasn't talked bad about Tazer, yet. It's probably because he's working for his father.

I lie and tell Che my cousin Manny is gay and I love him to death. I ask him, "So, what event in *your* life caused your hetero-sexuality, and why do you insist on telling people you like girls?"

Tazer laughs, but Che just stands there shaking his head.

Out of nowhere, London, better known as Luscious Lez, drives inside the gates in a black Jeep. My jaw drops open. He gets off and introduces himself by shaking hands with everyone. "I'm London. Just came a sec to talk to Shai."

I look to Tazer, who seems as confused as me. What the heck could this guy be doing *here*?

He takes me to the side, away from everyone, under a tall coconut palm tree. "Soli told me you were working at this ad-dress today." He goes into his pocket for a rubber band and ties his long wavy hair back into a ponytail.

I look up at him and sway from foot to foot. "So?" My heart is racing something fast. I don't know why I'm giving scum the time of day.

"Just wanted to tell you how sorry I am. I didn't know Jon was spiking the drinks with X's." His dark eyes meet mine and they seem honest. "That was horrible."

I take a few steps back. "What a jerk of a friend. It's disgusting. Does he do that to *every* girl?" I've heard of guys drugging girls and riding them to their apartments then taking advantage of them. Sicko pervs aren't my idea of fun.

He shrugs his shoulders, lowers his eyes, and stuffs his large hands into his tight black jean pockets. "It was my birthday. I turned eighteen, and he gave me and all my friends free drinks." He stares at his red high-top sneakers. "I didn't know he was spiking the drinks with X's. Trust me, Shai. You've got to believe me. He knows I'm not into drugs." He shakes his head. "I've already cussed him out. I'm really sorry."

I take a closer look at him. Something about his large, dark eyes, plump red lips and flushed cheeks remind me of a boy I had a mad crush on for years, before Marlena. Thai Buenavista was one of my mom's best friend's son. Our families got together on holidays on his parents' boat for barbecues and cruises around Miami to watch fireworks. Once, I asked Thai out to a movie with my friends CC, Olivia and me. He said, "Okay. Can I bring Carina, my girlfriend?" My heart dropped.

I wonder if London or Tazer would still be into me if I still looked like I did just a few years ago.

I dig holes into his eyes. "It sucked." I don't feel much like talking to a guy who has a friend who's a perv, even if he looks like the biggest boy crush I ever had.

"I know. But you've got to believe that I had nothing to do with it." He kicks a rock out of the way. "Soli told me you're sixteen. I thought you were my age. You look older."

"So what? Does that mean it's okay for that imbecile to drug me without my knowledge?" I'm getting really pissed now. Who knows? Even though I highly doubt it, I might have tried X one day on my own, but not having a choice wasn't cool.

"That's not what I meant. I told Jon he could be put in jail for drugging a minor. He's really crazed. I'm not talking to him again." He grabs my hand and blurts, "I hope he didn't screw it up for me and you. Can we go out sometime?"

I'm taken aback. Suddenly, out of nowhere, this guy comes here to ask for my forgiveness *and* a date? Weird. What else can happen? Is Neruda going to start talking? Will Viva begin to bark and howl in the middle of the night? I tell him the truth. "I'm going through a breakup right now. It's painful and I'll probably be a terrible date."

He steps in closer to me and says with a twinkle in his eye. "I don't mind being your rebound." I feel I've been a tourist in a labyrinth with borders, and now I can step outside territories once closed to me.

If I date him, I bet it'll hurt Tazer's feelings, though. I don't think I should. I need to stop being a coward and ask Gisela out. That's who my heart really feels like spending time with.

I get back to the old topic. "Why did you walk away at Papaya's and not confront Soli?" I thought he was a punk-ass-chicken to do that. I wouldn't date such a wimp.

"You saw how Soli got. We work together, for crying out loud, but she hasn't even let me say a word to her till today. I thought I'd have a better chance at seeing you again if I left Soli alone so she could let out steam. I even had Jon call her and talk to her. He told her I knew nothing, that it was *his* fault."

"Oh." I don't know what to say. I guess he's being honest. If Soli talked to him it must mean he's all right. It's too bad we aren't allowed cells on the job and can't text anyone or I'd ask Soli what's going on.

Just as I think I might muster up some courage to call Gisela or even give Tazer a chance, this happens. A genetic *guy*, of all things, comes into my upside-down life!

There's a profound silence between us and he breaks the ice. "So, what's your sign? I'm a Libra. I bet we were meant to meet."

"I don't know a thing about astrology, but it seems to box and label everyone. I'm not a robot or a puppet of the cosmos. I'm a free spirit and don't want to know the course of my life on a daily basis. I prefer surprises." I won't give him an inch. "I don't act like my sign says I'm supposed to, anyway."

"I'm not really into astrology, either, but most girls are so I laid that one on you."

"Genius move, player."

As he speaks I think about walking with Gisela on the beach at night, until the sun comes up. We'll go on paths through wooded areas with a speckled sky and moon glowing above us . . .

I glance at my watch. "Hey, thanks for coming and explaining, but I need to get back to work."

"I've got Soli's digits. She says you're living with her. Can I buzz you?"

I veer my eyes away from his, toward the crew. "Yeah." I don't want to give him my cell digits. He can call me at Soli's house phone.

We say our goodbyes and walk toward his car.

As London is about to climb into his Jeep, Che grabs him by the arm. He slaps his back. "Dude, you're a lucky dog. You've got the prettiest girl in Miami."

London shoves his hands in his jean pockets. "Me?" I stare up at a cloud and watch the sun slide out from behind it.

Che winks at me. "My friend Pincho El Flaco was at Papaya's on Sunday." His friend Pincho comes here on his lunch breaks. He and Che smoke weed and shoot the shit when Angel or Marco aren't around. "Pincho goes to mixed clubs to try to pick up *tortilleras* and bi's for threesomes. He saw you kissing a thin tall guy with long black hair." He slaps London's shoulder. Must be you, no?"

London cracks his knuckles. "I don't kiss and tell."

Tazer's eyes show disappointment. He hadn't seen him kiss me.

Jaylene drives in with her little blue truck. Saved by the *belle*! "Hey, guys!" She's always cheery.

Tazer gives her a big husky hug. They slap each other's backs like football players do. They're becoming close friends. I kiss her cheek. "Hey, Keen Mean Jaylene." London introduces himself and they shake hands.

Jaylene greets everyone else. Che doesn't greet her back. I

guess she doesn't care *what* he thinks of her.

George pats my back. "So you and London, eh? Nice couple."

"What's going on?" Jaylene asks.

Tazer shrugs. "Your guess is better than mine."

"It's not what it seems." London tries to explain.

Everyone teases him. "Yeah. Yeah. We know."

He stops brushing aside the comments. I think he's liking the idea because he can't take the big grin off his face.

Everyone keeps teasing us, so I cave in with a triumphant smile. It feels great to be getting so much positive attention. I goof off. "A'ite. A'ite. So we kissed, okay? So what?"

London looks to me with gleaming eyes. I slowly look away.

El Tigre sings in Spanish, "Love is in the air!" He slaps London on the back a few times.

I'm feeling pretty damned accepted. I hate to admit it, but Betrayer was right. This beats being thrown out of the house. It keeps a big smile on my lips till I face Tazer. He stands with his hands in his pockets, staring down at his feet.

"Let's have breakfast. Follow me." Tazer waves his hand. "You too, London."

London grabs my hand and I allow it. "Show us around," he asks Tazer. "I've never been inside a mansion."

"All right. Let's go!"

We follow Tazer through the arched entrance of the coral rock mansion and walk through huge marble columns and carved wooden doors.

The long spacey hall opens into a living room with white marble floors, as large as a skating rink. Light sneaks in through lavender-colored windows. He takes us through a long hallway with tons of mirrors, hanging chandeliers and paintings, then upstairs. "It's got seven bedrooms. This is the library."

I look around. The dark wood ceiling, gigantic windows, and the floor-to-ceiling bookshelves filled with books makes me feel as if I'm inside a cathedral bookstore.

Everyone gasps. "Amazing! Outrageous!"

It's odd to be standing here, thinking some people live in cardboard boxes under the expressway.

I guess Mami and Pedri might now be living in a villa like this one. Jaime is wealthy. Mami was ecstatic he'd be taking us out of our old neighborhood. I wonder if Jaime is going with her, as I used to, to speak to Pedri's teachers. Without me there to help him, I'm sure Pedri's doing poorly in school.

Tazer takes us back down to the dining room. The central air's temperature is freezing cold. Sulima—the Nicaraguan housekeeper—takes everyone's backpacks. She places them on the sparkling floor next to an elegant, velvet bone-colored living room couch.

Crystal lamps hang by thin glass chains in different parts of the room, glowing a soft golden color. Bright flowers in glass vases are all around the dining room. The air smells like crushed gardenias. We sit at the table.

Our breakfast is *tortilla de chorizo*, *pastelitos de queso* and *jugo de naranja*. Sulima—dressed in white from head to toe—brings in fresh loaves of oven-baked Cuban bread that fills the dining room with smells of toasty butter.

There are plenty of Cuban millionaires in Miami. I guess in some ways, Tazer is lucky. This place is gorgeous and I'd live here in a jiffy. But if I had so much money, I wouldn't spend it on a mansion for two. I'd buy a modest house next to a wildlife reserve as my backyard and build little domes for the homeless. I know Tazer feels the same way, but it's his dad's "castle" and there's nothing he can do about it.

We share a pitcher of *café-con-leche* with condensed milk.

"Breakfast for men!" Che trumpets. "And two gorgeous girls." He looks to Camila and me, lifts his orange juice glass, and cheers. He's such a loser, this guy. I think men with little peepers have PMS too: the Peeper Monster Syndrome.

London tries to save the day. He lifts his glass. "Here's a toast to Jaylene and Shai. I'm psyched you girls are here because you guys are so ugly to look at." The boys agree.

"Girls and guys should be treated equal," says George.

I lay it down like I see it. "True equality will happen when straight guys start dressing and acting like girls." I point to the guys. "Girls picked up all your bad habits like drinking, smoking, hooking up with everyone, going to the gym to get muscles, wearing suits and ties to work, just to be equal. It's a beautiful thing for butches, kings, FTM trans and genderqueers to dress like guys because that's how they really feel. But for real equality, you males have got to start dressing in skirts, heels and putting on makeup."

I cause a real commotion. Everyone gets riled up. Jaylene agrees with me and starts talking feminist politics.

We begin piling food on our plates while talking politics in fast Cuban Spanglish, so El Tigre will understand. Luckily, Jaylene speaks and understands Spanish from having taken courses in school and now in college. Her accent is sexy. I'm going to have to teach her our dialect.

Che fights back about Jaylene hating all men, stamping her as a separatist. She puts him in his place and lets him know she's a liberal feminist "fighting for the rights of political and economic rights for women." She says, "Radical feminism understands that men in power rule the world and oppress others . . ."

As she and Che debate, Camila delicately unfolds a napkin and places it on her lap. She sits quietly to eat while the rest of us jump in.

Camila's pretty. It feels good to think anything I want without being involved with anyone.

Che shrugs in exasperation. He launches a large piece of food into his Alaskan-sized mouth and changes the subject. He kisses his diamond-encrusted gold crucifix. "Thank you, God, for this food, for freedom and for freedom of speech." He stuffs a stack of food into his mouth, gulps oceans of juice, and burps loudly.

Before I stick another forkful of food in my mouth, I close my eyes and make a wish to Sacred Nature. "I hope the millions of homeless here, and the poor who can't buy food, get to eat every day." I take a sip of juice.

Jaylene puts down her fork. "Yeah. And I pray for *real* freedom of speech and freedom for LGBTQIs to marry whomever we wish all over the United States and the entire world."

With London here, a fake gay cousin Manny, and nobody knowing about my past, I feel courageous to express myself. "That's for sure. Gay people don't have the same rights or privileges as straights. Look at all the gay teens committing suicide."

Che lifts his cruddy index finger in the air. "Let them kill *all* fags!"

We all glare at him. I peer into Che's eyes. "Why do you hate gay people so much? What have they done to you?"

"Okay, so *don't* kill them. Stick them all in jail so they can fuck each other. AIDS cures faggots."

"Man, you're warped," El Tigre mumbles in Spanish. With a frustrated look on his face he excuses himself to use the bathroom.

London keeps his cool. "You should try to get to know a gay guy, *mano*. They're not as bad as you think." I like that London is intelligent, and a thinker. He stays calm, but I feel all riled up inside.

Tazer wipes his mouth with a napkin. "What are you, in the anti-gay guy Klu Klux Klan movement? Are you an antigay guy Nazi?"

Jaylene grits her teeth. "He's just a disgusting ignorant idiot."

Che's cheeks are a bloody red. He places his glass down. "And what do *you* care about faggots? You're nothin' but a confused *gringa bisexual*." He tears a piece of bread in half, smears it with a truckful of butter, and takes a huge bite out of it.

I swig a sip of sweet *café-con-leche* but it slides down bitter.

Tazer stands next to Che. "Leave my house."

Che gets up, and just as I think he's about to slam his fist in Tazer's face, he grabs his hand and shakes it. "Sorry. I get carried away talking politics. I'm Republican and have strong opinions. That's what I love about America: freedom of speech. We're free to speak our mind." He knows Tazer's dad's got our paycheck. That's why he's shutting up.

El Tigre comes back looking refreshed, as if he's splashed

cold water on his face. The tension got released and nobody became violent. Jaylene doesn't hold her tongue. She starts in about attending an all-women festival where thousands of female musicians eighteen and over pitch tents and, for two weeks, live in the woods together. "I get to play my djembe on stage with my Afro Cuban percussion band, Cunga. Well . . . I mean, obviously I'm 'beige,' but they're girls of color and play like a dream. We kick ass."

I'm wondering what it would feel like to be surrounded only by girls for a week, listening to music, talking, playing instruments, painting, taking workshops, swimming in rivers, until she says, "We feel so free without men around some of us get naked."

My thoughts crash into each other. That's definitely a place I couldn't visit. I'm way too shy about my body.

When Che gets up to use the bathroom, Jaylene starts gesticulating and capturing his distinctive speech, body movements, voice and quirks in a highly exaggerated way. We laugh.

The one good thing about Tazer having stood up to Che is that he's kept his beak shut.

Before you know it, we're done with breakfast and with *casquitos de guayaba* dessert made with guava and cream cheese.

Tazer smiles. "Let me show you guys something before you get back to slaving."

We follow him up the marble staircase that leads into the third-floor terrace. You can see the waterfalls we made cascading into a pond we installed in the backyard. There's a stone path with swaying tropical fruit trees, coral rock gardens, a grotto, arches for climbing roses and a pond with large koi fish, just as I sketched it for Marco.

"Woah! We did *that*?" Camila slaps her cheek, not believing her eyes.

We stare at the beauty of what we built, in silent awe.

I check my watch. "Time to get back to work!" I clap my hands. "Last one down's a rotten mango!" In a fury, I'm running down the stairs and everyone's following.

We get downstairs, and I bid farewell to London. "I'm glad

you came by." Now that I know he's honest about his apology, I like and respect him more.

"I'll call you soon." I wave goodbye and he takes off.

Tazer yells to me from his bedroom window, "Shai, come here a sec!"

I dash upstairs to the second floor and find him leaning against the door of his bedroom with arms crossed over his chest. He walks into his empty bedroom, which is being remodeled, and I follow. The chartreuse-colored walls reek of fresh paint. Intense music from my ancient classic Doors CD leaks in from the boom box downstairs.

I stare out the window to see the crew taking shovels full of mulch and throwing it by the palm island. Jaylene is whistling up a storm.

"She met a really hot babe last night, Rosa. Jay's in heaven."

"I can tell."

Tazer squints and puts on a grave expression. "Look, I know you got thrown out of school for Marlena's texts. You know how word spreads in Miami. I never told you so you wouldn't feel so bad about lying to me about 'Mario,' the Betrayer."

I feel heat climbing up from my heels to my head. Memories of the Incident fill my brain. I'm nervous he'll tell London and everyone here, and the good times the crew and I have had at work will end exactly as they did in high school.

He doesn't take his eyes off mine. "So if you're also into girls, and I totally get you, why can't you be honest with me? If we're supposed to be friends, why do you keep lying to me like that?"

I swallow hard a bunch of times as I scan the empty walls. I tap my foot on the shiny wooden floor and it echoes around the room. "I'm sorry I lied and have kept important parts of my life from you. It's just too hard to talk about some things, especially because if I change my life, my mother will accept me back." I can't believe the whole world knows about why I got kicked out of school. No one really knows it's because I didn't tell on Marlena. Soon, the crew and London will find out too.

"But I thought we were friends. Are you just pre*ten*ding to be my friend?"

"We *are* friends. I'm really sorry," I repeat. "Please forgive me, Tazer, and don't tell the crew about Marlena and me. My mom hates me now and I've got to keep it on the down low. And don't tell Jaylene, either. Please. I'm not ready to tell anyone."

I explain in full horrific detail everything I went through. I hope he won't start spreading the word. Just when my life takes a good spin, something happens to make it chaotic.

"It's too bad about what happened to you. If you don't want to tell Jaylene, that's fine with me. But you could've talked to me about what went down. I'm your friend, you know. I would've understood."

"It's just that I've never even *liked* any other girl but Marlena, until recently." I don't say it's Gisela, even though I'm sure he knows. "I'm in a lot of pain. My mom doesn't care about me any more and is keeping me from my little brother. Even though Marlena dumped me and got married, if I tell on her, my mom will notify Marco first, then fly to Puerto Rico to talk to her parents and husband, Rick, personally. Then, she'll force me to leave this job. Marlena's mom and mine were friends. She won't want me associating with anyone who has anything to do with her. Honestly, it will ruin Marlena's life and my job which I desperately need. I can't do that to Marlena and to myself. If I want to live a great, happy life, I should never fall in love with a girl again." I look into his eyes. "They're trouble for me and my mom will never accept me. And besides, didn't you see what a commotion London and I caused when they found out we had kissed? I like being treated with respect, instead of the way Che treats Jaylene."

"Respect?" He juts his nose in the direction of the crew. "I hate to tell you, but no matter what the crew says, I doubt they'll ever respect you, except for Jaylene. None of them spoke up when Che said such an atrocity. They're probably all conservatives. And Che is nuts. All that loathing. And he's wearing a crucifix. Jesus would die if he saw such shit. That's not what he was about." He peers into my eyes. "You're going to let *jerks* rule your life?"

"No. It's not about anyone but my mom."

"What mother terrifies a child into not being who they are? What kind of mom throws a daughter out of their house for having a girlfriend?"

He's so right. It's all about fear and ignorance. But it's so easy for him to say. He never had a neurotic homophobic mom. And his dad doesn't give three royal monkey pubes about his life. Tazer can come and go and do whatever he pleases. His dad doesn't even know or care who Tazer's friends are.

As if slapped in the face, I have a realization. I've never felt this strongly about anything. London is my savior. Is it so wrong to want peace and acceptance with my mom *and* society and also want my family back?

I jam my hands into my pockets and kick away a bit of mud that fell off my boots. I cough and turn my eyes toward the crew. "I . . . I . . ."

He interrupts. "Look. It's *your* life. You think you can fall in lust and love with London?"

I shrug. "Maybe attraction grows." I remember Marlena's words about Rick and I cringe. She did the same thing I'm doing now. Funny, but I understand her decisions much better at this moment.

Tazer smiles, a wicked funny, twisted smile. "Well in that case, I'm not a girl so your mom shouldn't care. And besides, if you can fall in love with *any*one, then include me." His lips reach mine and he goes in for a much deeper kiss.

14—Up Yours!

I have an urge to be thrown into what I've never known and get rid of all the nostalgia for what I had.

Now, I've got the opportunity to change my life. No one can dictate who I'll date but me. I've only intimately known one girl. Our breakup isn't a life sentence; it's a chance to get to know others, and who I belong with, in a much deeper way. Girls who like girls aren't an endangered species. No one has the right to kill us off. I know what I've liked and loved but I need to destroy that because it didn't work for me.

Don't get me wrong.

I'm not a hypocrite. I just need to leave behind what I once considered sacred and delve into the unknown to see if it takes me to where I really belong. Personally, I know that's with my mom and Pedri. My heart is only open to whatever will lead me to them.

I ride fast and furious after work to Pedri's school. He has learning disabilities in English and had to enroll in an after-school program.

It kills me Pedri has no one to help him with homework or run to for support. I know he still sobs about my having been thrown out of the house. I hate that I'm not allowed to be there for him. My mom won't tell him, "Everything's going to be okay. Your sister's coming back soon."

I'd always find a way to get Pedri out of any sad mood whenever he was in trouble. "You don't want Mami to see you crying. If you act like a little man and tell her, 'I learned my lesson and promise to clean my room when you tell me to,' she'll come around and forget your punishment."

I long for Pedri to bury his little face inside the curve of my neck and tell me how much he loves me. What was I thinking? Why has it taken me so long to come up with this life-changing decision? Why have I been so selfish?

I reach the fence and park my bike. Pedri runs to me.

"Shyly!"

"Little Punk!" I swing him around. "You grew about ten feet since last week." I goof around and fill his little mushy face with kisses.

"Yeah!" He squishes his head against my stomach. "I'm big now."

In the distance, the roar of kids' playful screams fills the schoolyard. I'm never happier and sadder, all at the same time, than when I come to see my little love.

Red Road is jam-packed with cars stretching off to who knows where. It's growing cloudy and dark. Cars honk their horns and kids rush to climb inside parents' cars. I feel truly happy for the first time since Mami kicked me out. Around this time, the day starts closing in on me, and I can't think of anything but try to figure out a way to go back home to Pedri without throwing Marlena under the bus.

I sit on the steps and put him on my lap.

"Do you know I miss you more than the whole mysterious universe?"

"Me too." He wraps his arms around me and I allow his love

to soothe me.

"One day, when I'm even bigger, I'm going to take you to Italy." I point to Pedri's favorite Italian pizza place set in a building that looks like the Eiffel Tower across the street. The Tower has a tilted heart, symbolizing the way my heart is leaning.

"But you are big already, Shyly. Let's go tomorrow."

"I mean when I'm an adult. Look." I jut my chin and he turns his neck again. "There's a real place that looks just like that in Italy. I'll take you to see beaches with mountains and a place full of Michelangelo paintings." I used to show him art books from all my favorite painters.

"I remember him!"

"We'll eat all the pizza we want on picnics on a gorgeous park."

"Let's do it, Shyly. Let's do it today! Pleeeeeeeeeease."

"I can't so soon. I know Mami will be here to pick you up any minute, but I had to come to let you know something important."

"What?"

I kiss his sweet freckly cheeks. "I'm going to work it out with Mami so she lets me move back home."

He leaps off me and jumps up and down. "Really?"

"Yup. But it might take a few months. You know how she is and I have to do it slowly. Can you be patient and wait for oh . . . I don't know, about half a year?"

"Yeah, Shyly! I'll wait! I'll wait! But make it fast! Can't it be faster? Like tomorrow. Pleeeeeeease?"

"I'll try. But no matter how long it takes, I'm almost sure I'm coming back home."

I find Viva outdoors. She's watering the organic tomato and cucumber seeds I planted for her, wearing a large, multicolored two-piece bathing suit, and a pink shower cap so her hair won't get fried. I notice a garlic clove stuck inside her belly button.

I rush to her and pinch her butt. "Vivalini! Are you growing a garlic tree?"

"*Ay*, Shylita!" She lets out a silly laugh and throws her arms around me. "*Hola, mariposita*. Garlics keeps evil espirits and *vampiros* away."

Neruda leaps all over me. I squeeze her in my arms. "Nerudi Rudi!" She licks and bites my nose with the sweetest baloney breath. I scrutinize her fur, it seems way lighter. "You dyed Nerudi's hair?"

"No. No. I promise. She be out in the sun too much."

I see a bottle of hydrogen peroxide on top of the lounge chair and give out a sigh of relief. I point to it. "What's that?"

"*Ay*, it's only nontoxic *peroxido*." She crinkles up her nose. "I put a little in the floor of our crib because she pee inside. I use the rest to make Nerudi a blondie."

"Nerudi peed in our *crib*?" I want to die laughing when she says "crib," but instead I act upset and throw my hands up. "Teaching you how to train a puppy is like teaching a noodle to run."

"*Ay*, Shylita, you is such a pain in thee butt." She pinches my cheek.

I go indoors feeling as if it's a perfect day. I can be in high spirits even when things around me are falling apart. But today's different. I'm on top of the world and nothing is crumbling around me! I was stupid to have rather gone homeless for Marlena than live with my family. It seems incomprehensible now that the solution has been staring me in the face all this time and I didn't see it. I can't believe it took so long to figure it out.

I shower, then Soli helps me make *fricasé de* tofu with lots of chopped organic veggies, stir fried onions, garlic, salt, green olives, ginger, olive oil, tomato paste and dried spices. I serve it with a side of wild rice. After dinner, Viva goes outdoors with Neruda to chill on the hammock and read astrology and saint magazines. Soli and I are hanging out on the floor, facing each other, just chilling, listening to my primeval vinyl records on Viva's archaic record player. I don't know why I'm the type of person who doesn't like the music everybody listens to. I either go for primordial tunes or new sounds no one's ever heard of.

I bite off a piece of nail that tore from my index finger and spit it on the ground. "You won't believe what happened. London showed up at work today and Tazer—"

She smoothes down the hem on her spandex miniskirt and interrupts. "Shyly, later on *that*. Damn, I think I got an STD or herpes or something. I'm all swollen. It itches and hurts like crazy."

"Shit, Soli, you haven't been using condoms?" I can't even think about her being bed bound with AIDS and in extreme pain. It would be too much for Soli, Viva *and* me to bear. Soli's in my heart. I love her like a sister, deep, deep down to the core. I don't want her to ever suffer.

"Of course I *always* use protection."

The dark circles under her eyes make her face seem droopy. I see her worried expression and hug her to me. "Don't fret, Hootchi Momma. I'll go with you to the gyno. I'm sure it's nothing." I'm concerned, hoping the condoms she used didn't tear and it isn't AIDS. One never knows. It could only take one time to get it. On the other hand, I'm a bit of a neuro when it comes to sex. If Marlena had been with Rick, I'd have never been with her because I had no clue who he slept with. I'm sure Rick wasn't a saint and probably got some from a lot of girls in Puerto Rico.

I talk to her for a while about what she's feeling and about Diego. I hate she's so down in the dumps. She's madly into him and says, "I won't be with him again till I know what I've got. He couldn't have given me anything. I don't want to spread something to him either, in case it's from a past boyfriend." I've never seen her so upset. What bad luck. I want to make sure she knows I'm here for her no matter what.

After I make her call the gyno for an appointment, she says, "I talked it out with London at work. He's a good guy after all. I bet you freaked when he went to see you."

"Yeah. I wasn't ready for him."

"He's so into you. Did you like making out with him the other night?"

I throw off my sneakers. "Well . . . it was . . . hard, different.

He's got nubs. But he's so persuasive, nice and sweet. He's been texting me like crazy." Making out with a guy will never compare to kissing Marlena. Kissing Tazer was better than making out with London. Now that I've established who kisses best, it doesn't matter because I feel illuminated. I'm focused and don't need to keep exploring.

"Shylypop, when you talked about kissing Marlena you were on fire. But: *nice* and *sweet*? Nice is lying on the ground and kissing the grass. Sweet is kissing a ladybug. You need to suck face with a girl again so you can see what you're missing."

I slap her cheeks as if they were bongo drums. "Well . . . in *that* case, Hootchi Momma . . . Tazer kissed me today. I know he's not a girl, but unlike trans who get their breasts and ovaries removed, he still has breasts and everything else." I tell her the whoooooole story about how it started back at the restaurant.

"Halleloo!" She slaps me a high-five, a low five and sings out, "I can't believe you've kept it from me for so long. Shyly got kissed by a b-o-i!"

I have to let her know the truth, even if she won't like it.

As a kid, when I broke something in the house, and didn't want to get in trouble, I'd bury the figurine in my backyard. After days of my mom checking under chairs, beds, couch, searching cupboards, trash containers, closets and even the refrigerator, she'd ask me, "Where's the stunning glass fish I placed on the coffee table, Shylita?"

I'd give her a sideways glance and shrug. "It disappeared, Mami."

"It couldn't have vanished," she'd say. "Tell me where it is right now or you're punished without your iTunes, TV, comics or sketchpad for a week." Eventually, I'd give in and take her to the "cemetery" out in the backyard. When she found all her favorite collectibles broken into pieces and laid to rest, she convulsed with laughter. I then had to help her wash and assemble everything with Crazy Glue. Our home was a redesigned shrine to dismembered pieces put together with meticulous care, like the broken bone unit in a hospital with patients in casts, slowly recovering.

I won't lie to Soli or shrug my shoulders and tell her I don't know what my next move will be. I refuse to spend my life putting pieces of my heart together even if Soli will help glue me back together again.

"I made out with him, but I didn't get butterflies in my stomach. I couldn't see shooting rockets and planets didn't collide. It's true. Tazer is a fine kissing machine, he's got this smooth, wild tongue action. But the firecrackers never went off. I let him kiss me, I really did. I stayed there and kissed him back. We kissed and kissed and kissed. No one can tell me I didn't give Tazer a chance."

She shakes me by my shoulders. "Tazer is a guy, Shyly. Kissing him is probably just like making out with London. He's not your type. Now, if a feminine-looking girl you liked with luxurious hair cascading down to her shoulders had kissed you, you'd have melted on the floor; I'd've had to scoop you up and bring you back to life."

There's no hiding anything from Soli. She knows me better than anyone.

Beep-Beep! Someone honks and we rush to the door. It's Tazer the kissing machine. Soli zooms out the back sliding glass doors. "I'll keep Mima company and leave you two alone. Kiss him again and again! You might like it the one *hun*dredth time! Think of it as the first step to getting you on to the second step: making out with a girl, not a boy, your type." She slams the back doors shut.

I wish I'd told her my plans so she wouldn't be so excited right now. Once I utter the words, I know I'll feel lighthearted. My decision will bring months of loneliness to a halt. I know Soli will understand and support me.

I let Tazer in. His smile glows. It fills the room with warmth. "You bailed so fast after work."

It's true. After we locked mouths for about half an hour, I became jittery and practically ran out, telling him I had to finish working. After work, I rushed to see Pedri without even saying goodbye. If I had stayed longer, I'm sure I'd have fallen into a dreamy state, since he kisses so incredibly delicious. He's disarmingly charming and yummy but that doesn't mean he'll help make my life better.

"I had to come home and cook."

We plunk on the couch, facing each other. I notice that his chest isn't flat. He didn't bind his breasts, and he's got medium-small breasts like mine. They stand out because he's wearing an extremely tight white tank. He's letting his bangs grow longer and keeps tossing them away from his face. It takes me a few seconds to get used to him looking so different.

I cross my left leg over my right and tap my thighs. I don't look at his face and don't know what to say so I blurt, "Your hair's starting to look beautiful."

"Be careful," he jokes. "You might start developing a weakness for me." He uses his hand as if it were a mirror. He stares into it and fixes his hair with his free hand. "Being genderqueer gives me the license to act like any gender I wish from time to time, whenever it fancies me and I can use it to my advantage. Maybe if I stop binding now and then and grew my hair a little longer, you'd like me better, eh?"

I'm touched by his ability to change into someone he thinks I might like, but this isn't the time for that.

I tap my foot on the floor: tippy-tap, tippy-tip. I uncross my leg and place my hands over my thighs in silence.

His eyes widen. "Hey. I've got a perplexing idea. What if you make me up like a girl, and I turn you into a guy, just for amusement purposes?"

Woah. He wants me to see he can transform into whatever I'd like. He gets I'm attracted to girls, not guys. This might keep his thoughts away from wanting to find ways to be with me. And, it might also contain his twirling tongue action away from my mouth. I can't deny I enjoy kissing him, but we must put a stop to it.

He lowers his brow. "You'll look like a drag king and I'll become a drag queen." He sticks two of Viva's velvet cushions up his shirt; it makes his chest look as if he's got two big balloon boobs. "I'm Booboola Anderson's confused grandchild, perplexed and baffled by my desire to mystify others with my knockers. Do you like me better now?"

"Absolutely! Come on, Tazeroni Spazeroni. Let's change clothes." I goof around and the tension flies out of me. "You can be Tazmina Mandarina and I'll call myself Sholo." I recall the time when some of my dreams were filled with abandoned outdoor markets where I'd walk around pinching, smelling and checking the fruit, alone, feeling lonely. Suddenly, boys and girls appeared. Boys were so busy with pretty girls they never even said hello. I'd look across the way and there were guys with arms draped around girls. I'd see the boy I liked but he kept getting farther and farther away. Sometimes, it's hard to believe anyone's so into me.

Before he can say, "I'm not wearing your miniskirt," I've changed into his clothes and he's got on my skirt and tiny stretch tank top. I've tucked my hair inside a baseball cap I found in Soli's closet and stuck a plantain inside my pants. We scrutinize ourselves in the mirror. "You'll never look like a boy, even while packing a colossal one."

"And you," I put on a gruff, thick male voice and exaggerate my tone. "You look like a sea wave, exquisitely clear, crashing into a new direction."

"Oh, my love. This takes so much nerve and bravery," he confides in an over-the-top dramatic way, in a contrived girly voice, with the palm of his hand over his heart. "I'm providing you with a raw glimpse into my romantic, private life. I'll bend, playact, wear anything and do everything you want. I'll even articulate my deepest love for you in my sweetest voice. I love you with all that I am, and more."

"I know, my precious. You're being so bold, transparent and self-revealing, for me, so I can get to know the many faces and facets of you."

I rush to Soli's organic makeup bag I gave her for her birthday before Tazer decides to start doing the tongue swirl with me again, and come back with all sorts of eye makeup, blushes and lipstick. I corner him against the end of the coffee table and layer his face with white powder. "I'm going to make you look like a geisha."

I want to see what Tazer would look like as a Japanese girl. Not that I want him to alter who he is, or that it'll change my mind about what I'm about to do with my life. And besides, I *hate* makeup. But sometimes flipping what society feels you should be like because it's not who you are and it doesn't feel right, can be freeing. Playacting is fun, it allows you get out of your own shadow; it makes you look outside yourself for a glimpse of an entirely new world and not take yourself so seriously, even if just for a few minutes. At the end of it all, I'd prefer Tazer as a guy for sure!

I can understand why he's a playwright and why so many people have a passion for acting.

Once his face and neck are ghostly white, I go to his eyes. I brush gold powder on his lids before outlining his eyes in black slants. "You're starting to look like a *real* girl. Shit. Now you'll have butches after your butt!"

"Are you getting a hard on?" He grabs my banana and I leap up.

It's been a long time since I've been able to let go and have a blast like this.

If you're caught between two worlds, exposing fragments of yourself can be rewarding if it doesn't intimidate you. Some people are threatened if they can't be themselves for one instant, and that's okay. It amazes me Tazer isn't like that, and it makes me like him more.

I place fake eyelashes on him as he blinks up a storm. I put mascara on his lashes and before you know it, I paint his lips bright cherry red.

I walk him to the nearest mirror. He flaps his eyelashes, grins and turns to me. "Am I good enough for you now?" He leans into me, grabs my face with both hands, kisses my lips, and goes into that wild tongue action motion that's smooth and soft but passionate. I start to melt and love the way his slippery tongue feels in my mouth. But I've got to stop this. It's just so delicious. I need to concentrate on what I've got to do. *Focus, Shai. What are you doing?*

Soli walks indoors and surprises us. "Hell yeah! You guys look amazing!" She sticks her hand into my pants, takes out the ripe plantain, peels it and takes a bite out of it. "Tazer, man, you look like a real girl. That's wild." She turns to me. "You look cute, but still femmy. But hey, don't mind me. Keep struttin' your stuff. I'm out of here."

She makes a U-turn but Tazer grabs her by the arm. "Don't worry about it. I've got to get going anyways. I should have already picked my dad up at the airport. He might throw a party when he sees my girly makeover. I'll tell him to not get his hopes high, that it's only a momentary lapse of good judgment and I'm being a drag queen, not a genetic girl."

He presses his lips against mine for a pop kiss. "I'll call you tonight." Soli slaps him a high-five, and Tazer rushes out the front door.

Soli gently smacks my face. "He's a hunk as a guy, and a striking girl."

"Drag queen," I correct her.

"Whatever. You've got the best of both worlds. Unbelievable. Was kissing Tazer better when he's playing a girl? Huh, huh? Was it?"

"It was exactly the same. His kissing definitely makes me feel like crawling the walls, but I can't see my life with him right now." I wipe my mouth clean from the lipstick with the back of my hand and slide the visor part of the cap toward the back of my head. "You'd think I was a hornball like you at the rate *I'm* going." I would never have thought I'd kiss a guy and then a boi, all in the same week. I'm just not the type to be carousing.

"Will you give him a chance? I know he'll be into being a girl for you."

"I wouldn't want anyone to not be themselves for me, ever. This was just a game. He's my type as Tazer, because of who he is as a person, but I don't want to be with anyone who's sexual, like you, not romantic and sensual." I'm making up a million excuses, but nothing will veer me from what I need to do.

Tazer is the type who grabs you and kisses you and throws you on the bed. Feminine gay girls can act assertive too—it doesn't take a butch girl, trans or boi for that type of behavior. But I like equal partnership, where nobody takes roles and you and the person you're with are free to do what moves you. Tazer's aggressiveness toward me, though, lets me know he's into wanting me to be submissive, unless, of course, we're playacting. That just doesn't fly with me. I need to be free to be what I want whenever I wish.

Soli squeezes my cheeks together, making my lips puff out like a fish. "Sissy stuff, that making love thing. You need a *real* lesbian, or someone like Tazer, Shyly, to show you how gay you really are. With Tazer, you've got it all: a boi who's still a girl underneath. You just have to keep giving him more chances. I bet he's super hot in bed."

Soli's starting to irk me. She won't leave it alone. It's time to tell her my decision.

"I'm sorry to say I'm forgetting about girls and anyone who was born female and still remotely resembles a girl underneath it all; it's just a big hassle that'll destroy my life even more. Tazer and London both kiss about the same, but only one of them won't bring me heartache. Can you imagine explaining to my mom that Tazer *is* a boy? She'll die. The hiding will be worse than it was with Marlena. No thanks. I'm sticking with the one that will free up my life of trouble."

Soli stares at me with her mouth wide open. "You're *not* giving Tazer a chance?"

"Nope. I'm going out with London till I fall for him. I need peace in my life. I've got to get my family back."

At this point, I don't care if I live a life of loneliness. I'll never resent having changed for Pedri. He's worth it. I've spent the majority of my nights, before getting to sleep, writing in my journal, crying, sketching and trying with all my might to feel better. I still have fun at work and with Soli and even by myself, learning my schoolwork. But I'm sacrificing my true happiness. I won't wait till Pedri turns eighteen. I have what it takes right now to bring peace and love back into my life

"Christ, Shyly. You know you like girls. You're going to push those feelings away for a mom who threw you out of the house? You can't give up on yourself. You've got to find the right girl. I get it that Tazer doesn't do it for you. But there are a million girls-who-love-girls who will. Going out with London is stupid and unless you're into him, a huge lie. You're doing a Marlena just to please your mom."

I don't care what Soli thinks. No amount of coaxing will keep me involved with a girl or boi or bi or anyone Mami won't accept. I must focus on Pedri and keep my priorities straight. Soli used to have a lot more sensibility and logic about her. True friends are supposed to be supportive. Suddenly, everything to Soli is about feelings and emotions and how it will affect one personally. Sometimes, life isn't all about me, me, me or how *I* feel about this or that. There's a bigger picture and Pedri needs me.

She keeps on and on about my dating girls. I'm not listening. I nod, but what I'm actually doing is looking outdoors from the corner of my eye.

Although it's late, the sun is still streaming in, boiling the duplex. Everything looks bright, and I won't allow Soli to keep me stuck in this bleak period. If I really mattered to her, she'd stop being in my face.

I rummage around the floor for my small sketchpad. I find it under the TV and start sketching galloping horses without looking at her. I want her to go away and stop the noise. Just when I know I've made the best decision of my life, Soli comes and stomps on it.

She keeps at it. "Forget about London. Go out with Tazer as just friends. You'll meet girls you'll like that way. He's knows tons of smart and pretty lesbians and bi's. I've cut the hair of a few of them and thought how much you'd love them. You're just traumatized because of what happened at school and because the Betrayer screwed you up." She repeats, "Hang with Tazer and his friends, till you find the right girl. He'll understand. He's got plenty girls after him. Let London do his thing with a *real* straight girl. I know you guys have been texting and you keep making excuses about why you won't go out with him now. Just tell London the truth. It's only fair to him."

I throw the sketchpad and pencil on the floor. "The truth? The truth is that everyone should be left alone to decide what they want to do with their lives without someone hounding them. You're beginning to sound like my mom who wants me one way. Didn't you hear what I just said about not dating anyone of my same sex or anybody who's different or looks gay? No one listens to me. When I told this to Tazer, he kissed me." I place the palm of my hand in front of her face. "Stop already. I swear, I'd rather get an enema from a gorilla than keep listening." I search the pile of CDs on the floor for something loud.

"You don't have to get so testy, okay?" She tugs at her nose ring and calmly lays her head on my thigh, hands clasped behind her head.

I scrub my face with my hands and place the CDs on the floor. "I just need to be left alone so I can figure out my life. I know you care about me, and you're trying to help. But I must make my own decisions, regardless of the consequences, all right?"

She stands and stares down at me with fists on her waist. "You've changed. You're suddenly becoming the *biggest* liar. Lying to others about you and Marlena was okay because she would have been disowned. But lying to yourself and to a guy? And you never used to get so pissed at me for any little thing."

I look up at her. "You're nuts."

She peels a piece of cracked polish off her fingernail. "You've never had such a strong personality. What's happened to you?" The peel drops on the tip of my big toe and I leave it there. "You used to be the most fun girl alive. You listened to everything I said. You're a different person since Marlena left you."

My frustration is mounting. Soli should get how hard it is

to be caught up in something irrational for my own good. I need to stay on course without any interference. She's pointing her finger at me as if I'm about to commit a crime. So *what* if I'm manipulating my own life to shape my mom's opinion of me? I must get rid of "my true self" and never, ever, give her a chance to emerge again.

It would be great to get a little support and sympathy right now from Soli, since I'll be losing so much. I mean, who chooses to kill herself? Doesn't she see I need to be in denial? Why is she forcing me to feel guilty before I embark on a new life that'll eliminate all my pain and sorrow, forever?

Her words insult me. In a heartbeat, I spring up. We're *this* close, facing one another.

"Are you *toasted*? I'm *still* the same person, just someone who knows what she wants to do with her life."

"No you're not. You're going to be doing strange things like dating a guy when you know you want to go out with girls. Before Marlena, you were crazy about two guys, but after your first kiss with her, you didn't even remember they existed. You told me so yourself."

"They dated me on a dare. Remember? I was the bony bookworm. I didn't even *know* how to kiss. If I'd known they were playing a joke with friends, I'd have never kissed Lorenzo. You know that the guy I really liked, who looks like London, wasn't into me. If he'd been, we wouldn't be having this conversation right now."

"You wouldn't have felt anything for him either."

"Yes I would have. I had a mad crush on him. I'd shake when around him."

There's a sad silence in the room. I stare at the painting next to the flat TV on the wall of the three of us we did last night, after I jogged around the neighborhood, picked up some groceries and an empty canvas. Viva, Soli and I are holding hands under an aqua sky with billowy clouds surrounded by palm trees.

I expect it to make me feel better, but it just pulls at my heartstrings. I'll soon be leaving here for good. This might be

Soli's last attempt to keep me as part of her little family. She should tell me she doesn't want me to go instead of putting me through hell.

We've never had an official fight. I don't want to argue, so I change the subject.

"I think you've got a mustard stain on your top."

"No, it's mango. Diego and I . . . er . . . well . . . forget it."

"What? Tell me."

"You don't care, anyways." She walks to the living room window. I jump over the piles of CDs, trying hard not to step on anything, and grab her arm.

"Soli, I *do* care." I don't like it when she acts this way. She knows I love her. I can tell she's hurt about my choosing to go back home to a mom she thinks doesn't deserve me. She wants me to teach my mother a lesson, but in doing so, I'll be hurting Pedri.

She presses her forehead and nose up against the window-pane and fogs it up. "You don't care what I think anymore. You won't listen to me, and you get pissed at me for everything. I don't need you anyways, Shyly."

"You *do* need me, you turkey. It's not that I want to leave. I swear. I could live with you and your mom till forever. It's just that I miss Pedri. I have to be there for him. He needs me. I know you'll miss me too. Just relax on the gay thing, okay?"

I grab my Cuban architecture book from the floor, sit down, and leaf through it. She picks up one of my organic gardening magazines, sits far away from me, and looks at the photos as if she were into it.

I put the book down. "Ever since my mom threw me out, and Marlena left, I've had the worst times of my life. You and your mom are the only two people in my life who've been there for me." I scratch the tip of my nose. "You're the best friend any-one could ever have, so stop the crap and let me live my life as I want to. I don't tell you how to live *your* life."

She looks up from the magazine. "Shyly, you're my *best* friend. You *know* I'd chop off my dreads for you."

"I know. I'm sure you'd rip out your eyeballs for me."

I smile, but she doesn't. Instead, she says, "But it's ridiculous and insane that you like girls and you're going to live a lie for your mom. Look at everything you sacrificed for Marlena and where is she now?"

I wring my hands. "You know I hate labels. If you want to brand me, then I guess I was lesbian when Marlena and I were together. I was wholeheartedly in love with her. I felt complete and I was never attracted to another girl or guy. The truth is that I'm drawn to London. It's not emotional yet, because I don't know him well, but everything else is there. If I were to fall in love with him, I'd consider myself straight. It's no big deal."

"Straight? You were deeply in love with a girl for two-and-a-half years, Shyly."

"I know. But I'm telling you the truth. That's the way it really is for me. The thing is that I don't know if I can fall in love with London. If I don't, I'll stop dating him. I won't use him. If I do, I know I'll never look at another girl or guy in my entire life. That'll mean I'm het."

"I get not using confining labels. But I just know you're not like most of my girlfriends at work into guys *and* girls. Labels don't exist in my world. I wouldn't tag any of my work friends. They're not gay, bi or straight. They just are. But I know you better."

"I need to go with my better judgment this time, and not just with my heart and feelings. That got me into serious trouble. Get it?"

"Nope."

"Look. For the one hundredth time: I need my mom and Pedri in my life. I'll do *any*thing to have them back. I'm in so much pain without them, Soli. I just have to clear this mess of my life up for good, on my own."

She wraps her arms around me for a hug. "Oh, I get it. It's about giving your mom, who threw you out of your house, the satisfaction of letting her see you with a guy." I loosen my hug and back away from her. "It's about lying to your mother so she can love you. Way to go, Shyly! But don't say I didn't warn you."

I peel off my cap, throw it on the couch, and my hair comes tumbling down. "Didn't you hear or believe anything I said?"

"I heard you, but no way do I accept it as truth."

"F you!" I belt out as I reach for the front door.

"Up yours!" she blasts as she slams the door behind me.

15—Get Me Out of Here!

Autumn marks its transition from summer into winter (Florida's two seasons) with the arrival of nights appearing earlier. Regardless of what season it is, it barely gets dark in Miami until after seven p.m. You'd think the days have started to grow cooler. That's not Miami. September is our hottest, most asphyxiating month.

Five months have passed since my one and only fight with Soli. We were upset ten minutes. I jogged around the block. When I got back home we put on my Brazilian CDs and started jumping around, bopping our heads up and down, side to side, pretending to be punk/goth groupies, as if nothing had happened. The following morning I went with her to the gyno. Luckily, she only had a yeast infection. And if that's not *fabulous* news, listen to *this*: Marco promoted me to part-time landscape designer/sketcher and part-time tree installer. He gave me a colossal, juicey raise!

I've also been dating London on weekends. I started seeing

him a week after the day he visited me at work. He's a fun guy who also likes things I love. We've spent time snorkeling off the Keys, bicycling around the Everglades, mini-biking, swimming with the dolphins and skateboarding. He's taught me how to surf, windsurf and sail. Luckily, his uncle has a windsurfing school/shop right on Key Biscayne Beach where he sells catamarans. He's told me, "All my exes hated water sports because they'd break a nail. I'm so lucky you're not like them."

Several times, we've been water skiing with his uncle, aunt, Soli and Soli's aunt who's a water sports freak, too. It took me a while to learn, but I got the hang of it and love it! Thanks to London I'm living the life, and having more fun than I've ever had with any of my old friends. But still, I miss CC and Olivia. I can't help it. They've never returned a single text or call.

London and I get along pretty well. I like his friends who've become my friends too. It feels good to be so accepted. I want to keep taking it slow, but he's driving me crazy about needing to see me more often. I'm going to bend because he's so good to me.

It's September eighth, Astro Viva's fiftieth birthday. Marlena, whom I'm one hundred percent over, called a bunch of times and left messages on my cell (I managed to keep my old digits). She seems to want to be friends, now that it's all behind us. "I'm so excited! I'm coming to Miami. I'll be staying at my uncle Marco's house. Rick isn't coming. I'd love to see you and talk in private. I hope you've forgiven me."

She talked as if nothing had ever happened between us. I haven't called her back nor do I plan to. I don't yearn to be Marlena's friend. After the way she ended it, something in me died. I'm sure if my mom and I were talking, Mami would be ecstatic to see her, since she never found out who the "culprit" was, and she really cared about her. She'd wrap her arms around Marlena and welcome her back, thrilled that she's married.

Early this morning Soli and I dropped off Viva and her best friend Adela at the Imax 3-D theater in Ft. Lauderdale. It's La Caridad del Cobre day. Traffic was horrendous because of a procession carrying the Virgin statue on Calle Ocho. Although worshipping virgins isn't my cup of latte (except for Marlena's body, that is, which was my shrine), I get the significance around the reverence and adoration behind the ritual: believers in our community get together to pray, ask for help, and celebrate with music and dance. I believe in something so strongly also that I too join a procession with others on April 22: Earth Day. Venerating plus taking action in caring for the earth gives you back so much more than praying to a statue, but I'm sure some might argue that.

Afterward, we headed to the dog pound. I bought Viva what she's always wanted since her dog Pelusita died of old age (21) two years ago: a bulldog mutt. Our neighbor is keeping the pup at her duplex till tomorrow morning, for an even *bigger* surprise.

Diego comes by to help Soli and me clean, organize and prepare our place for the most electrifying party *ever*. We're working away when Tazer walks in. I open my eyes wide. He stopped talking to me, cold, the day I made him up as a geisha. I called him that night. I let him know I just wanted to be his friend, and I was about to start dating London. He said, "I'm not into being *just* friends." No matter how many times I called, texted or e-mailed him, so we could talk things out, he wouldn't answer the phone or write back.

I've missed him. He has great ideas and opinions about the world and everyone in it that I enjoyed hearing. He challenged me to think outside the box. I miss our long talks, fun texts, book recommendations and hearty laughs.

He pulls me by the arm outdoors. We stand next to a pregnant banana tree. I'm excited to see him and hope he doesn't chew me out.

He buttons up his fancy white shirt, pulls on his black suspenders, and sticks his hands in his khaki baggy pants pockets. "Sorry I became so upset when you said you were going to date London," his eyes avert from mine, "a male with a penis, who, according to Jaylene, are the lowliest animals among us, thus why I've decided to be the poster boy and give them a good name."

"I didn't want to hurt you."

"I know. I get the motives behind your actions. To some extent I agree with them. I'm not in your shoes, so I don't have the urge to make it right with my family."

"Thanks for understanding. I wish we could have stayed friends but I get it." I can't lie to myself and deny that there wasn't a single day I didn't think about Tazer and wonder what he was up to. There were times when I wanted badly to read texts from him. But after he stopped communicating, I stayed away to respect his wishes.

"It's not as if seeing you with London would have been a heart wrenchingly, utterly devastating experience. I just wanted to be spared the torture of wanting you and being dissed for a genetic guy. I won't allow it to be the story of my life. I moved on immediately. I'll never let that type of negativity pervade my psyche too long. I'd rather live it up without turmoil or drama. You get it, right?"

"Absolutely." I grab a long banana leaf, pull it toward my nose, and sniff it. "I never saw it that way. It seems so insensitive now. I'm so sorry." I have to make sure he knows I never wanted to play with his feelings.

"It wasn't you. I'm the one who was after you. I got all your messages, texts and e-mails. I should've called you back, but I was upset you chose *him* over me." He stretches his neck, squints, and checks out the scene indoors. "Is he here? Are you still seeing him?"

"Yes, but he's home with the flu, so he's not coming today." I peel a piece of the leaf and tear it into a few strips. I tell him everything that's been going on and the truth about why I'm trying to fall for London. If he wants to be my friend, he's going to have to accept my life as I've chosen to live it. "Do you think we can ever be friends again? I mean, *just* friends?"

He hugs me to him really hard and slaps my back. "For sure, *chica*. That's why I came today when Soli called me last week. I recently met Elicia, a girl who works at my optometrist's office. She's studying to become an oculist. She's also a writer, like me." He fixes his purple tinted glasses and lets out a shining smile. "I dated a few girls and had blast going to the theatre, seeing plays, bungee jumping and things like that. But something different happened when I met Elicia. We instantly hit it off. She finishes my sentences; we listen to the same type of underground music; it's as if we've known each other all our lives. Finally, after Dori, I meet someone I'm really into. We go out on goofy, nerdy dates, like bowling, fishing, to the library and horseback riding. Soli said I could bring friends. I came early to help. Elicia is working, but she'll be here later."

"Fantastic." I feel happy and a little sad. I'm not sure why. I think it's because I'll never know what could have become of us if I'd given him a chance. He has all the qualities I'm fiercely attracted to. I'm sure we would have made an amazing couple. It's not easy letting go of someone who could have been part of your life in a deeper way. It's a sacrifice one must pay in order to do the right thing for your future with your family. But I'm psyched we can stay friends.

Tazer confides in me, "You know, when London came into the picture, he became my competition. I never felt intimidated, but I thought you were making a grave mistake to associate with a dense, superficial and intellectually inferior guy." He lifts an eyebrow. "I hope you know I'm joking."

"Of course." I smile. He hasn't lost his sense of humor.

"Granted, I'm sure he's exciting, but nothing like I believed I could be for you. I felt a little possessive of you. I kept hoping he'd make your life monotonous and dreary so you'd text me things like, *I was wrong! Come save me!*"

I laugh and the sadness leaps right out of me. "The truth is, Shai, once I got to know you, I couldn't help but love your sarcastic sense of humor, personality, and different way of thinking. You're not so bad on the eyes, either. And besides, you grew on me like testicles. But for my own selfish reasons, I didn't want you dating another guy. I wanted to be the *only* male you fell hard for." His vision swings toward the bananas and back to me. "I was ecstatic about you from the get-go. I guess if you'd allowed it, I could have fallen hard for you. I know that you too would have felt the same."

Soli screams from indoors. "Yo, dildos, we need some help!"

Tazer slaps my back. "I'm over you, though. Come on, *chica*. Let's go!"

I pull on his streaked bangs. "You're all right, Tazer. I'm excited you're back in my life."

We walk indoors arm in arm, just goofing off.

I bought party hats, balloons and crepe strips to hang from the ceiling, along with games, gifts and an organic guava and cream cheese cake. Soli bought a Santa Barbara *piñata* with a large red cape covered with fake pearls. Soli's super slick in her lime green dress, so tight you'd think she'll soon die of asphyxiation.

"Listen up, guys," she announces, tugging at her nose ring. "Once Mima pulls off the cape, little chocolate saints and teeny chocolate dicks will shower the floor."

Soli has always been generous to her mom and vice versa. If those two didn't have a penny to fall back on, they'd still make sure to give each other lavish surprise birthday parties. Last year, on Viva's birthday, Soli took us on a trip to St. Augustine to visit Viva's cousin Andreita.

Viva, Marlena, Andreita, Soli and I roamed the streets talking and laughing. We went on a carriage ride, entered cozy cafés, bookstores and swam at the beach. The azaleas and orange blossoms were in full bloom. Marlena and I were so in love the colorful flowers made the world around us a scented paradise.

Soli did the unexpected that day. Andreita, who's got a coconut oil suntan lotion business, invited Viva to a spa massage, then to dinner. She paid for a five-star hotel for all of us to stay in. After a feast, Soli took them to a play, then to watch the stars. Marlena and I had the hotel room to ourselves for five hours. Soli told Viva, "They want to go watch a lecture from a famous author at the bookstore down the road."

Marlena and I loved each other that day to the bone. We were so overwhelmed with passion we talked about having our honeymoon there.

The doorbell rings and my memories disperse. I let the

caterers in. They leave globs of pink cheeses, *croqueticas*, greasy chicken wings, fried green triangular sandwiches, deep-fried glazed *churros*, ham and cheese balls, *empanadas de carne*, *papas rellenas* swimming in fat, neon-orange pudding, *flan*, and custards. This is Soli's gift to her mom: clogged arteries.

I found organic recipes online and made hummus, egg salad sandwiches, *bocaditos*, black bean dip, baked plantain chips and huge exotic fruit bowls (star fruit, litchis, papaya, mango, finger bananas, *mamey*, *sapote*, etc.). Diego brought a truckload of chips and sodas. Tazer bought crates of organic juices, guacamole, crackers, and fancy food I've never eaten like caviar, truffles and other delicacies. We're ready.

Viva's video home phone which doesn't work after it fell and the screen broke, and never, ever rings, rings! I make a mad dash for it, in the privacy of Viva's bedroom, thinking it's probably Pedri and I didn't want to miss his call. I shut the door behind me.

"Pedri?"

"Shai?" Mami's voice is at the other end. I fumble and drop the phone. I pick it up with shaky hands. She must have gotten my phone message. I said I had changed and wanted to introduce her to my new boyfriend. I waited a long time to let her know about London. I needed to be certain my relationship with him would work out. With my mother, I must be completely sure she believes I've transformed, or there's no going back home.

"Is everything okay?" I don't know what to expect.

"Not only did I get your message, but I know it's true about you dating a boy. Graciela recently told me she saw you with a tall, thin, dark-haired boy around Miami." She speaks fast Spanish, in a high-pitched voice, as if she were the happiest woman in town. "Is he *really* your boyfriend? You have a boyfriend, Shai? Tell me this is true!"

"Yeah, Mami. I do!"

A flashback of the day my mom was thrilled about setting me up on a blind date with a friend's son slams my brain. The week before, she had told me, "All your friends have boyfriends except you." Marlena was upset I was forced to go out on a date with a guy who looked like a movie star. The boy and I barely talked. He kept texting people and receiving text messages. Since he was playing that game, I texted CC, Soli, Olivia and Marlena and let them know what a horrible date I was on. It seems his mother had forced him to go out with me too. Roque wore more cologne than a group of girls at a perfume shop. I turned him off when I asked, "Would you mind getting off at that gas station and scrubbing your neck? I'm allergic to scents. They're made with petrochemicals that seep into your glands. Not only are they terrible for everyone, but for allergic people, they're hell and I don't want a migraine."

I wasn't joking, but I laid it on thick so he wouldn't be into me. No lie. The kid picked me up with a gleaming smile and starry eyes. After he obliged, he came back with the corners of his mouth drooping. That's when the texting started. He must have thought I was a freak. And, of course, Marlena was over the moon about my behavior. After watching a violent thriller, Roque dropped me off at my house. I was so tense I made myself a tuna fish sandwich dripping in mayo and was taking big bites out of it when my mom walked in the door.

She called me into her room. "Follow me and tell me all about your date."

I tossed the sandwich on a plate and stormed into her bedroom, licking my fingers clean. Mami plunked herself on her bed and started slipping off her stockings, complaining about how tired and inflamed her feet got from working so hard.

I leaned into the doorway and exclaimed, "My date went great! Incredible! Unbelievably perfect! I've fallen in love with him!" Then turned around and marched back into the kitchen.

Mami came to me. She asked why I was shouting like that. "Are you sure you had a good time? You never scream."

"I told you not to introduce me to random guys, Mami." I explained the terrifying, gory movie he made me watch. "I didn't have a say. I was stuck watching it. Afterward, all he did was talk about himself and how he's going to be recruited to be a pitcher for the major leagues one day. Oh, and he smelled like a girl, and all he did was fix his hair in the car mirror. I think he might be gay." I lied about the gay thing, but not about anything else. I knew that would make her never want me near him again. "Don't ever set me up on a blind date."

The memories stop and I hear my mom's voice. Something inside me collapses, and I don't feel so blissful talking to my mother. I thought I'd be ecstatic. The idea of her calling me back was so intense I believed I'd be the happiest person alive. What a letdown.

She lets out a long sigh of relief. "Have you been seeing him a long time?"

I deepen my voice. "Five whole months." I want it to sound powerful, as if a century has passed by.

"Five months?! This is serious. I can't tell you how happy I am!"

I play with the phone cord, feeling upset my mother hasn't even asked me how I'm doing. She doesn't have a clue I quit school or that I'm working full time. All she cares about is that I'm dating a guy. I should have known to expect this from her.

"That's the *best* news I've ever heard in my life!" She pauses a moment. "What's his name?"

"Francisco Bustamante," I say dryly, "but everyone calls him London."

"*¡Qué cosa más grande la vida!* In Cuba the Bustamantes were wealthy, high-class people before Fidel, *el hijo de puta*, took their wealth and turned them into poverty-stricken animals. The grandchildren of those Bustamantes came to Miami and are very well off. I bet you his great-great-grandparents are people my great-grandmother knew."

I don't comment about politics or anything that will enrage her. I've learned my lesson. Being mute with my mom, never expressing my true feelings, or saying the truth about things that will upset her, is the best way.

"Listen, we finally moved into our dream house in Coconut Grove. We've just finished furnishing and unpacking. Jaime and

I are leaving to Europe for three weeks the day after tomorrow."
She talks for a while about her life and what she's been doing.
"We've been traveling on weekends with Pedri, sightseeing, and
doing all those things I was never able to do. Jaime is a blessing.
He treats Pedri like his own son."

"I'm so glad, Mami."

I ask her more questions about her life so she doesn't focus
on mine. As she talks, I can tell she's having a marvelous time,
and doing well. I wonder how I would have fit in with the three
of them.

"We'll be stopping in Spain to visit your aunt and uncle. I'll
pick you up tomorrow at noon so we can talk."

"Great!" I can't wait to go to their new house and see Pedri.
"Is Pedri going with you to Europe?"

"No. He'll be staying here with Zenaida. Jaime's sister adores
him. She's become like a second mother to him. He doesn't want
to go; he's terrified of flying and started having nightmares. I
trust Zenaida to take care of him. You can come see him to make
sure things are running smoothly. If you're still changed, and are
still with your boyfriend, we can talk about your moving back
when I return."

My hands get clammy, and I rub them on my pants. "Okay,
Mami." She gives me the address of their new house and I mem-
orize it.

Pedri hadn't known how to explain where they were living.
He just said, "It's no fun. I don't know nobody. There are no kids
in the street to play with. It's bad. I miss my friends and I miss
you too much." I knew it was somewhere in the ritzy Coconut
Grove neighborhood they'd been planning on moving to, but
exactly where, I wasn't sure.

Suddenly, my stomach feels like it's on fire. I almost wish I
had never called her to tell her about London. I want her to love
me unconditionally.

"Can I talk to Pedri?"

She hands him the phone. "Shyly!" The tiny candy voice at
the other end lifts my spirits.

"Little Punk! I'm going to see you every day now. We'll spend Thanksgiving, Christmas and New Year's together." I feel as if a party were going on inside me. "I'll be there early tomorrow morning. I can't *wait* to see you!" My call to Mami was all worth it now.

"Yaaaaaay!" he cheers and it melts my heart. Even though I've been seeing him a lot during lunch breaks, it's not the same as being with him every day.

"It's Viva's birthday party, so I need to go now. But I'll pass by Toys R Us tomorrow morning after breakfast before Mami comes to pick me up to visit you."

"Okay, Shyly. I love you."

"I love you more than all the deserts, rivers and even the sun, my Little Punk. I can't wait to see you."

"Me too." We throw each other kisses, and he hands the phone over to my mom.

"See how easy it would have been if you had taken my advice and dated a boy from the beginning?"

I say nothing. She keeps stabbing at my heart without even knowing it.

"Okay, Shai, I'll see you tomorrow. I've missed you, I love you, and I want you back."

"Okay. Bye, Mami. Have fun in Europe." We hang up. I've missed her so much too, and I love her deeply, but I couldn't utter those three words. I don't trust her to not hurt me again.

I could tell myself *she's my mom and everything will be beautiful*, like it used to before the Incident, but that's just not me. In her view, unless I'm with a guy, I'm worthless. If I don't achieve what she has (a good marriage and children) she may never see me as someone of value. Having a dick in one's life (a male) equals power to her. Females, regardless of how strong they are and even if they're CEO's, doctors, attorneys, billionaire business-women, they're still nothing without a man according to Mami. No one knows what the future may bring. In the meantime you can prepare so your mother can one day find you worthy and special, instead of a failure.

I slap my face a bunch of times. I take deep breaths, and walk slowly to the living room.

People pile in. Soli's friends from work, Viva's metaphysical friends and the neighbors. It's jam-packed.

Jaylene walks in. "Shai!" She hugs me nice and hard. "You look fantastic, girl." She turns to the wild-haired, cinnamon-colored girl with melancholy, poetic eyes standing on her right. "This is Gisela." She points to me. "And this is Shai, the greatest tree and landscape sketcher in the world."

"Hey, I know you from Cha-Cha's restaurant, remember?" Gisela says in a melodic voice. She's got on the same type of thrift-shop clothes I'm wearing. Her checkered pants are green and brown. Mine are checkered aqua and sea green. Her Indian print blouse is long and slinky. Mine is short, showing my belly button, with long, loose sleeves, '70's retro style. We've got on the same type of square-toed ankle boots.

She locks her dreamy emerald eyes on mine. "How's it going?"

I want to say, "Magnificent now, since you've just made my day and my whole life." But instead, I tell her, "Good, and you?" My heart is skipping beats. I don't know what I'm doing and I grab a vase from the coffee table to polish it with my hands.

Jaylene saves the day. "Gisela is Rosa's friend, you know, the girl I've been dating. She just graduated from high school and also enjoys foreign films. Since you love Italian, French, all types of foreign movies so much, I thought you'd want to meet her."

Jaylene talks about political films of historical relevance to women and how, when she was a child, they influenced her into becoming an activist. Gisela and I mention Cuban films and how, sadly, Communist propaganda rules the movies Cubans can watch. If they want to see an American film, they've got to buy it in the black market for an eyeball and a foot. We effortlessly jump to talk about other things. "There's a lake in Hialeah I went to last week on my day off," Gisela says. "I was swimming with the ducks when a snake slithered past me."

Jaylene and I listen with widened eyes as she explains that

her friend took a heavy branch and hit the snake over the head till it swam away. If it had been poisonous, I wouldn't be talking to Gisela right now. From one second to the next, life can either get you good or gift you.

I'm enjoying Gisela way too much. Just what I needed: the girl of my dreams to also love the same types of films, be into solar energy, retro music, organic foods, water sports, politics and fun in the sun right after I tell Mami I'm straight.

I speak to her in my broken Italian I've learned from a travel handbook and from watching Italian films. *"Come stai?"*

Her braces have made her teeny teeth so perfectly lined up you'd think the dentist chiseled them down just before she got here. *"Bene."* She smiles sweetly and my insides go all mushy, like melting, chocolate kisses. "That's about all I know." She smiles again, smoothly as a placid pond and holds onto her colorful beaded necklace. She has a suave demeanor as she gives her curls a distracted push away from her eyes.

We realize interests we share in common: architecture, music, novels, electric cars, hiking, camping out, riding bikes and traveling. When she speaks about environmentalism, it creates a shine around her that leaves me stunned. I shift from foot to foot and try to pull myself together.

"How long have you been Green?" I ask.

"Since I was a fetus. I came out of my mom's womb scolding her about the way she was destroying the planet by polluting and hurting humans with the choices of chemicals she used on a daily basis."

She grabs a bottle of sparkling grape juice off the coffee table next to us and takes sips of it while I speak excitedly about exotic fruit trees. "I'd like to fill the yard with them. One day, I want to be completely off the grid, use no emissions and make zero footprints."

She grins. "Me too."

I carry on about how even during bad economic times, millions who don't have much line up outside stores on Black Friday, and on the day after Christmas, and collectively purchase billions of dollars worth of gifts. "I know we're bombarded with advertisements about unnecessary items we need to buy, but shouldn't people be spending their hard-earned cash on paying debts and on necessities?" She agrees. We have so much in common it stings.

We mention new and classic Italian films we love. She adores Lina Wertmuller, Fellini and other dead directors from a distant era as much as I do. She mentions global warming, tsunamis, snowstorms, earthquakes and other types of storms. I say, "Solar storms affect Earth. Part of the reason they happen is due to the relative position of the outer planets and the effect electromagnetic forces have on the sun relative to the earth." I recently watched a documentary on the storms and am poised to impress, but hell, it's so complicated I'm not sure if I confused the facts or got them right.

"Yeah. Ancient people were aware of all types of celestial connections without NASA's huge telescopes, and other pioneering technologies only the elite can afford."

Jaylene jumps in. I'm sure she'll relate everything to women power or men's behavior.

"That's for sure. Take the moon, for instance. One day, the first girl bled like her mom and didn't die. Suddenly, all females in the tribe started having periods at the same time. This got males to view bleeding girls as goddesses, and more powerful than them, because they'd die if they bled for a week straight. Our pre-history was matriarchal. Those first girls noticed the connections between their bodies and the moon cycles affecting weather. The moon not only influences the tides. It affects certain stars when they rise, especially in the Nile River, where Sirius rose in the east and announced floods."

Gisela says, "Scientists take full credit for figuring that out. The first who understood the power of stem cells weren't doctors and pharmaceuticals; they were the ancients and witches who took the blood of animals and women's menstruation to heal their patients . . ."

Being around Gisela so long slaps me into reality. I hear

Pedri's little voice, "Shyly, I love you. I miss you so much. When are you going to move back?"

Something inside me rattles. The vase slips out of my hand and shatters into a thousand pieces. Jaylene, Gisela and I start pushing the glass with our shoes into a small pile. I insist I alone will pick it up.

As I'm about to head off for a broom, Tazer comes around with his arm over the shoulder of a thin, long-haired girl. I guess it's Elicia. He sings loudly to Jaylene, "Hey, Jay, what do you say? Can't get them both inside your O.J.? So glad you made it!"

Jaylene slaps Tazer's back. "Yeah! Good to see you here."

Tazer introduces Elicia to me. "My beautiful date."

"I've heard so many great things about you, Shai." She's got large teeth, a long face and vibrant golden eyes.

"Thanks," I say. "Tazer told me about you, too." We talk about school, her studies, how she comes from a family of op-tometrists and the script she and Tazer are writing. "It's a drama revolving around a teen girl with the natural ability to set fire with her eyes, but she ends up burning the boi she loves to death." Tazer speaks of planning on having a lot of eye problems to visit her at work more often. Elicia seems smart and feminine-looking with a multicolored skirt and blouse, a touch of makeup and small earring hoops. She's right up Tazer's alley, that's for sure.

"Hey, where's Rosa?" Tazer's sparkling eyes roam around the duplex.

"She had to work late," Jaylene says. "She's coming later."

Tazer's eyebrows leap upward when he sees Gisela. "You're the waitress at Cha-Cha's. What's up?" They all start talking and I send them outdoors. I need to clear my mind. I must erase Gisela from my brain. When a girl's scent, words, smile, intel-lect and everything about her captivates you but you can't do anything about it, it's probably like being homeless and starved and someone offers you a painting of a bed and a plate of sand molded to look like a steak just to watch you suffer.

As I'm heading to get a broom, Soli comes over with a bag

and a broom. "*¿Que pasó?*" She starts sweeping.

I tell her the entire conversation I had with Mami, but leave out that Marlena is trying to contact me.

"Your mom's a nutcase. I wish you hadn't told her you were seeing London. She should love you no matter what." Soli's right. Her words tear right through me.

I change the subject. I don't want to feel pain. "Listen, why is this party filled with lesbians? Are you getting back at me for the fight we had ten million years ago? I thought we were *to*tally over that."

"Shlylypop. Don't be rid*i*culous. I just keep meeting gay girls at work. That's why the dozens of lesbos here."

"Oh. I see. I guess straight people are too geeky to like your haircuts, eh?" I nudge her in the ribs and wink.

She raises an eyebrow. "No one can pull the wool over your eyes, Shyly, that's for sure. So, yes. I've got an ulterior motive, but can you blame me?"

"You're too much, Hootchi Momma." I can't get mad at Soli anymore. She goes out of her way to do outrageous things because she loves me so much and thinks she knows what I need and what's best for me.

She sweeps everything into the bag, places it on top of her CD player, and stands with a hand on her hip, the other holding the tip of the broom, peering into my eyes. "I saw the gleam in your eyes when you were talking to Gisela. It's the same type of shine you had with Marlena. Give her a chance. You hardly ever feel that intense attraction." She starts sweeping again.

I grab her arm. "She's not into makeup, perfume or plastic shit. She's one hundred percent Green. And she's into the out-doors, animals, politics and foreign movies, too." I talk low and let it pour. "Being around her makes me want to fly. I feel like I'm going to hyperventilate and explode."

"Shit! Shyly, it's about *damn* time." She musses my hair.

I lower my head. "But dating her will ruin my life. I just talked to Pedri." I tell her *every*thing. "I can't live without him anymore. I just can't. It's either Gisela or Pedri. You know girls come and go. Look at Tazer. You thought he was really into me. Now he's all riled up about Elicia." I take a deep breath and let out a long, slow exhale. "I need Pedri now more than anything in the world, Soli. I'm this *close* to moving back home and having my family back."

I get a dustpan from the closet and place it on the floor. She sweeps the dust left from the glass pieces inside it with such a serious face I think I've finally talked some sense into her. I pour the contents into the bag.

"It's so sad you can't follow your feelings because of your crazy neuro mom. I know how hard it's been for you to live without Pedri. I hate your choice, but I guess I'm forced to accept it."

I kiss the tip of her nose. "Thanks so much." I let out a sigh of relief.

That she understands me, makes a cheerfulness come over me. I know I'm making the right decision to bring a horrible period in my life to a close. I have the will to shut the door to girls for good. If I were swimming right now, I'm sure I'd have started floating.

I glance over at Gisela on the crowded dance floor, swaying her hips from side to side in a belly-dancing style, realizing I've made the right decision. I can actually put a stop to my feelings. I'm leaving behind all my troubles to look forward to a better, chaos-free life.

With broom in hand Soli walks away from me and comes back with a *limonada*.

"Cheers to our friendship. I'll miss you if your psycho mom takes you back. Here. It's organic. No alcohol, just like you love it. Lots of mint leaves, honey and lemon."

I take a sip and hand it over to her. "I'll miss you too. I love you Soli."

She takes a mouthful. "I love you too, Shyly."

Soli grabs the bag filled with glass from on top of the CD player, throws it in the trash, stashes the broom in the closet, and goes to find Diego.

Music blasts. Elbows and feet are going this way and that

way. Everyone seems to be having fun. I haven't even *thought* of London for an *in*stant. In a way, I'm glad he's not here. And the same goes for Marlena. I'm definitely not calling her back or seeing her, ever. She's history. That's what she wanted. So be it.

Jaylene comes to me and we hang around talking. "Fun party. It's like a lesbian bar in here."

"Yeah. Thank Soli for that."

She takes a sip of the mango fizz juice and licks her lips. "Too bad you're not at least bi. You'd have a lot of girls to choose from." I never told her about Marlena and me at work. We text a lot. Mostly about how she enjoys debating with Che and winning each time. After Tazer's job, Marco bounced me around all over Miami because of my landscape sketching design skills. He's got four different crews, one for South Miami, North Miami, the beach and the westernmost parts of Miami. Every once in a while, I work with the same crew, crazy Che included.

Diego comes around. He talks about music videos and recites an on-the-spot poem about Soli as we watch her dance with Gisela, Elicia and Tazer. I can hardly watch Gisela's movements; she's so delicious. I love the way she sways her whole body in that smooth, sensual way. I look away and hope Soli's telling Gisela I'm about to get married to a guy on skid row with six kids.

Soli leaves to pick up Viva and I dance up a storm with everyone *but* Gisela.

Everybody's eating, dancing and getting to know one another when we hear, *Bang! Bang! Bang!*

People in the backyard zoom through the back doors and we cram into the kitchen. I hear Viva's key in the door.

Adela, Viva's pudgy best friend, and Soli walk indoors as we rush forward. "*Surprise!*"

"*¡Ay, Santa María madre de Dios!*" Viva cries out. I drape my arms around weepy Viva and give her many kisses. She looks adorable in her flowered polyester pink and green dress and pink flip-flops. She checks out the *piñata*, pulls the cape, and down comes a shower of saints and teeny penises. "*¡Jesucristo!*" The candy flies all over the place and everyone goes wild. Neruda flies to the treats and growls as if the saints were alive.

I put on a salsa tape—a mix of old-timers she loves: Olga Guillot, Albita, Celia Cruz and Tito Puente—Viva's favorite. Hands are up in the air, hips are moving all over the place. Feet are shuffling this way and that way. People twirl around and around. Soli pulls Diego by the suspenders to the dance floor. He looks dapper with baggy pants, a tight pullover and slicked-back hair. She presses herself against him so tightly, you'd have to peel her off him in order to unglue them.

Gisela comes around and I walk the other way. I've got to cut the thread of passion that easily flowed between us so the need to be with her won't feel unbearable.

A tiny, plump man with bushy gray hair, wrinkly face, sweet wilting eyes, big belly and a twinkle in his smile arrives. He's wearing a *sombrero de guano*, a *guayabera* and pleated pants.

Soli peels herself from Diego. "Mima, this is Diego's dad."

Viva turns rosy red, as if she'd swallowed a beet and it's leaked inside her cheeks.

"It's Gabriel. Gabriel Eufemio." His eyes are glowing, as if he's seeing Cleopatra rise from a sarcophagus. "Pleased to meet you." Viva's face glows.

The party is grand! I spend the rest of the night talking and dancing with everyone except you know who. Jaylene, Tazer and Rosa manage to keep Gisela company all night long. For once in my life I'm headed in the right direction.

16—Stinking Liar

Beep-beep-beeeeeeeeeeeeeeeeeep! Beep-beep-beeeeeeeeeeeeeeeeeeeep!
I hop off the hammock, place my banana oatmeal nut breakfast bowl on the ground, and dash to my mom's new glue-smelling green Jaguar, leaving Neruda fenced in, in the backyard.

"Mami!" I lean into the passenger seat and press my cheek against hers. She hugs my face hard to hers and kisses it many, many times. She smells familiar, like home. Tears stream down our faces. I look away, trying to control my overwhelming emotions.

"I couldn't wait to see you and came early to pick you up. Let's go." She wipes her tears with the back of her hand. She must love me.

"Get down a minute, there's no one home." I want her to see how I live.

"Your neighbor," she says, still sitting inside the car, "the one with the Santa Barbara tattoo that looks like a criminal, was eye-ing my Rolex. I took it off and stuck it in my purse."

"Babalao Carasco is a nice guy, Mami." I roll my eyes.

Babalao Carasco is a *Santero*. Although he's a respectful neighbor, he kills roosters and goats to sacrifice them to the *Orishas* when purifying people of their ailments. I begged him to spare the animals' lives the other day. "Can't you use dead animal spirits or maybe animal fur or nails?" He insisted only animal blood works.

He and I sat on rocking chairs on his porch. We rocked back and forth, back and forth, debating religion and gods. I don't believe in gods, and he worships many *Orishas* and believes spirits of dead ancestors surround us at all times. He told me, "Animal sacrifices are the only way to appease the gods so they can change the course of nature. Your people slowly murder poor bulls in bullfights. The blood we use holds the *aché*, the life force. It's used for spiritual and physical healing. Everything possesses life energy. My practice is done with utmost respect for the animals and only when *Orishas* permit."

Even though I still hate the killing, I respected his religion when he explained, "I use animal sacrifice to communicate with the *Orishas*; it's ingrained in *Santería*, my ancient Afro Cuban religion. People eat chickens, lamb and goats all the time, yet nobody questions *their* slaughter. I'd never disrespect you by asking you to sacrifice something you believe in. I'm a good man. I worship my *Orishas* and cure people's bad luck and purify them of evil spirits and illnesses. That's a good thing."

Mami continues to complain. "Only you, Shai Sofía Lorena, would choose to continue living in this *barrio*. It looks as if the Castro family, *los hijos de putas*, opened the doors to more jailed criminals and they all moved *here*."

I *love* this *barrio*, and Soli's duplex, close to my old home. And besides, it's not as if I had a huge choice of places to go to when she kicked me out. But I don't say a peep.

I swing the door open. Mami bolts through it speaking Spanglish, words flying around ten miles a minute, rearranging our furniture.

"*This* chair doesn't match *this* wall." She shoves the

kitchenette table from the middle of the dining area closer to the wall. She takes down my two framed paintings of the Cuban mountainside. "*Uy*, I don't know why you paint *la jungla cubana* when you can fill your walls with colorful art. All this brown and green will make you depressed."

As Mami moves everything around, I think about soon wiping Pedri's runny nose and putting him to sleep at nights reading him storybooks I know he'll love.

I smile as Mami reminds me of something. A lady from our *barrio* started coming around every Saturday afternoon when Papi was off working and Mami was doing chores. One day, the woman went around our house, moving things around, saying she was an interior designer and wanted to help us.

"Remember when Maylie sat on our sofa and wouldn't move until after she'd had lunch with us?" I nod. "When she got up to leave with a full stomach, you slapped her butt and told her, 'Stop coming over. We have very little food to eat and you only come to stuff your face. We like our house just the way it is. Why don't you invite *us* to eat over at *your* house?'" We laugh, remembering how Maylie never stepped foot in our home again. I recall my mom telling the story to neighbors and laughing at my antics.

"I *like* brown and green, Maylie, er . . . I mean, Mami." She cracks a smile as I walk behind her, trying to grab my framed paintings from her. She darts and shoves me aside with her super-dooper BIG beach ball butt.

She hangs my Cuba paintings in our bathroom, over the toilet bowl, on two of the four lined-up empty towel hooks.

"Want some yogurt?" I ask, in an attempt to get her to calm down.

"*¿Estás loca?* I weigh one hundred ninety-nine pounds. I'm going on a *caldo* diet until I lose fifty pounds."

"Mami, you're forty-nine! You can't live on broth."

"Forty-five! And if *that* doesn't work, I'll need to start eating air to lose weight."

I chuckle and stuff a spoonful of yogurt in my mouth. "Eat more veggies." In some ways, I'm glad it's the same old mom in front of me. She's hilarious and tons of fun, except for her homophobia. If I could just peel off the phobia, she'd be the greatest mother in the universe to have fun with. I really miss the good old days and can't wait till things get back to normal.

"Vegetables give me a hernia."

"Veggies have nothing to do with a hernia, Mami." She continues to move things around as if it were her own home and as if nothing terrible had ever come between us.

"Your grandfather died of diverticulitis. I can't eat tomatoes or lettuce or anything with skin on it. I inherited that illness."

"What you inherited is called gluttony." I stay serious and she cracks up.

"I just got my cholesterol checked and it's a perfect two-fifty without my ever having eaten a *single* vegetable."

"Two-fifty!?"

"*¡Ave María Purísima!* Shai! That's *normal* for a forty-two year old, my doctor told me."

"A minute ago you were forty-five. *What* doctor?"

"Dr. Benítez."

"Mami, Dr. Benítez is three hundred years old!"

"He was the greatest doctor in Cuba. All my friends go to him. He's giving me a face-lift."

"A *face*-lift? Him? Mami, *por favor*, don't get a face-lift from *him*. By now he can't even hold his ding-dong to pee."

"Don't worry. I know what I'm doing. My friend Sylvina just got one from him and now looks *exactly* like a twenty-something Liz Taylor."

"Damn, Mami! That's terrible. She used to look like J. Lo." I wash and throw the empty yogurt container in the recycle bin and sit on top of the kitchen table, swinging my feet. She throws herself on the couch and poooooooof, the air slowly comes out of it. A flash of the day she met Marlena appears before me. Mami told her, "You'd be stunning if it wasn't for your nose. Have your parents fix the cartilage that got broken." Marlena turned all shades of red.

"When's the operation?"

"*El mes que viene.* When I get back from Europe."

"Next *month*?" My stomach does cartwheels.

"*Uy*, Shai Sofía Lorena, you worry about *every*thing. You're too sensitive, just like Papi was."

"Mami, nurses have to tie you up with ropes when they give you shots. I can't believe you're allowing someone to give you a face-lift. You're too young for that. And your face is *beau*tiful."

And it's true. My mother has gorgeous dark eyebrows, and large almond-shaped eyes with long lashes. Her teeth are moon white and straight. She's got a killer smile with two dimples. As a teen, she was a face model for soaps, creams and toothpaste.

"When you get to be forty, and you start sagging, you'll tell me a different story."

"Forty? So, who do you want to look like?" I'm intrigued.

"A twenty-five-year-old Sofía Loren." She pats her face with both hands. "I named you after her, my beloved mother's favorite movie star." She spins the subject around. "I've been on a high-sugar diet. Sugar eliminates wrinkles."

"*What?*"

"*Sí*, Shai Sofía Lorena. Your body needs sugar or you go into a coma."

"That's outrageous. Where'd you get *that* from, *Hola* magazine? Mami, won't you *ever* listen to me? Ditch the diabetes-causing sweets, and eat some veggies?"

"I'm *your* mother. *You* have to listen to *me*," she joked.

Loud bouncy music sweeps into the duplex through the opened windows. She stands abruptly and looks outdoors into the backyard.

Our neighbor, Maribel, is dancing around to salsa music, getting her high heels stuck in the earth as she throws clothes to hang on the line. Her parrot, Chuchito, is flying around the backyard, squawking, "¡*Ay*, Miguel! ¡Miguel!"

Miguel's friends are standing around him, drinking beers and barbecuing. "*Oye*, Chuchito's been listening to you and Maribel doing the *fuiqui-fuiqui*, eh?"

Mami pulls me by the arm. "What a *barrio*! *Uy*. To think we used to live like this. Come on! Let's go to my new house. Pedri is home. Jaime and his sister are in the pool."

"Take me first to buy Pedri some toys. I promised him."

"Later! We'll all go together. That way, he can choose what he wants."

We climb into her glossy car and in a *heart*beat, we're in my mother's new two-story fancy house with an Olympic-sized pool and immaculate landscaping.

After Pedri shows me all his new toys, I slide a bathing suit on him and off he goes to the pool. My mom gives me a tour around the all-white spacious house.

I follow her around the stark white, shiny marble floors. The living room is colossal, unlike the cozy, small rooms I loved in my old home where everything was crammed into a tiny space. A high-backed, peach-colored sofa, velvet love seats, marble coffee table, tall floor lamps with handblown glass lampshades, are placed in strategic spots, unlike the jumbled fashion at our old home. Large, colorful, modern paintings dominate the walls.

"I've got to pack for my trip," she says. "Get something to eat, and let's talk before I show you your new bedroom." She walks into her room. The thought of my own room here puts a smile on my face.

I open the sliding glass doors. An early September storm zoomed in this morning and cleared the bumpy black sky of clouds. I take a whiff of the salty, green and flowery smells and I almost feel whole again. I look toward the canal to check for the manatees Pedri says look like cuddly baby elephants from afar. I can't *wait* to go down there and see them up close. Pedri said one almost got hurt by a motorboat yesterday. How can some people just not care?

They are nowhere in sight.

I walk into the huge white tiled and stainless steel kitchen and find my mom here. She sticks her head inside the refrigerator and picks at *flan* leftovers. With my thumb and index finger, I flick her big bootie two times really fast. "*Flan* is excellent for losing weight, Mami." She lets out a musical laugh that permeates the house. It fills me with happiness she's back to laughing with me.

I'm not hungry and don't eat anything she offers.

We climb up the winding marble staircase, go out to the second-floor balcony, and sit on rockers, facing the bay. Mild warm breezes gently sway the Alexandra palms.

Without warning, flashes of Gisela's face fill my mind. I shut my eyes and push thoughts away to a place from which I hope they never resurface.

I wish I were robotic, indifferent to humanity, feelings, and attraction so nothing affected me. It would be great to not take myself so seriously and approach life with a light heart, or maybe no heart at all. Robots don't get waves of emotions attacking them with pain and uncontrollable sobs. They don't have fear, confusion, conflicts, impatience, urgencies to kiss and make love with other girls and get in trouble for it. I shake my thoughts. What the hell am I thinking? I never want to be a robot.

I look downstairs and hear a loud *sploosh-oosh* as Pedri dives into the Olympic-sized pool. I wave at him. "Outstanding, Little Punk!" My heart feels full again.

He waves back, "Shyly, I did it!" He blows me kisses and I give him a thumbs-up. He's with Zenaida, Jaime's pretty and round-as-a-truck-tire sister. She doesn't take her eyes off Pedri for one second. Even though she's not old, she looks like a funny elderly lady in her one-piece flowered bathing suit and a green rubber shower cap.

Jaime, Mami's well-built, tall husband, is sipping a drink while sitting on the pool steps with his hairy white legs halfway inside the water. From the stories Mami is telling me, I realize he loves my mother and Pedri a great deal and enjoys spending time with them. I'm thrilled about that.

I sit on my mom's lap, kiss her cheek, and press my cheek against hers. She kisses me back. "*Uy*, Shai Sofía Lorena." Just as I think she's going to be sweet and affectionate, like she used to be before the Incident, she says, "You've put me through such hell. I thought of you every second of the day. I never stopped wanting you to call and tell me you'd changed. I prayed for you to finally let me know who the deranged girl was, the one who wanted to turn you into something you aren't. But you didn't. You fiercely protect her and love her more than your own family."

I have an instant gut-wrenching reaction as if a horse kicked me in the stomach. I quickly sit on my own rocker.

There's no way I'll tell her now, that things are smoother. We rock for a little while in silence.

I wish I could tell her about the fun and deep love I shared with Marlena and the loneliness I felt after our breakup. I long to talk about what *I've* been through and everything Mami put *me* through, but it'll make things worse. Isn't that what mothers are supposed to be for—for talking about important things?

I'm not in the mood to listen to her speak about morality. No matter what I tell her, I'll always disappoint my mother. Something inside me wants to be comforted by her but I know it's not going to happen. Fear is in the air. Since she thinks I'm at fault, and I can't speak to her about my life, I change the subject before she becomes enraged, and talk about Jaime.

"Do you love him?"

She glances up but avoids eye contact. "*Of course* I love him. I would *never* marry a man I didn't love. You know, when Papi died and left us without a penny, I took on three jobs, sewing coats in *factorias* for rich *Americanos*. For years I didn't have a life. I will never forget your father. But now I'm starting to live and love again."

I want to make her laugh. She always gets sad when she reminisces about the past.

"Remember when I was little? One day you told me, 'Shylita Sofía Lorena, you have a cold. If you put *one* foot on the porch, you're going to get it.' But I did it anyway." My mom laughs, remembering. "You ran after me. I kept screaming, 'Mami, I didn't *put* a foot on the porch, just a *toe!*'"

"You've always had a strong personality, Shai." She chews on the inside of her cheeks.

"I wonder who I inherited it from," I tease.

"*Definitely* not me!" She smiles and her eyes glow. "Ask my friends; they'll tell you I'm *suave y dulce*."

"If your friends think *you're* soft and sweet, they're on hard-core drugs."

She lets out a colorful laugh, like the splashes of waves Pedri makes when he dives into the pool. I love it when my mother cracks up; it makes me feel that maybe she still loves me.

"*¡Ave María!*" She points to a neighbor tanning in her backyard in a bikini. "Skin and bones. And you," she pinches my stomach, "you transformed from bony to slender because you came out like Papi's side of the family. They all have gorgeous bodies, not an ounce of fat on them."

Mami speaks about how fashionable I look in my shorts and matching top outfit. She talks about everything except important things. She can't handle anything deep. She starts on about buying this and that so she can keep decorating the new house. The only thing I'd purchase, if I could, would be understanding. I'd take it by the hand and bring it right here and sit it next to my mother. She needs a huge dose of it.

She changes the subject from buying things, to me.

"You have the figure of a professional dancer, or a model, but you chose a man's job . . . planting trees. *Uy*, Shai Sofía Lorena. If I had known you were going to turn out this way."

She searches her dress pocket for diet spearmint gum, unwraps two, throws me one, and sticks one in her mouth.

I chew fast, blow bubbles, and smack them shut inside my mouth, thinking I no longer need to blur the lines between fiction and fact. I can openly tell her the truth about my life now, but I must stay quiet about the years I lied. I used to make up so many stories about boys I liked. As smart as she is, she never traced the fibs to my real-life events: lovemaking with Marlena. My feelings and truths were irrelevant, as long as I wasn't deviating from the plans she'd made for me. Honesty would have brought me unhappiness, so it was important that truth be overshadowed by lie after lie. Now that I no longer have to fib, I'll prove to her she provided me with a moral compass I'm happy to follow. She'll be overwhelmed with joy knowing I'll never again stray from the one-way road she painstakingly designed for me.

She looks down at her freshly painted, long, rose-colored fingernails. I almost blurt something out about London, but it seems neither of us wants to bring up the topic. Maybe she's scared of what I'll say.

I play with the tips of my hair. It's too hard talking to my mother about anything serious. I wish I could tell her the entire truth, starting from the day I fell for Marlena, not just about my current reality. Wouldn't that be great?

She stands abruptly. "¡Madre mía! I forgot that while cleaning my closet before moving, I found a coat I used to use when I was skinny."

"And when was *that*, Mami Pastrami with the big culiwami, when you were in Abuelita's womb?"

"*¡Tu madre!*" She wiggles her middle finger in the air. What a great feeling to have my mom goofing with me again. My smile barely fits in my face.

I walk on what now seems even whiter marble floors into the colossal den. One wall is filled with wall-to-wall mirrors. On the rest of the stark white walls hang expensive colorful modern paintings in detailed thick golden frames. There's an antiquated rug under an antique coffee table. In every corner there are tall, green, exotic plants.

I plop myself on the plastic-covered peach velvet love seat wondering when she's going to show me my bedroom. I guess I could go find it myself but I want it to come from her. I'm sure she'd like to see the surprise on my face.

In a heartbeat, she's back, carrying a bulky coat she wants to force me to try on. "Winters are getting colder in Miami. Last year it went down to thirty degrees. You *have* to be prepared."

"That coat's for Alaska. Not now, Mami."

"*¡Ave María!* You were born with your hand up in the air, saying, 'Wait a minute!'"

"I won't try it on now; it's one hundred degrees out. Later.

I promise."

She plunks on the couch, grabs my hand, pulls me to her, takes a container of pins out of her purse, and lifts up the coat. "Remember when Papi bought it for me in New York?"

I remember clearly. Mami, Pedri and I used to hop on a train every summer to visit my dad when he worked in New Jersey at Monmouth Park racetrack. My best friend in the neighborhood aside from Soli, Gloria, her mom, and other neighbor friends, along with Soli and Viva, waved goodbye. My friends and I had tears in our eyes as they watched the train move forward, and I saw them get smaller and tinier from a distance.

We have trouble talking about my father without breaking down, but we try.

"Of *course* I remember this coat." I hold it in my arms, bury my face in it, and inhale all the memories of my loving father. I couldn't have had a better dad. There was no father in the world as sweet and kind as mine. I'm sure if he were alive now, I'd be safe and protected at home, where I belong. If my mom had made a stink about showing me a lesson, even though he had a passive personality and she wore the pants, he'd have stepped in.

I try on the coat, and it's a bit large on the sides. Mami has me stand in front of her, with my arms spread out. She sticks pins all the way from under the arms to the hem. I feel a need to blurt out something about London, to jump-start the conversation, to get it out of the way, but nothing comes out of my mouth.

Even though the central air is on, beads of sweat drip down my eyebrows. The thick fuzzy black coat is making me itchy, but I don't take it off. I want it on me. I need the memories of Papi's love around me.

My mother's eyes are watery. "Papi was so good to me, you and Pedri. Remember when he used to carry you, and lift you up in the air, and sing, '¡La chiquitica más linda del mundo!'"

Mami tries hard not to cry when she says my dad's words— The prettiest little girl in the whole wide world—but tears rain down her face anyway.

I feel like I've swallowed a golf ball and it got stuck in my throat. Everything I've lost flashes in front of my eyes: my dad, Marlena, my reputation, Mami, my friends, my school, my old neighborhood.

I want to console my mom, but instead I ask her if she has ice cream.

"There's *mamey* ice cream in the freezer."

"Want some?" It's my best effort at making her feel good, even though I'm adding to the expansion of her two-ton bootie.

"*Sí.*"

I carefully take off the coat and give it to her. I scoop the ice cream into two white porcelain bowls and hand her one. I plunk next to her on the sofa, hoping we can slowly build a bond of closeness, mutual respect and love again. I just have to be perfect and try not to ever upset her or say anything about my *real* feelings.

She devours her ice cream, scrapes the last drop from the bowl, and licks the spoon. "Ahhh, I'm going to open a can of chicken broth and heat it up for dinner. I can't keep eating like this." She goes to the sink and washes our bowls.

I bite my nails, thinking that soon one of us will need to bring up the conversation about my being completely changed and in love with London. I'm scared of my mother's reactions. We're getting along so well, I don't want to spoil anything.

She comes back. We talk about what color she wants me to paint a fruit tree mural inside one of the walls of her bathroom. "Pastel ochre-yellow and salmon," I say.

"*¡Qué horrible!* That's the color of monkey shit and diarrhea. Neon orange is the 'in' color. You *have* to paint the fruits bright orange, with many hanging *mandarinas*."

I agree, just because I'm about to explode. I can't keep it in any longer. Without thinking, I blurt, "I'm trying to fall in love with London, Mami."

Her jaw drops open and her eyes widen. "Trying? You mean you *haven't* changed?"

"No. No. That's not what I meant at all." My heart is pounding hard. I look out the glass doors toward Pedri and then back into her eyes.

She arches her eyebrows something big. "Then what *did* you mean?" She breathes fast and heavy. "You've been with him five months. You're either *in* love with him or *not*, but *trying* isn't good enough. Which one is it?" Without giving me a chance to speak, she says, "Tell me *once* and for *all* if you've really changed or not."

"Of course, Mami. I wouldn't be here if I hadn't." I should have known better. What an idiot I am to not have worded things perfectly to her satisfaction. One more slip and I'm a goner. Things were going so great. I'm a stupid, mindless, dim-witted, idiot!

"So what did you mean about *trying* to fall in love with him?" She doesn't get off the subject.

"What I mean is I'm *falling* in love with him." I say plastic, empty things I know she'd love to hear. "You should see him, Mami, he's six feet tall. I'm five feet five now. He's so gorgeous in a skinny, model-type way. His muscles pop out all over the place. He's kind of like a thin, strong, superhero. You'll love him."

My mom doesn't give two cucumbers if a guy has a brain. She just cares about my being with a male, and that he's good-looking so our kids will be beautiful. She still hasn't even asked me a thing about my life. She might not even care that I dropped out of school as long as I'm on the "decent" road to one day in the future getting married and having kids.

She smiles big. "Oh, well, then, that's fantastic, Shai. He sounds like a hunk who just needs a little fattening up. Don't you worry about that. Bring him here for dinner every night after we get back from Europe and soon he'll have pecs to die for." Her smiles fades away. "I'm sorry to tell you I can't have you back until I'm *absolutely* sure you've changed. I won't go through the pain and humiliation you put me through again, especially not in front of Jaime. He can never find out."

My heart drops in my chest. I look to Pedri and wonder how he'll take the bad news. I promised him I was moving back. I never want him to stop trusting me. I'd like him to feel he can always confide in me and know I'll always be there whenever he needs me. If he loses trust in me, he'll feel I've left him out in the cold. I'd rather die than have that happen between us.

My mom keeps on. "I told everyone you're living at a friend's house in Ft. Lauderdale whose mother is seriously ill. I said you take care of her every day after school, for pay. Our family, friends and new neighbors all think you're very responsible. Don't you *dare* let them find out otherwise."

I feel my eyes watering and blink many times to make sure I don't shed a tear in front of her. I stay quiet, looking down at my feet. She must be blind. I'm one of the most respectable, trustworthy, loyal and overly responsible girls around. It's surreal I'm such a failure to her.

"Right now your feelings for London are iffy. While living here you can't go back to immoral behavior. Pedrito could, by mistake, have read one of those texts." She repeats, "The day you move to this house is the day you're *absolutely sure* you're in love with a boy." She shakes her head. "Tell me more about London."

I stay far away from my feelings of hurt and disappointment in order to not get her riled up. I talk about London, how I met him at a nonalcoholic teen dance club, and how he has a few acne scars I think make his features interesting, in a rugged-type way, and so I don't want him to laser them away. All the things she wants to hear. I leave out that the dance club was Papaya's, and whenever London kisses me, I miss girls more than ever. She obviously wants a stinking liar for a daughter. And that's what she's getting. A colossal, hard-core, stinking liar!

17—Inside Out, Upside Down

Every weekday these past two months I've spent time with Pedri, after work. After helping him with homework, we draw while playing a stream-of-consciousness game I invented: he says everything on his mind, all his thoughts and feelings even if they're sad, while creating a story on the sketchpad. We sit facing one another with folded legs in front of the coffee table, drawing, while the little storyteller with the lingering scent of bubblegum talks nonstop. Surprisingly, he's got a photographic memory. His troubles with English grammar I always helped him with probably stem from his pent-up feelings about my mom having thrown me out of the house. He invents stories, about green and yellow striped flying snakes that rescue sisters from colossal gorillas and barking roosters, that crack me up. Then he swears up and down, "They're for real. Why don't you believe me?"

I have to put on my more serious face and tell him, "Of course I do."

We're both sad Mami is taking so long to take me back, but

happy to see each other so much.

My mom came back from her vacation and London has joined us for dinners every night at her house. She's started telling people the ill woman I was taking care of moved to Miami and she allowed me to continue working for her. Jaime is a friendly and good man. He's never asked me a single personal question. He couldn't give a rolling tomato about what I do for a living, or where I live. He just talks incessantly about his boring businesses, or he'll tell a few work jokes that make Pedri and me yawn. Then, he laughs at business one-liners I find online to make him happy, like, "A backscratcher will always find new itch; a brown-noser will always find new sense." I guess as long as we're joking, we get along.

Mami adores London but no matter how hard I try to make her believe I'm in love with him, she tells me, "I *know* you're not." I think she's waiting till London gives me a promise ring and I accept him as the guy I'm committed to until we're older and I become his fiancée. Either that, or, she wants to further test me for another one hundred years, to make sure I'm completely straight. I guess she smells something still isn't quite right, and she hasn't forgiven me for humiliating her. And it's true. My head is somewhere else, lost in the flowering bushes, thinking about Gisela. No matter how hard I try, I can't shake her out of my mind. If I keep daydreaming about her, I may never pass my mother's sniff test.

Marlena is still texting, e-mailing and calling me, trying to get ahold of me from Puerto Rico. Her texts say things like, *I'm back home. I can't believe you wouldn't see me when I was there.* Her e-mails read, *My uncle Marco asked me not to visit you at work because you needed to focus. I wondered if he'd caught on and so I stayed far away. Do you think he figured it out? I hope not.* Her calls on my cell say, *Why won't you talk to me? Call me back.*

I've never responded. She got ahold of Soli and Soli said she shouldn't go to her house to find me because "that's disrespectful. If Shai wants to talk to you, let *her* call *you*." Soli was friendly until Marlena tried to give her a guilt trip about getting together to talk about what happened with me. Soli told her she didn't want to meet with her. "I love you too but after what you put Shai through, I must pick sides. It's nothing personal."

I don't want to hear how sorry Marlena is about having dumped me in such an insensitive way. I'd like her as far away from me as possible.

I'm still sleeping at Soli's. I spend weekend mornings with Pedri and Viva at museums or at the beach, and weekend nights with London, Soli and Diego. Sometimes, I spend time with Tazer at his house alone or with Elicia. We tend to the organic garden, cook, play computer games, listen to blasting music and dance, and goof off on Facebook. We've become close. He gets I can't be seen with him out in public right now. If my mom finds out, she'll *never* let me move back in.

Around London, my emotions are like April: never too hot, too humid, or too cold. Physically, though, I've recently been like June: hot, hot, hot! He's always like July: scorching! I told him to chill, to be cool like this month, November, and he promised he would.

London and I made a dinner date. We finished eating a meal of lentils and rice, tomato and onion salad, and *yuca con mojo*. I thank his sweet, frumpy mother as I finish helping her clean the table. "*Gracias*, Fina. It was delicious."

"Anytime, *mijita*." She wraps her mushy arms around me.

I love London's mom. She's so mellow for being Cuban. She hangs out at home in housedresses, painting neighbors' nails. She takes care of her kids, and she doesn't miss a Cuban soap opera on TV. Their little apartment is impeccable, and she's always doting on London and his brothers, who are great guys.

London takes me to the backyard shack he just turned into his bedroom; it's an all-cement room with tall ceilings and hanging black light retro lava lamps. The walls are painted deep purple. The only furniture is a velvet black armchair in front of a stereo system next to his bed, a little fridge where he keeps sodas and beer and a desk for his laptop and CD. There's a guitar in its case standing up along a wall, a bunch of *claves, timbales, tumbadoras* and congas are littered all over the room. He's serious about music. I love that.

I see his favorite photograph of his *Santero* dad on the wall next to friends in Cuba, wearing a white *guayabera*, white baggy pants, and many beads around his neck. Next to him, are pictures of London and me.

I smile. "That's miraculous the way you made this old crumbling place into your amazing new room."

"It's coming along." He grabs a beer from the fridge and slides on a CD. Soft *son* music comes on.

It started getting hot and heavy last month. Recently, my body's had an urge to go all the way. I almost lost my head yesterday, but a voice inside me snapped me into reality: "Wait until you're sure he's the one." I can't help but know my mom wouldn't have acted the same way if the texts had been from London. I'm sure she would've been upset, but I can't imagine she'd have kicked me out of the house. I'm positive my teachers would never have reacted so maliciously, either. There wasn't a single girl in my class who hadn't slept with her boyfriend.

I must admit I have a great time exploring his body, but it's frustrating I can't feel emotionally close to him. Just knowing we can't be tight in that deep, intense way, leaves me feeling empty and deeply alone. But maybe that's normal for girls who've been with girls. Maybe it's more emotional with girls because that's our nature.

I lean against the open window and look outside toward the cages filled with colorful cockatoos—the birds his older brother sells for a living. He holds me by my shoulders and peers into my eyes. "Listen to what I've got to say."

My heart thumps fast. "What?"

He's got a glow in his eye that speaks loud and clear. "I want you to be my girl and only mine."

I zip up my jean jacket, clear my throat, and look deeply into his eyes. "But I'm not seeing anybody else."

He takes a swig of beer. "Why can't you answer about being only mine?"

"Isn't my answer enough?"

"No. I want you to tell me you're madly into me like you were with Mario. I need to hear you're *all* mine. Haven't you forgotten him yet? Is that it?"

I told him about "Mario" when he asked about my ex. I couldn't bring myself to explain the truth. A Cuban guy doesn't want someone who can fall in love with other girls. He'd like a girl all to himself, and he wants to feel secure that another female isn't lurking in the corner somewhere, ready to get my attention. I also keep thinking it'll get back to Mami since they talk about everything.

"It's not Mario. I just think I can never fall in love again." I remember how it used to be with Marlena before everything slid down the edge. Even though I'm intensely attracted to him, nothing with London comes remotely close to what I felt for her.

He bites his thick bottom lip. "That's crazy. Why can't you feel for me the way you did for that fucking Mario guy? What, did he have a bigger *chorizo*?"

My heart pounds in my chest at his unexpected anger and disgusting response.

"Maybe you should be dating other girls. If you want, we can be just friends." I can't force my heart anymore. I've been trying hard for too long, and all I feel is an intense physical attraction and a great deal of care. Emotionally and intellectually there's very little there."

"Don't be ridiculous." He sucks on his beer. "I hate this Mario guy. He's ruined you."

I wish he didn't have to bring this up; it just reminds me of the truth I've been keeping from him.

He takes my face, brings it closer to his, and kisses me. His nubs chafe my skin. He's a great kisser when we're rolling around in bed, but way too harsh when I want to feel intimate and not sexual.

Suddenly, making out with him is making me feel lonelier than ever. There's a dark hole, deep, deep in my heart. I can't help my eyes becoming watery.

He takes his lips off mine. "Hey, what happened?"

"I'm trying to fall in love again, London, and it's just not happening." I'm as honest as I can be. "I don't want to hurt your feelings." I can't tell him I miss the closeness of being with, and kissing, a girl.

"You'll fall for me. It takes time. You'll see." He kisses me deeper and harder.

Maybe I will. Maybe feeling so alone the more time I spend with him is all worth it. I finally have my family back.

I stop kissing him and grab the beer from his hand. "Why do you always have to be drinking? It's dis*gus*ting."

He snatches the bottle from me, guzzles it up, and throws it in the trash bin. "A few beers is no big deal." He drops his husky voice to a whisper. "Maybe when we go all the way you'll fall hard for me. But I'm glad you don't ever want to go there."

"Why?" I'm confused.

He tilts his head to the right and his long black hair falls over his left eye. "I want the girl I marry to be a virgin, to be all mine. If we'd have done it, I might not be so crazy about you."

"You're so weird. You speak like an old man." He's talking like the type of Cuban grandpas you hear grandmas speak about who wanted to possess them, for them to be virginal and virgins. But look who's talking. I used to feel that way about Marlena. I loved that I had been her first. We felt like one, as if we belonged to each other. And for sure, I despised that she had sex with Rick the Dick.

I recall the times she told me, "Promise me you'll never be with anyone else." What we lived was a dream that turned into a nightmare because Rick could encroach at any given moment on our lives. Having wanted her all to myself seems so hypocritical now.

He presses his chunky mouth against mine, goes into his pocket, plucks out a small velvet black box, and hands it to me.

I open it slowly. It's a little Cuban coin hanging on a leather string matching the one I gave him. "Beautiful!" I'm glad the conversation is going in a different direction. I place it on my neck, securely clasp it, and feel the coin with my fingers. I love everything Cuban.

London knows my grandfather was a tortured political prisoner over fifty years ago because he was in Batista's army and one of the men who tried to kill Fidel Castro. My grandmother took him out of prison by paying the guard all the money she'd saved. Since my grandfather was a pilot, the guard took him dressed as a priest straight to a plane. He flew the three of them to Miami. The following morning in Cuba there was a street protest with gunfire. Fidel gave a speech about how anyone interested in stealing a plane to leave would be executed in cold blood.

My grandparents are heroes here. Everyone knows I was the granddaughter of Ignacio and Edilia Amores. That's made my life difficult because of expectations most Miamians have of me. I'm required to be an outstanding citizen, like my grandfather (may he rest in peace). Eyes seem to be on me. That's probably why my mom is so paranoid and always hyperaware of "what will people think." Being me carries a big responsibility. I want to do the right thing for everyone involved.

London throws the gift box in the trash, and rubs his hands together. "I have secret ways of making you fall for me and be with me in the near future. A guy can't wait *that* long." He licks his pretty lips and brushes his hair away from his forehead. It falls back over his eyes.

I give up trying to break up with him. I must continue forcing myself to feel emotionally connected. I never want to lose my family again.

I throw myself on the cushiony armchair and sink into it.

The slow dance music is still on in the background. He tears off his leather jacket, throws it on the bed, walks to me, and pulls me to him. I allow myself to be taken into his arms and rest my face on his chest. He smells salty. He's a good dancer, a soft mover.

From the half-opened windows come soft sounds of bamboo chimes and wind-bells. I feel his heartbeat on my body stronger and stronger. Before I know it, he's whispering into my ear, "I want you." His lips come close to mine, and he finally gives me a soft, passionate kiss.

I feel my body craving more. I squeeze him to me and get into the rhythm of kissing. Our lips are locked in a smooth dance, but then he kisses me extremely hard and I fall, fall, fall out of desire.

I stare out the window at blazing stars, wondering if I'll ever feel close to him, or if it'll always be *just* physical.

I'm dizzy with thoughts crowding my brain. Maybe I should tell him about Marlena now, and get it over and done with. No. He'll tell my mom.

I slam on the brakes and separate myself from him. "I've got to tell you something." I feel shaky inside.

"What?"

My hands get sweaty and I wipe them on my jeans. "Uh . . . nothing. I need to leave."

"No, tell me. What's going on?"

"Nothing. It was ridiculous anyways."

He gently grabs my hands. "I'm not letting you go till you tell me."

"Hey. I told you it's no big deal." I pinch his rock-hard stomach. "It's just that I wanted to thank you again for the gift. That's all. Really. I must go and finish my studies."

"What's *wrong* with you? Stay a little longer. Come on. We can go dancing at a club or see a movie. Don't be that way," he pleads. "You don't have anyone hovering over your shoulder. You can do anything you want. You don't even have a professor waiting for you to hand him your work."

"Just because I won't go to school again doesn't mean I can't educate myself online or buy books used in university courses I'm interested in or that I haven't got ambitions. Besides, I want to stay home tonight. I need to feed Neruda and walk her, then I've got to finish work I started from Yale U School of the Art."

I keep busy some weekdays after work, which upsets London. He'd like me to spend all my spare time with him.

He continues trying to coax me into staying.

"Seriously, I'm tired." I'm being a pain. I'm surprised he isn't sending me to hell, but I realize I *have* to put an end to this relationship no matter how much I've grown to care about him and enjoy parts of him.

"Listen," I go on. I'm more serious than ever. "We can't continue being together. Let's just be friends. You're a great guy, but you're moving too fast and my heart isn't keeping up."

"Too fast?" He groans. "Don't be silly. You're just the sensitive type. I know you'll fall for me in time. Chill. We're staying together."

It's as if he's not listening or he just doesn't care. "No! We need to end it now and become *just* friends."

"Don't be so delicate. You're so damned emotional. Trust me. You'll grow in love with me. I've been in your shoes. Just give it more time. I'm not letting you go. I'm in love with you."

Those words give me a jolt. When Marlena said them they melted me. Right now, all I want is to run the other way. "No London. It's not fair to you if I keep this up. I don't feel the same way. It's better if I leave now so you can go on with your life and stop spending time with me. There are dozens of girls out there who'd want you. You're amazing."

He points to his big banana. "No worries. *I'll* keep *this* up for both of us!" He chuckles.

"You're not listening!"

"Well, if we're *just* friends, then I'll come over to Soli's and we can play computer art games, the ones you love. We can draw something and make it into a cartoon. You're at it all the time, why can't we do it together?"

"Why aren't you taking me seriously?"

"We've been through this many times." He kisses my lips. "Okay. Okay. Go ahead. Go home. Choose art and design over me. I'll see you tomorrow."

"No London. This time it's for *real*. We've got to end it now, okay?"

"Sure, sure. We're *best* of friends." He plants a kiss on my cheek. "Ride safely."

I put on my helmet, grab the handlebars of my bike, hop on it, and ride into the silvery night, not knowing which way is up or down.

18—Untangling

I'm riding home from London's place, poking around my thoughts, digging for ideas about how to give my mom the breakup news.

I chose to veer into a black hole, a place nothing, not even light, can escape. It's not about London, the guy who was my savior for a while. I actually liked him a lot until I started missing girls. It's about sacrificing my entire life just to please my mom. Her belief system is the black hole sucking me in, killing me slowly. It's like poisonous rat traps that lure you in. The sticky surface won't allow you to move. Eventually, you die trapped, without nourishment.

I saw a documentary about a surface around the black hole which marks the point of no return. I was slowly arriving there.

I put my foot to the pedal and ride through the neighborhood I grew up in. I find our old home and park across the street from it, at the shoe factory, and stare at the front yard. I see myself as a little kid, playing slip 'n slide with Gloria, my best *barrio* friend who lived next door. I recall us laughing at every little thing.

I rode my bike here last month, so I could see my old friends. That was the craziest thing I could have ever done.

I knock on Gloria's front door. Her mother answers, "Never set foot in here again. My daughter will grow up to get married and have children as God intended for girls." She stabs at my heart. "I'll pray to God he straightens your path. You're a closed chapter in Gloria's book. As for my daughter, she isn't allowed to ever speak with you again. Don't ever come or call here."

She slams the door in my face. I gulp down pain and it settles in my stomach.

I get home and tell Soli what happened. Soli confides in me. "The night your mom kicked you out, I heard through the grapevine that somebody left an anonymous letter at your front door. It said you couldn't go to any of your neighbors' houses again because their children 'need to be protected from turning homosexual.' They signed their names in X's. Your neuro mom had a fit."

I can't bear the memories any longer and bail.

I feel like I'm blindfolded, riding through a dark tunnel, in search of light. Out of nowhere, a taxi hits the back wheel of my bike.

Bang! Crash!

My bike is skidding out of control and I can't stop it! It's spinning around and around and it slides into a sidewalk and *wham!* I hit a post. I look at my arms and body. I'm still alive and in one piece. I'm on the ground, holding my aching stomach. I'm so nauseous I feel like throwing up. There's blood on my left shoulder, where my jacket was torn. I cover my eyes with my arm.

The passenger in the taxi runs to me. "You okay?"

"My shoulder," I answer, looking up at him.

"Don't worry. I called nine-one-one. That idiotic driver almost got us killed." He blinks nervously. "You're lucky you didn't get run over. Don't move, stay put, in case you've broken something."

• • •

At the emergency room I give the nurse my home number and she calls Soli and Viva. I don't feel like seeing my mom right now. She'll just be upset about my riding a bike late at night. She might ask me a million questions about London because she's like a spy and will sniff trouble. I don't need the extra pressure. And besides, I don't want Pedri to worry.

I have a bandaged, scratched-up left shoulder, a swollen bump on my left thigh, and an archipelago of scratches and bruises on my legs. But I can move my left arm, and I didn't break anything. My bike is an accordion, though.

Soli speeds into the room like a locomotive with a new guy, and Tazer trails behind them.

"Shyly, what happened?" She kisses my forehead, uncovers me, and scrutinizes my body to make sure I'm okay. She takes my hand to her heart. "You all right?"

"I'm fine—just this." I shrug my bandaged shoulder.

Tazer searches my face. "You look like you're still in one piece." He covers me with the bed sheet.

Soli purses my lips together by holding my cheeks, and smacks me a big one. *Muuua!* She faces the new guy with a gleam in her eye. "Paublo, this is Shai."

Soli's new boy is a husky, short-haired, sort of conservative-looking guy. I find it odd that his hair isn't spiky, he's not in black leather, and he doesn't have a tongue ring or silver earring hoops, the way Soli normally likes them. I'm sure his arms aren't filled with tattoos, either.

"Hey, Shai," he whispers in a deep sensual voice. "I met you at Viva's birthday party. Remember?"

"Yeah, hi." How could I forget Gorgeous Godzilla among a room full of girls? This guy could easily be a spokesperson for a modeling agency or a university, since he's severely good looking and speaks perfect English.

"I've just stayed away. You know." He looks to Soli. "She was dating Diego." He grins. "I can't wait until you get better so we can all spend some time together." He pats my hand. "Excuse me. I need to use the bathroom. I'll be right back."

Tazer sits on the corner of my bed and stares at me, as if I were a painting. He breathes in and lets go of a big exhalation. I can tell he's relieved nothing happened to me. I appreciate the fact he's here. I'd be there for him, too. He texts Elicia to let her know I'm fine.

"Isn't Paublo a hunk?" Soli squeezes my hand "Shyly, he's the *hottest* and most brilliant guy I've ever gone out with. He's in U of M medical school, studying to become a doctor. Do I look sexy? Shylypop, look at me." Soli takes a spin. Her tight spandex red minidress sticks to her curves like a corset. Her large breasts spill out of the top. It could be snowing and she'd still be wearing her minidresses.

"You look as if you just came from taking your first holy communion." She lifts an eyebrow and releases a thunderous laugh. I throw her a piercing stare. "I can't believe you dumped Diego." I clear my throat. "I really liked him. Paublo's a great catch, but you're an ass to just get rid of Diego from one second to the next." I'm pissed she threw Diego away like an old rag even if this guy has a brighter future. I know what *that's* like.

She whispers into my ear. "Diego dumped *me*, but I don't want to talk about it now. Later." Her voice rises. "Damn, Shyly, I'm such a jerk. Here I am talking about *my* life and *you* almost got killed. You okay? Is there anything I can get you?" I shake my head no. "I went to pick up Tazer as soon as I heard. If anything ever happened to you I'd die. I mean it." She takes my hand. Tears well up in her eyes. Eyeliner drips down her face, leaving long streaks. "I know I'm a pain, but I can't live without you. I'm so glad you're alive."

I pull her toward me. "I can't live without you either, Hootchi Momma. You're my sister for life." And it's true. I can't imagine my life without Soli.

"When you coming back home?"

"Tomorrow. They want to keep me for observation. My head got slammed around a lot. My helmet's all banged up." I point to my cracked and warped helmet on the chair.

"Shit!" they both belt out.

There's a loud racket in the hall. Viva whizzes in like a tornado. Gabriel trails behind her.

"Shylita, thank all my *santos* you be alive!" She fills my face with *besitos*. "*¡Ave María Purísima! ¡Gracias, Dios!*" She makes the sign of the cross on her chest. "I call your Mami to tell her what happened. She not home. And thee message machine be not working."

"I didn't want to tell her, Vivalini. I'm fine. Please don't call her again."

She hands me the cutest stuffed gray and orange polka-dotted elephant.

I kiss the tip of Viva's round nose. "What? They didn't have a stuffed saint?" I cuddle the smiley elephant in my arms.

Viva gives out a sweet smile. "*Uy*, Shylita . . . you is always eating what thee chickens nibble. When frogs grow hairs and birds grow teeth, you will estop being such a pain in thee butt." Her tiny birdseed eyes slant. "The *elefantico* is Ganeshito, the Indian God, who opens paths when they is closed."

Gabriel leans over and gives me a soft peck on the cheek. He winks at me and tells me in Spanish, "Glad you are okay, *mijita*. If there is anything I can do for you, let me know. Gabriel Eufemio Fernandez is here at your service."

I'm ecstatic he and Viva are together. He's got to be the kindest little old man in the world. It's just odd that he's Diego's dad and he'll soon meet Paublo. I hope he won't feel hurt.

I take hold of his tubby hand and squeeze it. "Thanks."

Viva can't keep her trap shut. "My goodness, Shylita, you is going to kill me of a heart attack. Don't drive a bicycle on the streets no more, *mijita*. You and Soli Luna never listen to me. *Uy, mi madre*. Is you feeling okay, Shylita?"

"I'll live. My only problem is that I can't pinch your *culito* till my wrist and arm heal."

Viva points to the heavens. "This is a punishment from God. He no want you pinching my butt no more." I pinch her butt.

"*¡Uy, Dios mío! ¡Santísimo sacramento!*" Her eyes veer up to the ceiling. "Thanks so much, my *espíritus y santos* for not letting anything happen to my Shylita."

"I'm going to take you to Hollywood, Vivalini. You'll make Salma Hayek look as if she needs acting classes."

Paublo comes back all smiles. He shakes everyone's hand as he's introduced as Soli's friend. I wonder if Gabriel knows Diego broke it off with Soli. He must. His expression is wilted.

London unexpectedly walks in with a hurried stride. "Viva called me and told me you were here. Are you okay?"

"Barely alive," I goof.

He hands me a bouquet of red roses. As he comes to kiss my lips, I gently turn my face and kiss his cheek. I know *exactly* where I'm headed, and I don't want to lead him on.

I take a whiff of the flowers and smile. "They're so pretty. Thanks."

Viva and Soli hug him. He shakes Tazer's and Gabriel's hands and they pat each other on the back. He reaches Paublo. "Hey, man, what's going on?"

Soli explains to us, "Paublo cuts his hair with me or London, depending on who has less clients at the time." They all talk as Soli leans into me and whispers into my ear, "I miss Diego so much."

I do to her what she did to me when I was missing Marlena at Papaya's. "Forget about him, girl. I'm taking you to a club so you can meet lots of other guys right away. No wonder you look like you're going to a funeral in that dress." I roll my eyes. "I didn't realize you were grieving."

She squeezes the tip of my nose. "Shylypop, you're such a dildo. I guess it's payback time, huh?" I nod.

I squeeze her hand and whisper to her, "Sorry, Soli. I know it sucks. I'm here for you."

Soli and London talk about doing a girl's hairdo for her fifteenth birthday party. My mind drifts off to Soli's *quinces*.

"Remember when your mom spent her *entire* savings just to buy your gown?"

"*You* had a *quinces?*" Tazer grins.

"Thanks a lot, Shyly," Soli complains and lets go of my hand.

Tazer bugs her. "You don't look like the traditional type. You're just waaaaaay too hip for that."

"Well . . ." I keep talking even if Soli's going to be really pissed at me. "A month later, Soli wanted to burn her old fashioned *quinces* photo album. She said, 'I'm sick and tired of Mima showing it around the *barrio*, at work and to people she's never even met.'" I put on my best impersonation of Soli and her lively, sexy voice. "'I'm going to burn those suckers to a crisp. Shyly, I swear on all the saints, if any of my friends see these pictures I'll *kill* myself. Mima won't find out. She thinks they're stashed away in the closet.' Remember, Soli?"

"How could I forget if you're always reminding me?"

"I told Soli she was nuts to want to burn the pics, since the memory wasn't recorded on a DVD. I said I'd keep them for her and one day, when we're *viejitas*, we'll crack up looking at them. But she wouldn't let me have them."

"I've got to see them, please!" Paublo begs. "Where are they?"

"No way!" Soli booms.

Viva has on a wicked smile. "I show you. I keep them in a secret place at home."

"*Sí.*" Gabriel smiles. "She already showed me." He kisses the tips of his fingers all at once. "Soli Luna looked glorious, like a saint in heaven."

I crack up at the thought of Soli with a halo around her head. She pinches my stomach and I smack her hand.

I go on. "That day, Soli showed me the album and said, 'Shyly, swear to me you'll *never, ever, ever* tell anyone you've seen these pictures. If you do, I'll never talk to you again.' Remember, Soli?" I *love* to tease her.

"Yes. You swore to *la Vírgen María*, Shyly, but I didn't realize you didn't believe in her at the time!"

She's right. I got away with a lot when I swore on saints and virgins I think are part of a religious myth.

I look at Paublo. "Soli's *quinces* was the first in the history of our culture without teens. The *only* way she would have the party was if *no one* our age was invited. She told her mom, 'Mima, if you invite *any* of my friends, I swear to God, I'll take off the gown and run away from home!'"

Soli and Viva reminisce. "Yeah, the party was filled with Mima's adult *barrio* and work friends who don't even know how to use a cell to take a picture."

"But knowing Shai," Tazer says, "she just *had* to show up, right?"

"I like a good challenge," I admit. "She banned me from her party, so what *else* could I do but show up? When she saw me, she snatched my cell and yelled, 'Why'd you *do* this to me? Leave *now!* Don't look at me, I look like a clown in this dress!'"

We laugh heartily. Soli's good mood is back. "Hey. Remember *your quinces*?" She's trying to get back at me.

"Oh, god! Who could *ever* forget?" I don't mind talking about my tacky *quinces*.

"Her mom and uncles went into debt just to throw her a wild party." Soli puts her whole body into her explanation. "She was lowered from a helicopter into the street in front of her yard. Her ball gown was pink and ruffled with sequins. It was *so* wide she didn't fit through the front door. She had to be *pushed* inside!"

"That's true!" I crack up.

Soli keeps on. "Her aunts, uncles, and cousins came from Hialeah and Spain, just for the event. Her uncle led her into a huge pink shell glued with fake pearls and sequins. Later on, a white horse galloped in and she sat on it for photographs!"

"What a scene that was!" I can't stop laughing.

"I'm glad my dad never made me change my ways and have me behave like a sissy Cuban girl," Tazer says. "I would've died if he'd forced me to have a *quinces*. Can you imagine me in a puffy *quinces* dress?" Everyone bursts out laughing. "But still, I'd love to see *those* pictures."

"Definitely!" London and Paublo agree.

Viva holds on to Gabriel's hand with one hand. With a

rosary in her other hand, she grabs on to my right hand, praying silently over me. Soli sits on the bed holding my left hand. Tazer sits on the corner of the bed staring into my eyes and smiling, as only a good friend can. London stands beside me. Paublo hangs around looking at me with a sweet face. He keeps asking me, "Are you sure you don't want anything? Any coffee or food from the cafeteria?" I guess I can like him after all.

Most of us have people in our lives who come and go; some are far in the distance and don't matter at all, but I've found a bunch I can't live without. I look to Soli, Viva, London, Gabriel and Tazer. I wish Diego was here too. I feel a warm sensation in my body, like I used to feel when Papi hugged me. For a long time now, people I've loved have hated me for no reason at all. These folks love me and I love them back. In a strange way, I feel renewed, as if a drastic transformation is coming, as if I know I can make my life into something terrific.

19—Silence Shouts

It's a glisteningly bright November morning, but inside me, it feels like spring is bursting out in full bloom. I see it from every direction, leaping like a gazelle through the bushes, in wild colors. The world around me smells like mango fruit salad and tart green apples. I'm alive and everything is stunning and glistening. It seems as if such a long time since I was suffering and conflicted. I'm sure my whole world will change for the better. I know *exactly* what I need to do to make my life fan*tas*tic. And I'm going to get it done right away!

Today we're starting on the front yard of a large landscape job in a ritzy Miami Beach mansion. Marco forced me to take the week off to heal, and I did. I shopped around for a new bike and helmet. Marco wants me to be careful with my shoulder, so I'll sketch the back landscape, while the crew works up front.

London decided to take his two-week vacation from work early, starting last week, thinking he'd spend time with me at his place. Soli and other haircutters split the customers he'd booked, and everyone gave him the thumbs-up. He didn't pay attention to what I said about us being *just* friends. When I wouldn't budge, he left with his uncle for the Bahamas on a fishing trip. His last words to me were, "I won't be calling or texting you so you can see how much you'll miss me. When I arrive, things'll be back to normal and hotter than ever."

I get to work with a juicy grin, not having seen the old crew for a long while. I hug everyone, and just as I'm about to kiss El Tigre's face, a black vehicle screeches up to the curb and Marlena climbs out of it. My heart skips beats. She sits on the hood of the car and looks to me with a loving expression in her eyes and a wide smile.

I avert my eyes but do a double take when everyone, especially Che, talks about the beautiful girl. "Man, she's blazing. Look at those sexy lips and curvy hips. Just looking at her is making me horny."

I park my new red mountain bike with tall handlebars next to a tree wondering what she wants. She stopped texting and trying to get ahold of me, so I figured she'd never contact me again.

Che comes to me and spits out, "That's my dream girl. Do you know her?"

"Yes, but she's married."

"That never stopped me." He snickers.

"*¡Hola!*" Marco drives into the driveway. I stand up straight and try to act calm and collected. "Everyone get to work, except Shai." They leave and I walk to Marco. I'm not sure what to do or say. I'm still acting as if I haven't seen Marlena. If she wants to talk, she's going to have to come to me.

We get to the backyard. "Marlena is here. She came to say hello. When we're done, go see her. I told her last night not to bother you until you're on a break, but she came early anyway. You know how she is. She better not distract you from work. This is a very important client. He's the president of my bank. I really need your talent, especially this week. We've got several mansions to attack. Stay focused."

"I will."

Marco takes out his thick colorful plant, tree and shrub book and leafs through it. I grab my sketchpad, charcoal and colored pencils from inside my bag. "Our client wants shade, color and many exotic palms in the front." He shows me pictures of the plants we can use. "Let's give them a Southern magnolia tree over there," he points to the spot, "and a live oak north of it by the side of the house."

My heart keeps pounding fast.

I nervously sketch the three-story mansion with shaky hands, and paint the magnolia with heavily overlapping large leaves and the live oak with tons of tiny vivid green leaves.

I draw the outline of a stone path leading from the back porch to a pond surrounded by a semicircular hedge of white gardenia plants. Overlooking the pond, I paint a seating area with wooden benches.

To the left of the pond, I sketch a tall trellis threaded with climbing red roses.

With large strokes I paint tall, skinny Alexandra palms in a row on one side of the pond, and red salvia plants circling them.

I sketch the exotic palms he showed me in different locations. I fill in splashes of color by adding pink, orange, red and yellow flowers in circles all around the palms.

"¡*Maravilloso*, Shai!" Marco messes up my hair. "I'm off to show Angel. I'm taking Jaylene. She's a computer expert and knows how to computerize the sketch. She'll place it on a CD portfolio for a more professional feel while Angel and I work out an estimate."

I walk him to his truck, but don't see Marlena anywhere in sight.

He calls to Jaylene with a whistle and a wave of his hand. They climb into his truck, and Marco searches into my eyes. "Look." He points to his wife's car. "My wife let her come in it to see you. I've told Marlenita how outstanding you've become at drawing landscapes. She's proud of you."

"Great."

"Don't do any digging or lifting today. Take an hour off to

hang out with Marlena, then come back and water the plants. Tell her to take care of the car. And remember, don't make plans with her in the mornings this week. I know you two are old friends and dying to see each other. But this is business and I need your total focus. Don't let me down." He takes off.

I see Marlena walking toward me in long hurried strides.

She reaches me, "Scrunchy," and spreads her arms wide for an embrace. I take a few steps back. What an awkward thing to call me after what she did.

"Not even a hug?" Her eyes show concern.

I shake off my anxiety and give her a quick hug then back away instantly. She smells exactly the same as when I last saw her at the airport: watermelon candy.

"I've missed you," she says. Confusion stirs within me. She's missed me?

"Come on," I tell her. "Let's go to the back so we can talk in private." She follows me as she lights up a cigarette, which grosses me out, but it's not the time to talk about that.

She leans against the back porch. "You're more beautiful than ever. I can't believe I'm here with you again. It's been so long." Her eyes become cloudy. "Why didn't you call me back? Why wouldn't you text me? I've been dying to see you, and it's been hard giving you your space. I broke down today and just couldn't stop myself from coming over."

I feel my muscles tightening around my jaw. "I wish you hadn't."

"I'm so sorry. I didn't know what I was doing when I broke up with you. As time went on, I realized you were right. Love of any kind is a good thing. You made me think long and hard. I'll never forget the lessons learned."

"Good for you."

I don't want to stay on the topic of us and ask her about her life. She gets to talking about how much freedom she's got now that she's not living at home. She asks about me. I tell her I just broke up with London but he still thinks we're together. "He never takes me seriously." She tells me she's pregnant with a girl.

"I'd like to call her Elless, a secret name no one will decipher. The name is comprised of your initials: L and S's, for Shai Sofia Lorena."

I gulp hard and try not to show any emotion. "That's such a pretty name."

She states she's happily married without drama or emotional upheaval, but she can't forget me.

"You're always on my mind. Even though my life is great, I can't stop thinking about you. Rick's been offered an excellent job in Miami with triple the pay he's getting in Puerto Rico. We're thinking of coming back. If we do, I'll be going to U of M. They accepted me!"

"Great," I state with a half smile. I definitely don't want her back here, now that I'm getting my life together.

"I told my family I prayed every night so you'd find a boy-friend and you did. They think you've changed too. No one hounds me anymore. They believe I'm in love with Rick, and what I went through was a phase of confusion. This means you and I can be together again."

"Really? Don't I have a say in this matter?" I let out a nervous chuckle. "What if I'm not interested in you anymore?"

"I know you still love me, Scrunchy." The sides of her mouth curl up in a confident smile. "Love between your first girlfriend never dies. I still adore you with all my heart. I've never stopped thinking of you. Stay with London. You've got to go back with him. We'll go on double dates and no one will need to know our secret. When Rick's not home, we'll make love. I really miss being with you. There's no one like you."

I turn my face away from her, not sure how to respond.

"You'll baptize Elless and be her godmother. We'll be together like we always dreamed of."

Before I can respond, she grabs my arm and pulls me with her inside the house. "My uncle said these people are away two weeks. I'm glad the door was left open for him to come and go."

She puffs the cigarette and walks a few steps toward me. "So. You haven't missed me?"

My insides tremble. "I . . . I . . . I did at first but not any-more." I take a few steps back from her. "The cigarette stinks. It's terrible for Elless. Put it out." I'd never date or even be remotely attracted to anyone who smoked. That's disgusting.

"I barely smoke. I'm just nervous about seeing you and stole one from my aunt," she says with eyes as beautiful as gleaming daggers. She presses her lips against mine for a sensual kiss.

I allow myself to let go for a moment, but then separate my mouth from hers. "I can't do this right now."

She flicks and shoots the cigarette outside the open door a few feet away from her. Marlena's mannerisms have changed so drastically I barely recognize her. It suddenly hits me she's wear-ing a blouse I'd given her for her birthday a while back and violet pants that match the color of her eyes. She's gained weight and being a little pregnant looks stunning on her.

"Let's go for a drive. We need to get some fresh air. My uncle told me I could steal you away for an hour only. He's such an obsessive businessman. I can't believe he wouldn't give you the day off to spend time with me." She peers into my eyes. "I heard about your crash and couldn't stay away. I'm glad you're still alive and looking better than ever. I don't know what I'd have done if I would've lost you. I'd never forgive myself for not tell-ing you everything stuck in my heart and for not apologizing."

We walk out the back door as she talks about how I should stop riding bicycles on the street. "It's so unsafe. I hope you learned from this . . ."

I climb into the passenger seat and wave to everyone. "Back in a few!" They wave back.

We fall silent as she heads into back roads without the usual traffic jams.

We drive down the Rickenbacker Causeway with the tur-quoise sea on our right. To our left, the water is speckled in surf-boards with colorful masts. Windsurfing is something I'll miss doing with London. In order to break the silence, I tell her all about the water sports I've gotten to love.

I stop talking and fill my lungs with the smell of the ocean's saltiness, but it doesn't soothe me.

"I'm taking you to Rick's mom's house. She won't get home from work until six. He's off with his uncle, fishing." She talks about her fun life in Puerto Rico, clubbing on weekends and how she wishes she could be dancing with me instead of Rick. "Remember when I didn't know how to dance and you taught me?" I nod. "You taught me how to kiss, too. I can't believe I had the guts to kiss you that day at your house. I had such a crush on you. It took me a whole year to muster the courage to get that close. I'm glad you didn't push me away. If it wasn't for me, you'd probably be in love with a boy right now."

I shrug. "Maybe."

"You don't sound like you anymore, Scrunchy. What's happened to you? Why aren't you excited to see me. How do you feel about us?"

"How can you expect me to be ecstatic? What we *had* was beautiful." I make sure to focus on the past.

Once we get onto the main road I turn on the air conditioner and she flicks on some tunes. I always imagined us driving together, blasting music and holding hands, heading toward hidden secret places all over Miami to make love. I was never happier than with her. So much has changed.

The city thickens around us as we speed on toward Kendall. She places her hand on my thigh. I place it back on the steering wheel.

We get to a squat, pastel pink house and she parks inside the garage. She cuts the headlights into the darkness and everything becomes cavern-like.

But I can see her ears and neck flush. "I've got the keys to the house," she murmurs in her sexy, dripping-in-honey voice. "We can be together. We'll be safe here."

Flashes of our last conversation disappoint me. I remember her clearly dumping me.

"I'm not into being with you any more, Marlena."

She goes on and on about how sorry she is she treated me so badly. "I was so confused. You mean everything to me. I swear.

I just needed out of my house. Once I got my freedom from my parents, I was able to think better. I've come to my senses. Come on. At least lie in bed with me to talk. Give me a second chance to prove to you how much I've changed."

She reminisces about our past together, revealing her most intimate feelings about me. I melt a little, but then she throws around details about how she thinks of me when she's having sex with Rick. My stomach turns and I want to cover my ears.

Her stare pierces me but I won't allow her eyes to have such a grip on me. "Don't you remember everything we did while your family was away?" She goes on to talk about our sensual encounters and how sweet everything was. "We didn't know what we were doing at first, but eventually, with all our experimenting, we became experts in . . ."

I turn off the CD player and interrupt.

"It's too bad you've got to lie to Rick like that for the rest of your life. You could divorce him instead of betraying him, you know."

She plays with the car keys. "I've got a baby on the way. I can't divorce him. What I feel for you is pure love and I can't help wanting to be with you."

I feel a wave of tenderness sweep over me and let out a genuine smile. She takes my face in her hands, leans into me and presses her lips against mine. We end up in Rick's mom's bedroom.

Our world spins into a mouth-watering blur . . .

Everything felt so rushed. Marlena was very aggressive. Her kissing was harsh and desperate. My old Marlena is completely gone. We'd make love for hours back in the day. This took about twenty minutes, as if she needed to get something heavy out of her chest. She was rugged and forceful and, don't get me wrong, I enjoyed every delicious, exquisite second, but it was so different and fast that it's as if she'd been replaced by another person.

We stretch out on the bed under the covers to talk about details of what we've been through since we last communicated.

As time ticks by she doesn't hold my hand and isn't as affection-ate as she used to be. I guess it's because Rick isn't that way and she's gotten used to him. I place my arm under her neck and pull her closer; it feels weird to be this far apart after having been so intimate.

"Rick can't make love to me the way you do. You're the best. Our bodies belong together." She talks about the times her uncle, aunt and cousins left to Key West for the weekend. I'd buy votive candles and fill her room with them to make sure it was dim while I worshipped her body. She says Rick isn't romantic. "He doesn't even like taking baths with me. Remember when you used to massage my back in the tub and even wash my hair?"

"Those were incredible times."

"Guys aren't into that. I've missed your touch so much. There's no one for me but you, Scrunchy. I'm so sorry this was so hurried. I'm nervous about being with you again and getting you back in time. I'm also sorry I hurt you. Please forgive me."

"I forgive you." I fill her face with soft kisses.

I turn my body toward her. She plops a leg over my thigh and everything feels so familiar. I smooth her hair away from her forehead and kiss the tip of her nose. "What will you do about Rick?"

She brushes her fingers over my arm and it gives me goose-bumps. "I have to go back to him tonight as if nothing's hap-pened. I won't want to be with him after being with you, that's for sure. You're so passionate and fierce and yet so tender. You kill me. I needed this time with you so desperately. Tonight, having sex with him will be hard. I mean, I like it, but it's only physical."

Something inside me snaps. I pull her closer to me for a last, long, deep, make-out session. Time ticks by. I separate my mouth from hers. "I can't be with you again unless you break up with him." I don't need her in the way I used to, and it surprises me. She's got a husband and a baby on the way. What am I doing here? I was taken by the moment and don't regret it, but who am I kidding? This relationship won't work. I can't imagine going backward, but I also don't want to hurt her like she did me.

"You know I can't leave him."

I repeat so she gets it, "If you stay with Rick, I'll be dating a girl I like."

Her voice rises. She separates herself from me a little and starts arguing, wanting me to be with her and only her. "You can't go and date another girl after what we just did. That's so insensitive. It's not like *I'm* seeing another girl. Rick is a guy, for crying out loud! He doesn't count."

I glance at my watch and spring up. "Damn! We left almost two hours ago."

"Shit! Let's go! I don't want my uncle to get any ideas. Hurry!"

We leap off the mattress and start reaching down for our clothes littering the floor. She sits at the edge of the bed and quickly puts on her pants one leg at a time, as I hurriedly slide everything on.

"You're into another girl, eh?" The corners of her eyes sag. "Who is she?"

"No one yet. I don't want to talk about whoever I'm going to date, especially after our beautiful time together. It's not right. All I'm saying is I'm entitled to be in a relationship too if you stay with Rick. It'll be terrible for me. I need to date other girls until I find the right one. You have Rick and next year you'll have Elless. I want somebody of my own, too. Four's a crowd."

She flings her arms around me. "Please don't date other girls."

I help her up. My heart breaks. "I've got to." I embrace her as hard as I possibly can. "You still mean the world to me," I murmur. "You introduced me to love. You were my very first girlfriend. I'll never forget you. Never."

My cell rings, and she separates herself from me. "It's probably my uncle."

I check a text from Marco. *Shai. Where are you?*

"Tell him I took you to Ft. Lauderdale to meet with an old friend of ours who moved away."

I text him back. *ur niece took me far 2 meet with an old friend of ours. I told her not 2, but u know how she is. we're headed back. soon!*

We make the bed as meticulously as we possibly can and leave the room exactly as before we messed it up. Although we're completely dressed, we decide we should scrub ourselves down with lots of soap.

After a quick, frantic shower, we brush our hair and head back to the car. As she drives, she stays on the subject.

"I can't leave Rick. Elless needs grandparents, uncles, aunts and cousins. I wish you'd reconsider. No matter who I'm with, I know you're the only one for me," she repeats. "I mistakenly thought I was the only one for you, too."

"You did? That's so weird. I would have never known by your actions. I can't do it."

We drive in silence all the way back to the house I'm landscaping. No one's in sight. It seems they've gone out for lunch as a group.

Marlena won't leave me yet. I still have her scent around me and don't want her to go, either.

We climb out and with dragging hearts, walk to the backyard, where she feels safer. A large wooden fence around the property keeps neighbors from seeing us. We stand under the large mulberry tree.

Her eyes become two sad saucers. "If you won't be with me, I might talk Rick into not getting the job here. I can't live in Miami and see you around with your new girlfriend."

"Yeah. That'll be as weird as my seeing you arm in arm with Rick."

Marlena belongs with her family. Hiding our desire for one another from Rick isn't the life I want to live. I can't see myself doing that to him behind his back or accepting that she has sex with him every night but he's the only one who gets to sleep on the same bed with her and build memories together as a family.

The sun glares on her face. She stares at her hands, then at me. "You're the only girl I've ever loved and want to be with. I'll never be with another girl, ever again. I wish that were the same for you."

I've got to end this now or it'll be too hard. "Let's stop this. I'm one hundred percent sure I'll never be with you again unless you and Rick aren't an item. I've got to go." I fling my arms around her for a final embrace. "You should leave now. Take good care of Elless. Maybe one day in the future, we'll be able to be friends." My eyes begin to water. "Bye."

I break away from her and walk away, wiping tears from my eyes with the palms of my hands.

I get to the pile of coral rocks and look back at Marlena. She's standing as if she were in shock, still not believing my unexpected reaction.

Finally, she walks through the gates, climbs into the car and without looking back, drives away.

20—Temptation

Last week, after I succumbed to Marlena's advances, I had to face Marco after the crew came back from having lunch. "Where's my niece?" he asked.

"She dropped me off and said she needed to get going," I said.

She texted me once. I gave her the same response, "If u and Rick r ever not an item, call me. For now, stay away; it's the best thing 4 Elless and us. I'm going to start dating girls. I wish u & ur family the very best."

Luckily, she stopped trying to communicate with me.

At first, so many memories flooded my brain, but as the week wound down, I felt better and calmer about my decision.

London arrived tanned and refreshed, and with plenty of shark tales. He called to tell me he wouldn't let me go so easily. "You'll give me one last chance," he said with confidence in his voice.

I let him know we were definitely broken up, but I'd meet

with him *only* as a friend, because I needed to come clean.

He's driving me to South Beach pier, with the Jeep windows open. It's freezing, and my nose and ears are numb, but the wind feels good on my face.

I say to London, "I have something important to tell you."

But he insists, "We'll talk about everything later. Let's go for ice cream first, then dancing at Papaya's, where we first met."

There's nothing like ice cream on the most frigid day of the year.

He's also got something important to tell *me*, which makes me nervous. I suspect he didn't take my breakup seriously. He might profess his never-ending love, thinking a promise ring will change my mind. He says a little dancing first will make everything easier.

I ask him, "Tell me now." But he won't. London is that way. He likes things set a certain way, and he won't bend even if you've got a machete to his *chorizo*.

We come to Moo ice cream shop. The walls are filled with photographs of Cuba. All ice-cream cones are topped with tiny chocolate bongos.

London orders a triple-decker *guanabana, anon*, and chocolate on a cone. "*¡Delicioso!*" He radiates happiness and all I want is to blurt out what I must tell him.

I order two scoops of *tres leches* topped with flan cream.

We stroll the boardwalk savoring our ice creams and reach Papaya's at the end of the pier. The waves are crashing loudly underneath, but I feel them rolling inside me. I'm desperate to speak.

"Listen. Let's forget about dancing. I need to talk *now*," I insist.

"Later. I'm serious. I told you I've got a surprise for you. Don't ruin it."

We finish our ice creams and enter into a cloud of smoke and loud disco music. There's a bunch of people dancing. Tazer and Elicia yank me by one arm, and Jaylene and Rosa by the other.

"Holy pube! What are you guys doing here?" I slap my face in surprise.

"Soli asked us to come." They pull me smack into the middle of the dance floor and whisper to me, "We think Soli has something planned."

London follows. "I invited Soli and Paublo to come, and a bunch of our friends from work. It's great she invited you guys. The more the merrier." His eyes bounce around the club. "Is Soli here?"

Soli, Paublo and Gisela appear from a cloud of smoke and start dancing with us. "I asked Gisela to join us," Soli informs me with a twisted look on her face. She whispers into my ear, "This is your last chance. You know I'm on vacation. Paublo and I are leaving at midnight to Key West for two weeks. I won't see you till your birthday. Hope I come home to good news." She goes back to throwing her arms in the air and shuffling her feet to the rhythm.

"*Hola*, Shai." Gisela's smoothly swaying her curvy hips in front of me. Like a magnet, I move slowly around her. We watch each other's moves. London walks away to a table, to talk with friends he invited.

Gisela comes closer and smiles right in front of my face. "*Bella*, funny that fate should bring us together again, eh?" I get a glimpse of London, yakking away.

Once the song is over, I force myself to stop dancing.

"Hey, I really love dancing with you, but I need do something important. We'll shake and move some more later." I wave goodbye, and walk away.

Gisela follows me to the table. She hasn't a clue that London and I had been dating. London, being the gentleman that he is, pulls out a chair and invites Gisela to sit with his friends and us.

He introduces everyone to Gisela—I already know them— "This is Sarita, Morena, Taíno and Gitano."

We spread kisses. I sit next to London, wringing my hands over and over again. I excuse myself and take him to the side a minute. "Listen, what I need to tell you is that I'm not who you think I am—"

He interrupts. "Shai. You're always on this same note, then you change your tune. Once you see what I've planned at midnight, you'll never say those famous words, 'I just want to be friends' again."

It's as if I were talking to a pair of socks. He *never* listens.

"We're *not* a couple and we need to talk, *now*."

"You must be PMSing." He takes me by surprise and smacks me one on my lips. "If you keep this up, you'll ruin the surprise. Just have a good time and chill till midnight. Let's go."

"No. Wait!"

He walks away from me. I don't want to make a scene and I follow.

We get back to the table. He puts his arm behind my chair and starts talking with his friends about car races he'd like to see. I won't allow him to put his arm around me, but if he does, I don't want to make drama in front of his friends. I have such a strange mix of feelings. I think I'm finally going crazy.

I converse with his friends awhile. "Gisela is Jaylene and Rosa's friend." I point to them. "We met at Cha-Cha's, then at Viva's party." I talk about Astro Viva and her antics, and they enjoy my stories.

The conversation twists and twirls. "Let's get away from the blasting music, have drinks outside by the bar, and play pool." London's eyes veer over to his friends. "Shai hates alcohol, but it's a special occasion. Come on!"

Everyone stands up except Gisela and me.

"If you drink, I'm not going home with you. Remember that you're driving," I remind him.

"I'm just having *one* drink, Shai." I know he's lying. He turns to Gisela. "Let's go!"

"Sorry. I don't drink either. I'll take you up on playing pool later."

"Both your losses." He leans into me and almost kisses my lips. I abruptly turn my face and his lips smack me a big wet one on my cheek. "Go dance, have fun." He faces Gisela. "Take care of my one and only," he adds sweetly, yet strongly. I wish he wouldn't speak that way, especially not now that we're not together. "We'll be back soon."

I drastically change the subject. "Did you have a good time at Viva's party?"

"It could've been riveting if we'd spent some time together."

Damn. This girl is into serious confrontation. I tilt my head away from her, toward the dance floor and catch Jaylene, Elicia, Soli, Tazer and Rosa talking up a storm. They catch me looking and smile.

My hands are sweaty. I rub them back and forth on my thighs over my corduroy pants.

Gisela slips off her boots and places her feet on the chair. She hugs her knees and stares at me freely. I watch her from the corner of my eye. Her index finger and thumb are rubbing the turquoise hanging on a thin green strap from her neck. I find her eyes and fleshy shapely body so striking, and I'm so attracted to her I could die.

"Why did London call you his 'one and only'?"

"He still thinks we're dating." I come clean and tell her a bit about my relationship with him.

She sits up straight, holding her knees, looking deeply into my eyes for answers. "Soli didn't tell me you were seeing a guy." She puts one foot down and leaves a knee up. "I didn't realize you were bi. I thought you were lesbian, like me, through and through." She shakes her head. "I have nothing against bi's. In fact, all my friends are bi, but I'm not into dating bi's again. My ex professed having been born a lesbian and she left me for a guy. I get a lot of shit about this from my bi friends, but I know what I want. I'd like to be with someone who stomps their foot down and says, 'I'm a lesbian!'"

I grab a glass of ice water, gulp it down fast, and munch on some ice. I clasp my hands together around the glass and squeeze it hard. "I hate labels, but I know what I love."

"Are you confused?" she asks earnestly, examining my eyes, trying hard to figure me out.

"No," I answer fast and honestly. I explain why London and I were together so long. And I add, "I did everything possible to fall in love with him, but emotional closeness just never happened."

She stuffs the balled-up napkin into my empty glass and lowers her other foot onto the floor. "Maybe you could have fallen in love with him if you'd gone all the way, like he thought."

I look her smack in the eye. "Never." My heartbeat is so strong I can hear it. "I don't know why, but I just can't fall wholeheartedly for a guy. I always feel there's something missing."

Her eyes glisten with question marks. "So, why does he still think you're together if you're no longer an item?"

I place the glass down and fidget with a napkin. "In the past, I ended up letting him talk me into staying with him after I broke it off twice. After a while, he stopped taking me seriously."

She grabs the napkin I'm fidgeting with, rolls it into a ball, holds it in her hand, and splashes in. "The day I saw you at Cha-Cha's my heart took a flying leap. You had sparks in your eyes, too, but at Viva's party you pushed me away. I've been thinking about you, on and off, since we first met." Her sparkling eyes glow. "Soli shouldn't have invited me over to meet you if you're here with the guy you're no longer dating who thinks he's still involved with you."

"Soli wants you and me together. I'm psyched she invited you, because I haven't been able to get you out of my mind either. I was planning on going to see you Sunday morning at Cha-Cha's. I called them and found out the schedule of 'my favorite waitress.'" I smile. "I know *exactly* what I want, but first I have to tell London the truth. I need this time with him. Can I call you tomorrow so we can get together?"

She abruptly gets up. "Hey, if I've waited four hundred years and two days for you, I don't see how another day will make a difference, unless I die tonight, then it's your loss." I appreciate her sense of humor. "Okay. I'll expect your call tomorrow. I'm excited about seeing you again." She asks for my cell and puts in my digits. "Good luck." She kisses my cheek and bails.

I head over to London with a jumpy stomach. He's sitting at the bar talking to his friends, waiting for his turn at the pool table. I edge my way to him. He looks toward me with a loving expression.

I sit next to him and whisper into his ear. "I wasn't involved with Mario. Her name was Marlena."

There's an empty silence between us. Suddenly, his expression changes to confusion. "Are you *serious*?"

The DJ puts on loud, shrieky music. The smoke and noise bothers me. "We'll be right back," I tell everyone, and we walk outdoors.

He leans his back against a wall. His eyes dart around. The night is dark and windy. He raises his voice. "I can't believe you never told me."

I tell him the entire story, from when I got thrown out of school, till my wanting to fall in love with him so my mother would accept me. "I'm so sorry if I hurt your feelings. I should have told you from day one. I was conflicted because I was physically attracted to you. But in all honesty, I love you as a person, and will always remember the great times we had together. It's just that I can't fall in love with a guy. It's not you. You're incredible."

"You suck! Were you faking having a good time with me in bed, too?" I hate that sex is his only focus.

"No. I swear! Being with you that way was fant*a*stic. I loved every minute." I explain about my inability to profoundly and deeply fall for guys. I let him know it can only happen with girls.

"Oh. You used me so your mother would think you're straight and take you back?"

"No. I thought for sure, in time, I'd fall for you." I give him a friendly peck on his cheek. "Please forgive me. Believe me, London, I wanted us to be in love. I didn't want to hurt you on purpose."

He wipes the kiss with his hand. "Judas."

"London, please. Don't treat me so mean."

"I have news for you too," he blurts in a heated tone. "When you said you weren't coming with me to the Bahamas I invited this chick, Lorili, who's hot for me. We hooked up at a hotel and had the time of our lives on a boat. That's why I didn't call or text you." He would have never come clean if he hadn't wanted to hurt me back. "But it was just raw sex, and you're a better lover even being a virgin and all. I ended up missing you and I knew I'd never do that again."

"I guess we're even."

"We're not *even*. Asshole! The reason I wanted to come here is *this*." He takes out a silver ring from his pocket and shoves it in my face. "But instead, you took me for a fool."

"You knew we were broken up. But if you were in love with me as you say, and you slept around, it's weird you think *I'm* the only jerk here."

"We had great sex but you *never* went all the way. I'm a man, you know? If a beautiful girl throws herself at a guy, he's going to go for it. I don't care what any guy says. It's our nature."

"I hope you used protection."

"Shut up! Why'd you lead me on?"

I open my mouth to explain, but he growls, "Fuck you!" and takes off in the direction of his Jeep.

21—Digging Into Love

I called and texted London, but he didn't respond. When I went to see him after work, he wouldn't allow me in his house. Ending things in a friendly way, without him feeling hatred for me, or calling me horrible names, is what I wanted. I feel sad, but relieved for both of us. Now he can go on with his life and find a straight girl who really loves him. I finally did what we both needed, but I just wish I hadn't hurt him so much.

I called Gisela this morning and asked her to meet me at the beach.

I get to the edge of the pier and find Gisela. We embrace and sit, feeling the cool night air blowing on our faces. Our feet dangle down toward the crashing waves. I zip up my wool jacket and rub my hands together.

Her eyes gleam when she smiles. "I can't believe we're finally on a date."

"Yeah. I know I haven't acted as if I was into you, but I swear, there's something about you that hits me hard."

She takes my hand in hers and murmurs, "Now you're talking." Her breath tickles my ear, and I feel a tingling sensation sliding down my spine.

The pier starts to get crowded. My heart beats faster as her mouth comes closer to my lips. I lean farther away and let go of her hand. "I want to kiss you, but there's too many people around."

"So what. If they don't like it, it's *their* problem. If folks don't see more girls together, out and about, doing normal everyday things, they'll never get used to us."

"You're right. I'm just a really private person." I squeeze her hand and sense butterflies in my chest. "Let's walk on the sand to the water," I say, feeling a warm sensation inside. We take off our shoes and do just that.

A silvery light shines over the waves as I sit on the sand, facing the ocean. She plunks next to me, looking out into the horizon. Finally, everything inside me feels right. I'm at peace, one with myself, and all around me. I haven't felt that in a long, long time.

We ask each other many questions. She tells me more specific things she's interested in, such as sailing, scuba diving, kayaking, hiking, swimming and camping. And she's fascinated with Cuba, zoology and anthropology. She confides, "You know, the first day I met you, I wanted to impress you and I chose my words carefully."

"You could have babbled and you would've awed me."

I draw her profile on the sand as we talk about our lives. She tells me, "After my parents got divorced and moved to different states, they allowed me to stay in Miami, living with *Abuelita* Carmina and *Abuelito* Alberto."

"Can I meet your *abuelitos*?"

"Definitely. They'd love you."

I ask her about her relationships.

"I was involved with Sonia, the bi I told you about, for a year-and-a-half till she moved to New York. I couldn't leave my grandparents after my grandmother got Alzheimer's. She became upset and instantly found a boyfriend. I've dated for a while and it's taken some time to get over her. I wanted to wait until the right person came along."

Just my type of girl.

She asks me questions about my life. I tell her the important things that have happened to me from the day of the Incident, until this very moment, including my whirlwind, two-hour affair with Marlena, whom I still care about dearly but am no longer interested in rekindling our relationship.

"I've only been in love once, with Marlena, and we were both closeted. I don't know anything about being an out lesbian, or dating gay girls. From now on, I'm just doing what feels right for me." In the sand, I sketch her bushy wild locks flying about her head.

The sun starts to dip slowly into the horizon. Streaks of reds and pinks splash the sky. I press my lips against hers as the orange sun plunges into the sea.

Cozying up next to her, with our arms wrapped around each other, I feel all my pain and confusion melt away. I love holding Gisela in my arms, with her spicy scent around me.

We go into a much deeper kiss as I caress her face. Her kisses float me toward the water, where we're two waves, crashing as one. Now that I've found her, and she feels the same about me, I hope we can make it work.

Her mouth lands on my closed eyes for sweet kisses on my eyelids. "That was the greatest, most delicious kiss of my life."

I smile. "You're the best kisser in the history of the world."

"No. You are. I could make out with you all day and all night long until we both die. Do you believe in karma?" she asks.

"No. It makes no sense that some kids are suffering and dying, and serial killers are on the loose living a grand life. It's criminal to take vengeance on victims now, for crimes they don't even know they've committed in their past lives."

"Do you believe that everything happens for a reason?"

"Only for *ob*vious reasons. If you stick your foot in fire, it'll burn to a crisp. I believe we met because Soli, you and I, made it happen."

"You're a cynic and a free thinker. Just like me. I love that." She gives me a moist kiss on the lips. "I believe life is unpredictable, but it seems to be on our side right now."

I've never heard more beautiful words. I gaze into her eyes. Everything about her moves me. It's so true. Who'd have known life would bring us together?

Something comes over me. I feel as if I've finally taken off a tight iron mask and chest shield I've been wearing this year. The feeling of freedom is overwhelming; it makes tears pour out of my eyes.

Her lips catch the drops dripping down my cheeks. "You okay?"

"Yes." I wipe my eyes with my hands. "Just tears of bottled-up happiness."

The puzzle pieces of me haven't yet been put back together, but who can say they're whole and complete? I feel different, though, a bit happier. It's not about her; it's about finally letting go of the fear that didn't allow me to try to get to who I am: a good person, worthy of acceptance and love.

The day has turned into night. She holds me close and I breathe in her rainforest smell. Our faces are so close our noses touch. "I want to stay here forever, Gisela. This is our spot. It's got the memory of our first kiss."

We kiss and talk till three in the morning. "Viva's texted me ten times. She's worried. I've got to go," I explain and she understands.

We walk hand in hand on the cool sand, leaving behind our footprints to be washed away by the frothy waves.

We get to the parking lot and arrive at her hybrid car. She pushes my hair back behind my ears and fills my entire face with gentle kisses. I do the same. She tells me, "Let's get together again tomorrow."

Before I climb into her car, I say, "Tomorrow is ours." Her eyes gleam. "If it works, who knows? Maybe the following day will be ours too."

22—Gay Marriage?

It's December seventh, my birthday! I've been seeing Gisela for two weeks. When Soli called from Key West to find out juice, I told her about my breakup with London and lovemaking with Marlena. I didn't mention dating Gisela. I'd like to surprise her.

Gisela turned up at my place with a gift: an Italian film collection DVD set. I ran with her to buy myself a birthday present with the money I've been saving from landscaping: a 1982 mustard-colored, tiny retro convertible. I bought it cheap from a ninety-year-old wealthy environmentalist engineer who gutted it, made it like new, and turned it into an electric car.

Mami called to wish me a happy birthday. The day after I broke it off with London I told her about it. She screamed a bit, but calmed down quickly and said, "That eliminates your chances of moving in here any time soon. But maybe . . . ahhh . . . well . . . we'll see. I'll figure something out."

I didn't ask what she meant by that weird remark. We haven't talked about it since, but today she said I needed to be over her house at five p.m., before dinner. I let her know I also had a surprise for her.

My mom's front door is open and I let myself in. I sniff the air and it smells like Pedri's favorite orange gelatin. There's nothing like the scent of a little brother's love all around you.

I sit on top of her kitchen table, crossing and uncrossing my legs, drumming on the marble counter with the palms of my hands, tips of my fingers and knuckles, waiting for Mami to come out of the shower. I wonder what the surprise will be, but I sure can't wait to tell her mine. When a mother kicks you out of her heart so you can find safety, care and security on your own, you're forced to either make things work or you become broken. I'm trying to make it work, but I can't say I'm in one piece. I look around me. I've hardened but still feel the need to be accepted and loved by her. Feeling like an outsider whose mom doesn't feel you belong with her is the most difficult thing to deal with. I need her to love me unconditionally, is that too much to ask?

She rushes out of the bathroom in a silky aqua dress, dangling diamond earrings, pointy high-heeled shoes, her face drenched in makeup and her neck filled with talcum powder.

She spreads her arms around me and for a moment, we're both teary eyed. "*Te quiero, hija. Felicidades.*" She hands me two thousand dollars in one-hundred-dollar bills. "Woah! Thanks Mami!" I stuff them in my jeans pocket. "I really needed this." I can't *wait* to surprise Viva behind her back. I'll go straight to the landlord to pay our rent because she never lets me pay a cent. Then, I'll fill the fridge with food she and Soli love and pay all our pending bills.

My mom runs around nervously, making sure everything in her house is in perfect shape. "Silvina's son, Tony," she's out of breath, "the one who looks *exactly* like *Jesucristo*, is coming over to meet you, now that you're available. He's a lot handsomer than London. That's your surprise. I want you to date him and make him fall for you so one day he'll marry you and you'll bring a good name back to our family."

"*What?*" My heart drops flat on the ground. I should have

known better.

She sprays me with perfume.

"Yuk!" I grab the bottle and jump down from the table, coughing, running as fast as I can into the living room, away from the scent. Mami knows the petrochemicals in perfume makes me nauseous, but she doesn't care. I open the sliding glass doors for a breath of fresh air. I turn my neck to face her. "Are you insane about me dating and marrying a guy I don't even know?"

"Close those doors!" she yells from the pantry. "The neighbors!" I slide them shut.

"You've totally lost it!" I've got my hands on my hips, watching her searching the cupboards for María cookies.

She finds them at the very end of the shelf and lets out a sigh of relief. "*Ay, gracias a Dios.*" Then she's in my face. "You like seed-eating vegetarians and those strange environmentalists. He's got long blond hair and blue eyes. Your children will be blond with light eyes. I got married with your father at sixteen." She pushes me aside. "I got lucky with Jaime."

I dump the perfume bottle in the trash when she's not noticing. She plops onto her embroidered sofa with the María cookies on her lap and sews cuffs on Jaime's pants. The tiny glasses on the tip of her nose make her look freaky.

"You're nuts." I open the sliding doors wide and stand outside, looking down at the bay. It's pretty peaceful and quiet out, but I feel chaotic inside. My heart always hurts when I'm around her. That's not right. A mother is supposed to love her children no matter what.

She swallows the first cookie practically whole. "You know it's not healthy for a girl to not want to date boys. What are you going to do, live with those two females all your life now that you broke up with London?" She stuffs another cookie in her mouth and keeps stitching without looking up.

"Yes. I'll live with Soli and Viva for the rest of my life. At least *they* love me."

She sticks the needle inside the cuff of the pants, throws them on the couch, takes off her glasses, places them on the coffee table, and storms off to the fridge. I follow her.

"Don't tell me you haven't changed even after having had a boyfriend." She wags her head in disgust. "*Ay, mi madre*, you're going to kill me." The fridge door is open. She's picking at left-over *fricasé de pollo* bones, sucking out the marrow, and drinking orange juice straight from the carton.

Just as I'm about to tell her that yes, I *have* changed, but not in the way she wants me to, the doorbell rings and I freeze. She washes her hands in a fury and runs to answer the door. I feel like leaping out of the balcony into the bay to swim back home.

In comes a husky blond with icy blue eyes, dressed in a dark blue Italian suit, wearing a long ponytail. Mami plants a kiss on his cheek. "He's studying to be a brain surgeon, just like his father. Isn't he the most handsome boy you've ever seen, Shai? Didn't I tell you he looks *exactly* like *Jesucristo*? Didn't I?"

"Jesucristo probably had dark hair, skin and eyes, Mami."

"*Uy, chica.* You don't know anything."

Tony shakes my hand. Mami makes a mad rush to the fridge to bring him the *flan* she made for him. He accepts, eats it standing up, and raves, "*Qué delicioso.* You should open your own bakery." Mami's cheeks are flushed so rosy, you'd think she just climbed Mt. Rushmore. She hands him a pink *limonada* with a thin slice of lemon. "You're such an incredible host."

Mami leaves us alone, saying, "I've got to finish sewing Jaime's pants." Her beach ball butt disappears into the den.

We sit across from each other in the living room, talking about the weather.

He finishes his *limonada*, places it on the coffee table, scoots forward on the couch, and whispers, "Listen. I'll get to the point. I'm gay too. That's why I'm here."

"What?"

"Shh. Let's go out on the balcony. I don't want your mom to hear what I'm about to say."

We're on the terrace, looking at the smooth, peaceful waves of the bay. He scoots over to me. "No one knows about me; they think I'm straight. If you want, we can act the part. We'll get married. I'll have my private life; you'll have yours."

I scratch my head. "I can't do that."

He changes the subject. "Hell, Shai, you don't look gay at all. You aren't like those plastic gay girls trying to look straight. You're beautiful. I imagined a butch dyke with buzzed hair and a mustache." He moves even closer. I can smell his sweet lemonade breath. "I would have never guessed." He grins. "We'd make a gorgeous couple." We laugh.

"I was expecting a straight macho guy who'd be making passes at me. Snap, girl. How come no one's ever found out about you? My mom thinks you're God's gift to girls." He's definitely a hunk.

He squeezes his right arm muscle with his left hand. "No one knows I'm gay because I've had a girlfriend for four years and my boyfriend is a closeted married doctor."

I bite my thumbnail and spit it out. "Does your girlfriend know?"

"It's a cover-up. She's lesbian. The problem is that her new partner is supremely jealous and demanding of her time. Suddenly, she can't go out with me anymore."

We're leaning on our arms on the veranda railing. He comes so close our clasped hands touch. I bite my upper lip. "How did you know I like girls?"

"*Uy, mijita*, rumors spread quickly. Everyone in Miami knows." He lets loose and gets all queeny. In a high voice with a lisp, and with a bent wrist he whispers, "*Uy, chica*, I'll tell my parenths I've fallen deeply, passionately in love with you and I turned you thraight. All those thtupid friends of our parents will love that I've transformed you into a dignified hetero. We can walk the threets holding hands and people will treat you with rethpect."

I belt out a laugh. If Mami saw him she'd fly off the veranda to her death.

He clears his lisp and puts on a serious tone.

"Actually, the truth is, if we don't act as if we're together and one day in the future get married, Shai, we're doomed to live a miserable, empty life. People who matter, like professionals, will always point fingers at us. They'll never stop saying horrible things behind our backs. We'll never be respected like the straights."

I search the sky without answering him. I remember London and what I did to him. If I could take it all back, I would. I shake memories of him and prepare to speak my mind.

I grab my hair with both hands and face him. "That's exactly why we need to tell everyone about us. The more people get to know us, the more they'll respect us. We're everywhere. If an ER doctor is an 'out' lesbo, will a dying homophobic person stop her from giving him the immediate care he needs? I don't think so. If the lesbian doctor saves his life, he'll have more respect for gays. Anyhow, I tried being straight, and I hurt someone really badly. I'll never do that again. We can't let people keep hating us. We need to be in their lives and prove to them they're wrong."

"I wish I could be as strong as you." He blinks a few times with such tenderness I feel like hugging him. I come closer to him. He puts his arms around me and hugs me tightly.

We sit on two rocking chairs and talk a while about his obsession with the gym. "It releases all my tension and I can sleep like a baby. *Pero, mijita*, let me tell you," he waves a hand and snaps his fingers twice, "that's where I found Javier, my man." I crack up so loudly, Mami rushes out to us. Tony immediately controls himself.

"Act natural," I whisper, "unless you're ready to tell the truth."

Mami makes the sign of the cross on her chest. "*Uy, Dios mío*. You see? What did I tell you, Tony? I knew you were meant for each other."

"Mami, cut it out." She's embarrassing me.

Tony starts talking so manly, he sounds as though he took a testosterone shot and is about to sprout hairs on his chest and back. His back is straight. His hands are crossed over his chest, and he speaks in a particularly husky voice.

"You were right, Marisol; Shai is an absolute dream. She's so ravishing, she should be a model."

"*Uy, mijo*, I've told her that a *mill*ion times, but you think she listens? She has to do what *she* wants."

We hang around talking about Mami's and Tony's parents' friends for a while.

Tony checks his watch. "Goodness. I have a dinner engagement. I have twenty minutes to get there." I can tell he made a fake excuse. He can see I'll never change my mind.

We kiss him goodbye, and Mami invites him back soon. She walks into the elevator with him. I hear the elevator going down, then coming up again.

Mami comes indoors smiling wide. "That's the boy I want you to one day marry. I've known him since he was little. He's grown into a respectable young man. He's a great guy, and he comes from a decent, moral and respectable family."

I gulp hard, take a deep breath and let it out. "Please listen and try to understand. I'm never going to get married to a man, Mami." Next I tell her how much I hurt London. Then I finally say, "I'm dating a girl named Gisela."

"*¡Ave María Purísima!*" She walks into her bedroom with tears streaming down her face, and plunks on her bed. "What have I done to deserve a daughter like this?"

I stand next to the edge of her bed. "No, what have *I* done to deserve *you*?"

"I'm the *best* mother in the world." She bawls. "I had you go to an expensive private school even if it meant working till two in the morning. I took on three jobs just to put food on the table after your father died. I've never thought one minute about myself, only about you and your brother. You're the worst daughter in the world. An ingrate." She blows her nose with a tissue paper.

"The worst?" I pace the floor of her bedroom. All the memories of her throwing me out of the house fly back to me. "After you found out about my being with another girl, you never, ever cared about me. You kicked me out just because I was in love with her."

"Don't talk to me about those X-rated texts! Any mother

would have been horrified."

I shut my eyes really tightly. "I tried to fall in love with London just so you'd love me. That's not right." I repeat, "I can marry a girl and have kids with her. You can still be a grandmother."

"*¡Ay, Dios mío!* Why me? How could I have given birth to such a horrible daughter?"

"Horrible?" My voice quivers. "Mami, Mami. I'm your daughter. Why are you being so cruel? All you do is hurt me and hurt me. You have to stop."

She turns to me with such rage in her face I'm afraid she's going to slap me. "You're sick and disgusting."

"No, I'm not! I'm going to start supplicating to Santa Barbara so she'll turn *you* gay. How do you like *that*?"

"Shhh. The neighbors." She rushes to close the sliding doors.

I calm down. "I've always wanted a mother to understand and support me. But you just can't do it, can you?"

"No. I'll never support that. Two girls together disturbs me. That Soli is probably gay too, right?"

"Soli's *not* gay. I've already told you. You've never given Viva or Soli a chance. They *love* me. You don't *love* me. Admit it. If I were straight you'd love me." I'm talking right in her face but she's looking away. "Viva said I was born 'different' and that means great and she loves me no matter what."

"Don't talk to me about deranged people. Viva's insane. You're going to take me to my grave."

"Mami, I don't want you to suffer. And I don't want to feel any more pain. Let's stop this. Why can't you just accept me and love me for who I am? I'm a good person with good feelings. Why don't you love me, Mami, why?"

She softens up. "I love you too much, Shai, that's why I need you to change. You were never gay before that degenerate girl came into your life and lured you into another lifestyle. Change so you can come back and we can have a normal family life like we used to. I miss you."

"I've already tried, Mami. It's your turn now. Please, at least *try* to accept me."

"I can't. I don't understand how someone like you came out of me. I'm embarrassed about you, Shai. I can't have you being a *tortillera* in this house. I just can't. It's the grossest thing I can ever imagine. Two girls together makes me want to throw up." Mami walks to the door and swings it open. "When you get back to your old self, you can come back."

Standing at the door, I gather all the courage I possibly can and I muster, "I love you, Mami. I always have. If you can't accept me, that's your problem, but you can't stop me from seeing Pedri again. If you don't allow me in here to see him, or take him out, I'll tell Jaime the real reason you threw me out of the house."

"*¡Ay, Dios Mío!* You're going to kill me. Jaime better never, ever, ever find out."

I take a deep breath and calm myself. "Then that's your deal. I see Pedri, or I tell the world the reason why. I won't live a lie any more, Mami."

23—Sex Goddess & Lezzie Nun

I rush home from my mother's and fling the back sliding doors of Viva's house open. The smells of roasted pork and *cebollitas* saturate the yard. Gabriel is hanging out with his usual bunch of adorable *viejito* friends, barbecuing, playing dominoes, and listening to *son* music. Viva and her incredible open-minded metaphysical girlfriends are playing canasta, an old Cuban card game.

"*¡Hola!*" I boom.

Everyone bursts out singing, "Happy bird-day to you . . ."

Viva rushes to me with opened arms and gives me a bunch of *besitos* on my cheeks. "Happy bird-day, Shylita!"

Neruda and Sai Moomi—the fatty bulldog mutt I gave Viva for her b-day—leap up and down, barking.

Tazer, Elicia, Jaylene and Rosa greet me with hugs and good wishes. "Gisela's on her way," Jaylene lets me know. "They kept her at work longer than expected."

We're all talking about what happened with my mom when

Soli and Diego walk outdoors. "Sorry we didn't make it on time. Traffic was terrible." She rushes to me. "Happy B-day, Shyly!" She spreads her arms around me. I'm surprised she's not with Paublo.

"Wazzz shakin', little bird." Diego lands a soft kiss on my forehead.

I fling my arms around him. "Hey! I've missed you. So glad you could make it."

Viva lifts in the air a lopsided white frosting cake with chunks of pineapples, shaved coconut and cherries. "The first cake I ever make and it be organic. For Shylita *la mariposita!*"

I blow out the candles and make a secret wish. *I hope Mami one day accepts me, and Gisela and I keep getting along great.*

Gabriel starts serving slices of cake on paper plates to everyone lined up in front of the picnic table.

While everybody talks fast and gesticulates, as most Cubans do, I whisper into Viva's ear with a mouthful of the moistest cake I've ever tasted, "Hey, don't forget to use condoms." I love to bother her.

She slaps my hand. "*Ay*, Shylita, you is such a pain in thee butt. You know I is decent. Me no hooking up with Gabriel until we is married."

I lick my fingers. "Mmmm. This is so yummy." I sniff her. "Are you becoming a chef behind my back? You smell like garlic and chocolate."

"No. I is getting a cold so I eat raw garlic and blow-dry my nose with your hair blower." Her belly bulges out and so does her butt. She's on a diet and promised everyone she'd stop eating chocolate, her passionate addiction. She swears up and down and all around, "Me don't eat no chocolates."

Neruda paws her and a *turrón de chocolate* wrapper flies out of her dress pocket.

"Oh, and what's *this*, a salami sandwich?"

She grabs it from me, throws her head back, and shows all her tiny teeth when she laughs, just like Neruda.

With a swing of the hand, I call Soli to me. I need to talk to her in private. We run indoors.

I wrap my arms around her. "I've missed you *so* much! I couldn't *wait* till you got back home." We've texted a lot but it's not the same. I've never been so happy to see her.

"Shylypop, you on drugs or what?"

I'm out of breath. "Wass up with you and Diego? What happened to Paublo? I thought you guys were in the Keys together?"

She fidgets with her nose ring. "I kept a secret from you. I knew it would make you happy when you found out." She delves in. "I left early from Papaya's that night. I knew London was going to give you a promise ring and want a committed relationship with you. I needed so badly for you to say no. I couldn't bear thinking you'd marry him. As Paublo and I were leaving for Key West, we bumped into Diego. I couldn't stop talking to him. Before I knew it, Paublo left me there."

"So what *else* could you do but vacation with Diego, right, Hootchi Momma?"

"That's the *best* luck I've ever had! Diego and me got to talking. He broke it off because I wasn't serious about him. He said I have too many guys after me and I didn't treat him special." She tilts her head. "He sure was right, Shylypop. I kind of took him for granted. I don't ever want to lose him again."

I've never heard Soli being so emotional about a guy. I hug her. "I'm so psyched, Soli. It's about time you find someone you really love; it's such a great feeling."

"Here." She hands me a gorgeous purple photo album decorated with colorful dried flowers. "Mima and I made it before I left for the Keys. I have it on CD, but you know how old-fashioned she is. Mima thought it would look prettier as a real gift."

"It's so beautiful!"

They'd arranged our elementary school pics in order. I leaf through pages of us making funny faces, my pulling on her pigtails, and sticking my tongue out behind her back. Memories of sweet times fill my mind.

"Catholic school warped our brains, Shyly. Look at us now. I'm a sex goddess and you're a lezzie nun who was thinking of marrying a guy."

She never ceases to make me laugh. I can't *wait* to tell her what I've been dying to say.

I squeeze her to me. "This is the *best* birthday present ever." I take off one of the silver bracelets Papi gave me for my seventh birthday and hand it to her. "Just never lose it."

"What's gotten into you, Shyly?" Her smile radiates as she places it on her wrist. "I'll keep it forever. I know it's special." She looks smack into my eyes. "So, did you hook up with Gisela that night? That would be am*a*zing news." She snaps off her nose ring with a wild-eyed expression and places it in her dress pocket.

"I'll tell you later."

Dark clouds roll in and everyone rushes into the back porch. Thunder rumbles loudly and rain starts to pour. I go around opening all the windows. The electricity shuts off momentarily, along with Gabriel's music. All you can hear are hard raindrops, *tipi-tap-tipi-tap*, and Chuchito, our next-door neighbor's parrot, shrieking, "Happy bird-day to you!"

"Tell me *now*!"

With a huge smile plastered on my face, I fumble around the CD rack for a specific tune from the dramatic drag queen, Ambrosia, and stick it into our CD player. I take a brush from the coffee table, hold it over my mouth like a microphone, and sing along to an archaic song, while waving one hand in the air:

"Is it love or lust?/Or, is it just . . . /Another girl I text?"

Something inside me suddenly snaps, and I can't hold it in any longer. If I don't say it, I'll explode.

I leap up, throw my head back, and trumpet over the song, "I'm dating Gisela! I told my mom about it! I'm going to be with whoever I want from now on." I lift Soli up in the air and swing her around. "You know how much I hate labels. But Gisela makes me feel as if I want to shout 'I'm a homo, dyko, lesbo! I'm a *tortillera*!'"

"Wahooo! You finally came to your senses, Shyly."

The thump-thump of the rhythmic beat and the raucous stream of wild music sets Soli dancing, showing off her bouncy butt and fly moves.

Everyone comes around us and claps to the beat.

I pull Soli to me, spin her around and around, then let her loose. I swirl and twirl, like a vertigo machine. I take hold of her and steer her.

Soli follows the swinging motion of my body. "Tell me *everything* that happened while I was gone." Her teeny, perfectly lined-up dreads are bouncing all over the place. "I'm glad you told your mom. What did she say? I guess this means you had sex with, er . . . I mean, made love with Gisela, right, or are you just dating?" She can't stop asking me questions. "Tell me! Tell me all the juicy details."

I stay quiet. I *love* to keep her in suspense.

Everyone starts dancing. Nerudi and Sai Moomi run around us in circles, barking, *grrraaawwff-oof!*

I don't say a word until Gisela knocks. Finally, the moment I was waiting for.

"Come in!" I yell. She walks in, and I throw my arms around her and kiss her lips. We smother each other's faces with kisses. "I could hardly wait to see you again."

"Me too!"

"You two sure know how to keep a secret!" Soli blasts.

We all get into the groove of the music. Gisela undulates her hips, turns, and moves around me with arms graceful as a butterfly.

I grab Tazer's arm and pull him to us. Viva joins Soli, Gisela, Tazer and me in a dance by the wall I painted of her and her favorite saint, Santa Barbara. They're floating in neon-pink lounge chairs on aqua blue ocean waves, wearing small, square tangerine-colored sunglasses, and eating grapes.

While on tippy-toes, Viva wiggles her bootie out of control. "I no tell Soli that it was Giselita you be seeing. I wanted her to be surprised."

"Sneaks!" Soli laughs.

I tell them in full detail what went down at my mom's, then pull Tazer closer to me. "I'll hang with you in the streets now.

Sorry I was so dense to not have done that before. Will you ever forgive me?"

"No apologies. I totally get it. Tomorrow, we're hitting the town!"

An intense emotion takes hold of me as I wrap myself in Viva's and Soli's arms. "I love you guys. You're my family."

Viva's smile glistens in the dim light of the living room. "You is my little daughter, Shylita. Your mami will come around. You will see, *mariposita*."

"Sisters for life," Soli remarks.

I glance out the window and see the humidity fog begin to lift. I look at all my friends and Gisela's smile and feel a fog lifting from me, too.

A mild breeze with the smell of rain fills the room. I feel warm and deeply loved. This is where I belong. Finally, I feel understood and loved, right down to the bone.

Glossary of Cuban Pronunciations

Abuela \ah-boo-eh'-la\ grandmother

Apartamento \ah-par-tah-men'-to\ apartment

¡Ave María! \ah-veh mah-ree'-ah\ Cuban exclamation similar to "Holy Mary!"

¡Ave María Purísima! \ah-veh mah-ree'-ah poo-ree'-see-mah\ Cuban exclamation similar to "Holy mother of God!"

¡Ay! \i\ oh!

¡Ay, Dios mio! \i, or ah'-e dee-os' me'-o\ oh, my God!

Ay, gracias a Dios \i, or ah'e grah'-see-ahs ah dee-os'\ oh, thank God

¡Ay, madre mía! \i, or ah'-e' mah'-dreh mee'-ah'\ Cuban saying similar to "Oh, my goodness!"

Ay, mi madre \i, or ah'-e' me mah'-dreh\ Cuban saying similar to "Oh, my goodness "

¡Ay, Santa María madre de Dios! \i or ah'-e sahn'-tah mah-ree'-ah mah'-dreh deh de-dee-os'\ oh, holy mother of God!

Balsa \bahl'-sah\ raft

¡Bárbaro! \bar'-bah-ro\ Cuban saying similar to "Fantastic!"

Barrio \bar'-re-o\ Latino neighborhood

Bella \bel'-lyah\ Beautiful

Bene fine, in Italian

Besito \beh-see'-toh\ little kiss

Bocadito \bo-cah-dee'-toh\ finger-food, appetizers

Bolero \bo-leh'-ro\ a Spanish dance and musical rhythm

Caca \cah'-cah\ poop

Cacharro \cah-char'-ro\ old jalopy

Cafecito \cah-feh-see'-toh\ Cuban espresso shots

Café-con-leche \cah-feh' cone leh'-cheh\ Cuban breakfast drink of espresso, milk, and sugar

Caldo \cahl'-do\ broth

Caliente \cah-lee-en'-teh\ hot

Casquito de guayaba \cas-kee'-to deh goo-ah-ya'-bah\ guava in light caramel

Cebollitas \seh-boh-yee'-tahs\ fried onions

Cha-cha-cha sensual Latin dance with complicated rhythms

Chica \chee'-cah\ Cuban saying for "girl," literally means "A little girl"

Chorizo \cho-ree'-soh\ sausage. Cuban slang for "penis"

Churro \choo'-roh\ long, deep-fried doughnuts with sugar coating

Claves \clah'-veh\ Latino musical "sticks" that keeps the rhythmic timing in beats for the band

Comemierda! \co-meh-me-err'-dah\ Cuban slang/obscenity with similar meaning to "Asshole!" literally means, "Shit eater"

Come stai? Italian for "How are you?"

Croqueta de pollo \cro-keh'-tah deh poh'-yo\ chicken croquettes

Croquetica \cro-keh-tee'-ca\ little croquette

Degenerada \deh-heh-neh-rah'-da\ degenerate

Descargamos \des-car-gah'-mohs\ we jam (as in a "jam" session with a band)

¡Dios mío! \de-os' mee'-o\ my God!

Elefantico \eh-leh-fan-tee'-co\ little elephant

El hijo de puta \el ee'-ho deh-poo'-tah\ the son of a bitch

El mes que viene \el mess' keh ve-eh'-ne\ next month

Empanada de carne \em-pa-nah'-dah deh car'-neh\ meat pies

Enamorada \eh-nah-mo-rah'-dah\ in love

Espiritu y santo \es-pee'-re-to ee sanh'-toh\ spirits and saints

¿Estàs loca? \es-tah's lo'-cah\ are you crazy?

Fabuloso \fah-boo-loh'-so\ fabulous

Factoría \fac-to-ree'-ah\ Cuban slang for "factory"

¡Fantástico! \fan-tahs'-tee-coh\ fantastic!

¡Feliz Cumpleanos! \feh-lees' coom-pleh-ah'-nyos\ happy birthday!

Flan \flahn\ a custard-like dessert

Fricasé \free-cah-seh'\ fricassee

Fricasé de pollo \free-cah-seh'-deh-po'-yo\ chicken fricassee

Frijoles \free-hoh'-les\ beans

Fuiqui-fuiqui Cuban slang for sounds bed springs make when a couple is having sex

Gracias \grah'-see-ahs\ thank you

¡Gracias, Dios! \grah'-see-ahs dee-os'\ thank you, God!

Guarapo \goo-ah-ra'-po\ cane juice

Guayabera \goo-ah-yah-beh'-rah\ a man's shirt popular in Cuba and Latin America. It has four front pockets and two vertical lines of alforzas (ten vertical pleats that pass from above the top pockets down to the bottom of the shirt)

Hasta luego \ahs'-tah-loo-eh'-go\ goodbye

Hola \oh'-lah\ hello

Hola, mariposita \oh'-lah mah-re-po'-see-tah\ hello little butterfly

Invertida \in-ver-tee'-dah\ inverted, twisted, a derogatory slang Cuban word meaning "dyke" (*tortillera*)

Jamon y queso \hah-mohn' ee keh'-soh\ ham and cheese

Jesucristo \heh-soo-crees'-toh\ Jesus Christ

Jugo de melocotón \hoo'-go deh meh-lo-co-tohn'\ peach juice

Jugo de naranja \hoo'-go deh nah-rahn'-hah\ orange juice

La chiquitica más linda del mundo \lah chee-kee-tee'-cah mahs leen'-dah dehl moon'-doh\ The prettiest little girl in the whole world

La familia \lah fah-mee'-le-ah\ the family

La jungla cubana \lah hoon'-glah coo-bah'-nah\ the Cuban jungle

La luna \lah loo'-nah\ the moon

La semana que viene \lah seh-mah'-nah keh vee-eh'-neh\ next week

La Virgencita María \lah veer'-hen-see'-tah mah-ree'-ah\ the Virgin Mary

Limonada \lee-mo-nah'-dah\ lemonade

Machaso \mah-chah'-soh\ macho man

Malta \mahl'-tah\ non-alcoholic malt drink

Mamey \mah-may'\ reddish orange sweet custard-tasting fruit in the shape of a small football with thick brown skin

¡Mami, por favor, por favor! \mah-mee' por fah-vohr'\ mami, please, please!

Mandarina \man-dah-ree'-nah\ mandarin

Mañana \mah-nyah'-nah\ tomorrow

Mano \mah'-no\ literally means "hand," Cuban slang for "man." Example "No man! Hey man!"

¡Maravilloso! \mah-ra-vee-yo'soh\ marvelous!

Maricón \mah-ree-con'\ "Fag" or "Queer"

¡Maricónes de mierda! \mah-ree-co'-nes day me-err'-dah\ full of shit faggots!

Mariposita \mah-ree-po'-see'-tah\ little butterfly

Mariquita \mah-ree-kee'-tah\ literally means "plantain chips," Cuban slang for, "sissy"

Medianoche \meh'dee-ah-no'-cheh\ literally means "midnight." Cuban sandwich made with sweet Cuban bread, spread with mayonnaise and mustard to which ham, pork, Swiss cheese, and dill pickle slices are added

Mercado \mer-cah'-do\ market

Merengue \meh-ren'-geh\ the joyful, lively music and dance from Cuba, Puerto Rico, and the Dominican Republic

Merenguito \meh-ren'-gee-toh\ a confection of sugar and egg whites

Mijita \mee'-hee-tah\ term of endearment meaning "My little girl"

Mijito \mee'-hee-to\ term of endearment meaning "My little boy"

Mis santos \mees-sahn'-tohs\ my saints

Moi French for "me"

Muchachita \moo-chah'-chee'-tah\ term of endearment meaning

"Young girl"

Mucho \moo'-choh\ a lot, a great deal

Muy caliente \moo'-e cah-lee-en'-teh\ very hot

¡Niña! \nee'-nyah\ literally means "Girl!" An exclamation of horror, "oh, my God, young girl!"

No hablo ingles \no ah'-bloh een-gles'\ I don't speak English

¿Oigo? \oy'-go\ Hello

Orisha \o-ree'-shah\ a spirit that reflects one of the manifestations of God in the Yoruba religion

Oye \o'-yeh\ Hey

Oye, chica (o'yeh chee'-ca) hey girl!

Papa rellena \pah'-pah reh-yeh'-nah\ stuffed potatoes

Papi \pah'-pee\ dad

Pastelitos \pas-teh-leel'tohs\ puffed pastries

Pastelitos de guayaba \pas-teh-lee'tohs deh goo-ah-yah'-bah\ guava pastries

Pastelitos de queso \pas-teh-lee'tohs deh keh'-so\ cheese pastries

Pendeja \pen-deh'-ha\ pendejo literally means "pubic hair," Cuban slang for "chicken," or wimp

Pero \peh'-ro\ but

Pero mijita \peh'-ro mee'-he-tah\ but girl . . .

Piñata \peen-nyah'-tah\ jar or pot ornamented with fancy paper and filled with candy, hung from ceiling. Children pull its string to break it and get the candies

Pipi \pee-pee'\ pee

Plástica \plahs'-tee-cah\ plastic

Platanito maduro \plah'-tah-nee'-toh mah-doo'-ro\ fried sweet plantains

Promesa \pro-meh'-sah\ promise

Pulpo \pool'-po\ octopus

Por favor \por fah-vor'\ please

Puerco asado \poo-err'-co a-sah'-do\ Pork

Qué bueno \keh boo-eh'-no\ yhat's great

¡Qué cosa más grande la vida \keh co'-sah mahs grahn'deh lah vee'-dah\ Cuban saying for, "unbelievable!"

Qué delicioso \keh deh-lee-see-oh'-so\ how delicious

Qué horrible \keh or-ree'-bleh) how horrible

Qué loca \keh lo'-cah\ what a nutcase

Qué pasa, calabaza \keh pah'sah cah-lah-bah'-sah\ what's up pumpkin?

Qué rico \keh ree'-co\ how delicious

Quince \Keen'-seh\ coming of age party given to a Latina girl when she turns fifteen

Rumba \room'-bah\ Cuban percussive song and dance

Salsa \sahl'-sah\ a diverse and predominantly Caribbean dance and latin music

Salsita \sahl-see'-tah\ sauce

Santa Barbara, por favor, por favor \sahn'-tah bar'-bah-rah por-fah-vor'\ Saint Barbara, please, please

Santería \sahn-teh-ree'-ah\ religion combining African and Catholic elements

Santero \sahn-teh'-roh\ a person who's been initiated as an Orisha priest and is entitled to work with spirits and Orishas

¡Santísimo Sacramento! \sahn-tee'-see-mo' sah-crah-men'-to\ Sacred Sacrament!

Santo \sahn'-to\ saint

Sombrero de guano \som-breh'-ro deh goo-ah'-no\ a fine textured Cuban hat made from the Cuban palm

Son \sohn\ a style of music with roots on the island of Hispaniola. Cuban country music

Suave y dulce \soo-ah'-veh ee dool'-seh) soft and sweet

Te quiero, hija. Felicidades \te kee'-eh-ro ee'-hah feh-lees-see-dah'-dehs\ I love you my daughter. Congratulations

Tia \tee'-ah\ aunt

Timbales \tim-bah'-lehs\ percussion kettledrums or timpani instrument mounted on stand and played standing up

Tio \tee'-oh\ uncle

Tortillera \tor-tee-yeh'-rah\ Cuban slang for "Disgusting Dyke." Some political Latina/o gays use this word in a fun, light, and teasing way, just as a North American gay/queer would use the word "fag," but it's mostly used in a derogatory way by loathing Cuban heterosexual homophobes

Tortilla de chorizo \tor-tee'-yah deh cho-ree'-soh\ sausage omelet

Tortillera de mierda \tor-tee-yeh'-rah deh me-ehr'-dah\ full of shit, dyke

¡Tu madre! \too mah'-dreh\ literally translates to "Your mother!" Cuban slang meaning something similar to "Up yours!"

Tumbadoras \toom-ba-doh'-ra\ congas

Turrón de chocolate \toor-rohn' deh cho-co-lah'-teh\ nougat paste made of almond, pine kernels, nuts, chocolate and honey

Turrónes \toor-rohn'-nehs\ nougat paste made of almond, pine kernels, nuts and honey

Uno, dos, tres \ooh'-no, dose, trehs\ one, two, three

Uy \oo'-ee\ oh

Viejita \vee-eh-hee'-tah\ little old lady

Viejito \vee-eh-hee'-to\ little old man

Vírgen María \veer'-hen mah-ree'-ah\ Virgin Mary

Yuca con mojo \yoo'-cah cohn mo'-ho\ Cuban recipe for boiled cassava with sauce poured over made with garlic, onions, and olive oil

Bella Books, Inc.

Women. Books. Even Better Together.

P.O. Box 10543
Tallahassee, FL 32302
Phone: 800-729-4992
www.bellabooks.com